About the Author

Eleanor Agnes Berry is the author of 22 published books and says her first brush with literature was when she broke windows in Ian Fleming's house at the age of eight. 'He struck me as being a singularly disagreeable man, with no understanding of children,' she recalls. Of Welsh ancestry, she was born and bred in London. She holds a BA Hons degree (a 2:2) in English.

Eleanor specialises in black humour. In many of her books, there is a firm of funeral directors called Crumblebottom and Bongwit. The works of Gorki, Dostoevsky, Gogol, Edgar Allan Poe, James Hadley Chase, George Orwell, Joe Orton and William Harrison-Ainsworth have strongly influenced her writings. While at university she completed an unpublished contextual thesis on the Marquis de Sade (whom she refers to as 'de Soggins'). In her spare time she wrote a grossly indecent book, entitled *The Story of Paddy*, which she had the good sense to burn, and inadvertently set a garage on fire.

After leaving university she worked as a commercial translator, using French and Russian. She then worked as a debt collector for a Harley Street specialist, namely the late Dr Victor Ratner, and has since worked intermittently as a medical secretary. She was unfairly sacked from St Bartholomew's Hospital in London because she had been a close friend of the late Robert Maxwell's. (She had worked there for five years!)

Two of her novels are available in Russian and a third, which she refrains from naming, is currently being made into a film.

Eleanor is the author of numerous articles in *The Oldie* magazine and has appeared on television and on radio several times, including Radio California. Her interests include Russian literature, Russian folk songs, Irish rebel songs, the cinema, amateur piano playing, sensational court cases, the medical profession, entertaining her nephews, to whom she is extremely close, and swimming across Marseille harbour for kicks. When she dies, she will have her ashes scattered over Marseille harbour, her favourite place.

Eleanor Berry is the maternal niece of the late, famous, self-confessed gypsy author, Eleanor Smith, after whom she was named. Sadly, Eleanor Smith died before Eleanor Berry was born.

Books by Eleanor Berry

The Story of Paddy (A pornographic book – not published)
Tell Us a Sick One Jakey (Out of print)
Never Alone with Rex Malone (A black comedy about Robert Maxwell's relationship with a crooked funeral director – Out of print)
Someone's Been Done Up Harley
O, Hitman, My Hitman!
The Adventures of Eddy Vernon
Stop the Car, Mr Becket! (Formerly *The Rendon Boy to the Grave Is Gone*)
Robert Maxwell as I Knew Him (out of print)
Cap'n Bob and Me (Also out of print)
McArandy was Hanged on the Gibbet High
The House of the Weird Doctors
Sixty Funny Stories
The Most Singular Adventures of Sarah Lloyd
Alandra Varinia – Sarah's Daughter
The Rise and Fall of Mad Silver Jaxton
By the Fat of Unborn Leopards
The Killing of Lucinda Maloney
My Old Pal was a Junkie (Available in Russian)
Your Father Had to Swing, You Little Bastard! (Also available in Russian)
An Eye for a Tooth and a Limb for an Eye (A Story of Revenge)
Help me, Help me, It's Red!
Come Sweet Sexton, Tend My Grave
My Face Shall Appear on the Banknotes

MY FACE SHALL APPEAR
ON THE BANKNOTES

Eleanor Berry

www.eleanorberry.net

Also available on You-Tube

The Book Guild Ltd

First published in Great Britain in 2018 by
The Book Guild Ltd
9 Priory Business Park
Wistow Road, Kibworth
Leicestershire, LE8 0RX
Freephone: 0800 999 2982
www.bookguild.co.uk
Email: info@bookguild.co.uk
Twitter: @bookguild

Typeset in Baskerville

Printed and bound in Great Britain by CPI Group (UK) Ltd, Croydon, CR0 4YY

ISBN 978 1912362 899

British Library Cataloguing in Publication Data.

A catalogue record for this book is available from the British Library

MIX
Paper from
responsible sources
FSC® C013604

The Killing of Lucinda Maloney
'This is the funniest book I've read for months,' Samantha Morris, *The Exeter Daily News*

My Old Pal was a Junkie
'Eleanor Berry is to literature what Hieronymus Bosch is to art. As with all Miss Berry's books, the reader has a burning urge to turn the page.' Sonia Drew, *The International Continental Review*

Your Father Had to Swing, You Little Bastard!
'A unique display of black humour which somehow fails to depress the reader.' Craig McLittle, *The Rugby Gazette*

'This book is an unheard of example of English black humour. Eleanor Berry is almost a reincarnation of our own beloved Dostoevsky.' Sergei Robkov, Russian magazine, *Minuta*

An Eye for a Tooth and a Limb for an Eye: A Story of Revenge
'Words are Eleanor Berry's toys and her use of them is boundless.' Mary Hickman, professional historian and writer

Help Me, Help Me, It's Red!
'Despite the sometimes weighty portent of this book, a sense of subtle, dry and black humour reigns throughout its pages. The unexpected twist is stupendous.'
Stephen Carson, *The Carolina Sun*

'This is grim humour at its very best. The most challenging and most delightful novel I have read in six months.' Scott Mason-Jones, *The New York Globe*

Come, Sweet Sexton, Tend My Grave
'Breathtakingly black, a treasure to read from beginning to end.' Grace Ponsonby, *Newsweek*

My Face Shall Appear on the Banknotes
'Absolutely hilarious throughout.'
Alexis Lawrence, *The Dublin Times*

Sixty Funny Stories
'This book is a laugh a line.' Elisa Segrave, writer and diarist

The House of the Weird Doctors
'This delightful medical caper puts even A.J. Cronin in the shade.' Noel I. Leskin, *The Stethoscope*

The Most Singular Adventures of Sarah Lloyd
'A riotous read from start to finish.' Ned McMurphy, *The Irish Times*

Alandra Varinia – Sarah's Daughter
'Eleanor Berry manages to maintain her raw and haunting wit as much as ever.' Dwight C. Farr, *The Texas Chronicle*

The Rise and Fall of Mad Silver Jaxton
'This time, Eleanor Berry tries her versatile hand at politics. Her sparkling wit and the reader's desire to turn the page are still in evidence. Eleanor Berry is unique.' Don F. Saunderson, *The South London Review*

'This is a dark, disturbing but at the same time hilarious tale of a megalomaniac dictator by the always readable and naughty Eleanor Berry.' The late Sally Farmiloe, award-winning actress and author

By the Fat of Unborn Leopards
'Could this ribald, grisly-humoured story about a right-wing British newspaper magnate's daughter, possibly be autobiographical, by any chance?' Peggy-Lou Kadinsky, *The Washington Globe*

'Fantastically black. A scream from beginning to end.'
Charles Kidd, Editor of *Debrett's Peerage*

the top of the Buckingham Town Hall and erected the red flag. Eleanor Berry fits into the long tradition of British eccentricity.' Stewart Graham, *The Spectator*

Someone's Been Done Up Harley
'In this book, Eleanor Berry's dazzling wit hits the Harley Street scene. Her extraordinary humour had me in stitches.' Thelma Masters, *The Oxford Times*

O, Hitman, My Hitman!
'Eleanor Berry's volatile pen is at it again. This time, she takes her readers back to the humorously eccentric Harley Street community. She also introduces Romany gypsies and travelling circuses, a trait which she has inherited from her self-confessed maternal gypsy aunt, the late writer, Eleanor Smith, after whom she was named. Like Smith, Berry is an inimitable and delightfully natural writer.' Kev Zein, *The Johannesburg Evening Sketch*

McArandy was Hanged on the Gibbet High
'We have here a potboiling, swashbuckling blockbuster, which is rich in adventure, intrigue, history, amorous episodes and above all black humour. The story Eleanor Berry tells is multi-coloured, multi-faceted and nothing short of fantastic.' Angel Z. Hogan, *The Daily Melbourne Times*

The Adventures of Eddy Vernon
'Rather a hot book for bedtime.' the late Nigel Dempster, *The Daily Mail*

Stop the Car, Mr Becket! (formerly The Rendon Boy to the Grave is Gone)
'This book makes for fascinating reading, as strange, black-humoured and entertaining as Eleanor Berry's other books which came out before it.' It is to be noted that Eleanor is deeply embarrassed by parts of this book. *Gaynor Evans, Bristol Evening Post*

Reviews

Tell Us a Sick One Jakey
'This book is quite repulsive!' Sir Michael Havers, Attorney General

Never Alone with Rex Malone
'A ribald, ambitious black comedy, a story powerfully told.'
Stewart Steven, *The Daily Mail*

'I was absolutely flabbergasted when I read it!' *Robert Maxwell*

Robert Maxwell as I Knew Him
'One of the most amusing books I have read for a long time. Eleanor Berry is an original.' Elisa Segrave, *The Literary Review*

'Undoubtedly the most amusing book I have read all year.'
Julia Llewellyn-Smith, *The Times*

'With respect and I repeat, with very great respect, because I know you're a lady, but all you ever do is just go on and on and on and on about this bleeding bloke!' *Reggie Kray.*

Cap'n Bob and Me
'A comic masterpiece.' *The Times*

'As befits the maternal granddaughter of F.E. Smith (famous barrister who never lost a case) Eleanor Berry has a sharp tone of phrase and a latent desire for upsetting people. Campaigning for her hero, Robert Maxwell, in a General Election, she climbed to

To Sally, Charlotte and many others who took me out of the grave, after my beloved Peachey died

PART I

The Limbo of Miss Natalie Klein

The year was 2056. Highgate Cemetery was one of the few parts of Britain which was left intact after the Russian hydrogen bomb of 2054.

This was engineered by a certain Boris Apresky who had been the Russian ambassador to London. He was a stark, staring, raving madman. He was short and bald and had beady black eyes.

He had borne a private grievance against Britain for some years. He was enraged by the media's frequent mispronunciation of his surname with the stress on its first syllable.

Moreover, he thought that sections of the British public were, for want of a better phrase, taking the piss. He assumed that they were associating his surname and his personal habits with a life of decadence, with drunken moonlight picnics in the mountains, and with wild parties in chalets, at which fornicating couples got so drunk, after a day's ski-ing, that they could not hold their bile.

Outwardly, Apresky seemed to be calm and balanced. He hid his obsession about the mispronunciation of his surname so successfully from his bosses in the Kremlin, that no-one found out about his insane plans.

After standing down as Russian ambassador to London, on his forty-second birthday, Apresky became the captain of a nuclear submarine called the *Nikolai Gogol*. It was easy for him to violate the programming of the master computer on the submarine. His paranoia had festered even more within him. It had driven him to drink and had sharpened his homicidal tendencies.

He entered a coded message on the master weapons console* to the effect that Russia was at war with Britain. He had an accomplice called Sergei Sogrov who was a senior officer on the *Nikolai Gogol*. Apresky had a homosexual relationship with Sogrov who had his own security key to the master weapons console.

They both turned their keys simultaneously, to enable the nuclear missiles to be fired.

As a result, most of London became a mass of rubble and other British cities were piteous wrecks. Apresky and Sogrov had a lovers' pact between them. They both committed suicide.

* * *

Since the hydrogen bomb of April 2054, a large building was erected in Highgate Cemetery. This was known as "Maguire's Vault", in which the British Prime Minister, Jack Maguire, his wife, Hortense and their children had been laid to rest. Maguire's Vault was situated in the only part of Highgate Cemetery which had not been cordoned off.

Maguire had been Prime Minister of Britain for ten years. There had been two general elections and each time he had won on a landslide.

He had been extremely popular, because the inhabitants of Britain and indeed those of the entire Western world feared another Holocaust and they needed someone strong to look up to. Also, his prepossessing appearance and rough diamond charm endeared him to a large number of female voters in Britain as well as many male voters.

---

* Console: controls desk

4

Maguire's Vault was constructed on the instructions of an eccentric Welsh woman called Natalie Klein. Natalie had been sentenced to life imprisonment in 1981. She was in her early twenties at the time. She had murdered a woman who had tried to blackmail her. She had given instructions, regarding the design of Maguire's Vault, from her prison cell, using her mobile phone.

Some people considered her to be almost as loose a cannon as Boris Apresky. She was a crooked funeral director.

She hero-worshipped Maguire who had always been very kind to her. They first met on a motorway and he helped her when she had broken down.

She was once incarcerated in a lunatic asylum, where the staff had treated her with abject sadism. Maguire had rescued her from the asylum, and she had had an adoring relationship with him from then on. Indeed, she loved him ever since she had met him on the motorway.

He had admired her beauty. He had admired her for joining the communist party, when she had hailed from a wealthy, right-wing newspaper family. He admired her for having taught herself Russian, against her parents' wishes. Lastly, he had admired her for having gone to Russia alone, without telling her parents that she was going there. She lied to her parents and said she was going to stay with friends in Cornwall (She was in her late teens when she had done all these things.)

Natalie had employed a prestigious firm of architects and stonemasons to design Maguire's Vault. Her employees were intimidated by her Germanic manner on the phone, and feared her because they had found out that she had once been in a lunatic asylum.

Had it not been for Natalie, the vault would never have been built. It was said in some of the newspapers that she and Maguire had a lot in common and even that he saw himself in her. She wouldn't hear a word against him, whatever his faults may have been.

***

Maguire's Vault had a black, rectangular, marble base. It was approached by a flight of matching black, marble steps, edged with gold. At the top of the steps, was a giant, gold effigy of Maguire.

The vault was entered by a doorway, beneath the words HOUSE OF MAGUIRE, in gold letters. The doorway led, first to an outer chamber and then to an inner chamber. This was divided by a hollow gold block, higher than the rest of the vault.

It was within the gold block, that the bodies of Jack Maguire and his wife, Hortense, were laid to rest. Maguire's body occupied one side and Hortense's body occupied the other. At the top of the block, two giant hands, a man's and a woman's, were clasped in defiance of the dark grey sky, at which they pointed for the rest of eternity.

Jack's and Hortense's seven children had been laid to rest in the lower part of the vault. On Jack's side, lay the sons. On Hortense's side, the daughters. A replica of each child was sculpted in bronze and their hands were crossed like medieval saints.

Outside the vault was a black pedestal, on which a biblical quotation was engraved:

> *"They were lovely and pleasant in their lives*
> *and in death they were not divided."*

The results of Maguire's leadership were summarized in the words of Longfellow, which Natalie thought were applicable to the inhabitants of Britain under his rule:

> *"Alike were they free from fear that reigns with the tyrant,*
> *And envy, the vice of republics …*

Their dwellings were open as day and the hearts of their owners.
There the richest were poor and the poorest lived in abundance. "*

(Natalie was particularly fond of Longfellow's works.)

* * *

Sir Jeremy Klaytor was the Keeper Elect of Maguire's Vault. It was his responsibility to inspect its maintenance and cleaning, both inside and outside. A team of cleaners, known as vaultmen, worked under him. A foreman referred to as First Vaultmate Vernon, was responsible for checking the vaultmen's work. Klaytor's job was similar to Vernon's, although Klaytor was the senior of the two men.

Klaytor, Vernon and all the vaultmen were wearing white overalls, white gloves and white beekeepers' headshields. Their bodies were encased in radiation-resistant polythene over their overalls.

Klaytor's family had all died of cancer, except for his five-year-old son, Michael, who was fighting the disease. His doctors said that there was a chance that Michael's cancer could be cured.

The boy was incarcerated in an underground clinic called Harley Zone One. This was about a hundred feet below the area where the Harley Street Clinic had once existed.

The hope that his son might one day be cured gave Klaytor an incentive to live. This, combined with the honour of being Keeper Elect of Maguire's Vault, cheered his otherwise dreary existence. He looked sadly at the dour grey sky, and swung his arms in the air to protect himself from the savage gusts of wind, which lashed him through his radiation-resistant clothing. He approached the vault to inspect its cleanliness.

He found the vaultmen lined up in a row outside the vault, in order of size. They saluted him.

"Is the work done?" asked Klaytor.

First Vaultmate Vernon stepped forward and lowered his head. He made the sign of the cross.

"Yes, sir, the work is done," he said.

"Good. You may go to your shelters now."

"And you, sir?" asked Vernon.

"I? I shall stay here for a while."

"Yes, of course, sir, I understand." Vernon turned to leave.

"Oh, Vernon!" called Klaytor.

"Yes, sir?"

"I'd like you to have this."

Klaytor placed a gold coin worth two hundred pounds in the palm of Vernon's hand. Inflation had altered substantially over the years.

On the gold coin was a carving of Maguire's face in profile, intricate enough to show his acute, penetrating stare.

"My face shall appear on the banknotes, and my profile shall appear on the coins." These words were engraved on the coin.

They also appeared at the top of the front page of the newspaper, *Maguire's Voice* before general elections. They were Maguire's words.

Vernon looked at the coin in astonishment and kissed it.

"Why! Two hundred pounds, sir! That's ever so generous. I'll be able to buy a half-pint can of beer with this."

Klaytor turned away from Vernon and walked towards the vault. He knelt in front of the giant gold effigy of Maguire at the top of the marble steps, crossed himself and spoke out loud:

"Maguire, Master, don't let my son die. Make the doctors cure his cancer. Please be merciful as you were in life."

A snowdrift was suddenly blown through the entrance of the vault and into the inner chamber, which it had taken the vaultmen two hours to polish.

"Filthy Russian bastards! At least, have some respect for

what we hold sacred," shouted Klaytor. He shook his clenched fist in the air.

Although it was then summer, winter had come early to the wastelands that had once been London. A raging blizzard descended. Klaytor staggered through the brutal storm towards the nearest tow-cart terminal, which had once been the London Underground.

A nine-year-old boy in rags, unprotected from radiation, rushed towards Klaytor. He was weeping piteously: "Bread, good neighbour, bread! Bread for the love of Maguire!"

"I can give you a hundred pounds but no more," said Klaytor. He slapped a coin worth a hundred pounds into the palm of the boy's hand. The boy thanked him, kissed the back of his gloved hand and ran off.

The tracks in the tow-cart terminal could still be used but there were no trains. Like Harley Zone One, the carts were about a hundred feet below ground level. They were pulled along the tracks by heavy chains, which were manually operated by closely supervized convicts. These men had been caught selling secrets to the Russians. Part of their punishment was to have direct contact with the survivors of the hydrogen bomb, who used the terminals. Embittered travellers spat into the faces of the convicts as they wound the handles of the tow-carts.

Klaytor was about to get into the makeshift lift, which descended to the tow-cart terminal, when another blizzard whistled past him and knocked him over. He scrambled to his feet and got into the lift. He looked at his watch and noted bitterly that the month was June, which had been a hot and sunny month during his childhood.

"Where to, Mrs Mop?" asked a cheeky convict, who had opened the door leading to the lift. Because Klaytor was famous, the convict knew what his occupation was.

"Harley Zone One, you cock-sucking commie!" rasped Klaytor. "It will amuse you to know that my son's got cancer."

"What's that?" asked the convict, who had a brain the size of a sparrow, which was why the Enemy had used him.

"A disease," shouted Klaytor. The convict let out an involuntary village idiot's titter. Klaytor broke his jaw, without knowing initially that he had lost his temper. It was only when he saw the convict's dentures on the floor of the lift, that he realized what he had done. He felt much better.

* * *

There was an underground prison in the north of Scotland. Its location was known as "north- strip seventeen".

A slow, but rousing tune known as *Once to Every Man and Nation*, now the British national Anthem, was being played even more slowly than usual, that day. The tune was an old favourite of Jeremy Klaytor's. Whenever he walked to Maguire's Vault, he sang the words of the new national Anthem to give himself strength. He invited tourists in radiation resistant clothing, who visited the vault daily, to join him.

While the tune was being played in the prison in north strip seventeen, two warders were standing in the corridor, speaking in hushed voices. The oldest, Mrs Ethel Murray, who was forty years old, had worked in the prison for eighteen months. Her colleague, Mrs Beverley Pell, aged twenty-seven, had just joined the workforce. Both women had heavy Scottish accents. Ethel said:

"Our oldest prisoner's a hundred and one years old, just turned. She's a lifer. First degree murder. She's an extraordinary old woman, who hugs a large porcelain bust of Jack Maguire all day and never lets go of it."

"What's the woman's name?" asked Beverley.

"Natalie Klein. She was a close friend of Maguire's and his wife's."

"The Maguires?" exclaimed the younger woman. "You mean she *knew* them?"

"That she did. Mr Maguire and his wife were very kind to her and she loved them in return," said Ethel.

"When did Natalie first meet Maguire?"

"Oh, they'd known each other for years. She first met him when she had broken down on a motorway, apparently. He helped her. Later on, Natalie was incarcerated in a lunatic asylum. That's common knowledge. He rescued her. She had an adoring relationship with him ever since she met him."

"What were Natalie's parents doing at the time? Why didn't *they* rescue her?" asked the younger woman.

"Oh, I don't know. I think they were both ill in hospital. Natalie regarded Maguire as a surrogate father."

"How did Natalie get on with her own father?" asked Beverley.

"They say she and her father were very close."

"Why would a fine man like Maguire have anything to do with a common murderer, Ethel?" asked Beverley.

"Natalie committed the murder some time before she met Maguire. He knew nothing about it, until the Law came for her. She canvassed for him. I'm not sure exactly what she did, but whatever it was, it wasn't what he told her to do. It was what she thought ought to be done in his interests. Although he won on a landslide, and became Prime Minister, as you know, she helped him to win, but not in the way he wanted her to help him, as I said."

"What do you mean? You're not being very clear."

"Natalie committed many misdemeanours, all with intent to help Maguire, but he was bitterly disappointed when he found out what she had done. Even so, he still remained her friend."

Beverley ran her hand through her long black hair. "What exactly did Natalie do when she was working for Maguire?" she asked.

"I don't really know. I was ill at the time it all came out and I didn't see any newspapers. All I know is that he was angry with her, and told her so, but she still believes she did the right thing and is proud of it," replied Ethel.

"You said she committed a murder before she met Maguire," said Beverley."Whom did she murder?"

Ethel got impatient. "You don't know much, do you? She killed another woman in cold blood, called Dolores Murphy. Natalie was in her early twenties at the time. Dolores was blackmailing her."

"What was Dolores holding over her?" asked Beverley.

"She threatened to tell Natalie's common-law husband, that she had been having an affair with her brother, Seamus. That's not all, though. Dolores had personal information about the old woman, that was even more sinister than the affair."

"What information was that?"

"I'd like to tell you the whole truth but I can't," said Ethel. "Natalie knows she hasn't got long to live. One day, I went into her cell and burst into tears. She took pity on me, told me her whole story and swore me to secrecy. She said that once she's dead, I can sell her story to *The Sun*."

"What's that?" asked Beverley.

"Christ, you're ignorant! It's a newspaper – or shall I say, it's registered at the post office as a newspaper. It's read by filthy old men in black rubber mackintoshes."

"Why should they wear black rubber mackintoshes? They're not radiation resistant," said Beverley.

"Don't be so stupid," rebuked Ethel, adding, "I don't mean to be rude. I know you've barely been out of a shelter for most of your adult life. *Sun* readers read *The Sun* within the privacy of their shelters. They get a kick out of scandal and they play with themselves under their black rubber mackintoshes."

Beverley laughed. "Natalie told me I could sell her story after her death and not before," repeated Ethel, adding, "I got very friendly with her one day. I had been talking to her about my domestic problems. She's a good listener. I told her how bored my husband had been getting with me recently, and how he had threatened to leave me, unless he could be kept amused by a hologram-viewing room in our shelter. *The Sun* offered me ten billion pounds for my story. A hologram-viewing room costs something in the region of ten billion pounds. Natalie swore me to secrecy, as I said." Ethel continued,

"I went to the underground offices of *The Sun* in Wapping Strip Four, and finally asked to speak to the Editor. The Editor said the story was fascinating and gave me a written promise to the effect that his paper wouldn't print anything until after Natalie's death."

"Dolores's reason for blackmailing Natalie – is it very sordid?" asked Beverley conspiratorially.

"Yes, I think the story is what you might call pretty tacky. Can you imagine a newspaper like *The Sun* being interested in it if it wasn't?"

There was a tone of bitterness in Ethel's voice which confused Beverley. She was afraid of being snubbed again, so she decided not to ask any more questions. She paused.

"May I go and look through the slit in the door of the old woman's cell?" she ventured eventually.

"Yes. Go and make friends with her," said Ethel. "You'll find her a bit strange and conceited. She's extraordinarily serene and contented, despite her solitary confinement.

"You'll also find that she has delusions of grandeur and is very repetitive. She goes on and on about how she found glory in her youth. She seems quite happy but it's common knowledge here that she's pretty batty."

Beverley looked through the slit in the door of Natalie's cell. The old woman was smiling and was moving backwards and forwards on a rocking chair, to the accompaniment of *Once to Every Man and Nation*. She was holding a porcelain bust of Jack Maguire in her black-gloved hands. Her face was veiled. Her long, blonde hair had turned white. It was arranged in a plait, just as she had worn it in childhood.

She held the bust like a baby and spoke to it as if it could hear her. She had a strong Welsh accent. Beverley listened to what she had to say:

"I was called a coward in the days of old, first by my beloved brother and after that by my evil lover." Natalie repeated herself.

"I was called a coward in the days of old and the brand of cowardice is a cancer of the soul.

"I served a man once and I pledge myself to his supreme glory. I, too, found glory, by helping to bring about the attainment of power, by this man who was far more glorious than I, and who was far wiser than I, although that person did not approve of my methods.

"But I killed someone, long before I found glory, when a funny law existed and the taking of another person's life was called 'murder'. Natalie continued,

"A hundred and one summers have passed me by, and I am waiting for the Reaper to come for his pound of flesh. But I am not afraid, for he shall know how I found glory in the days of old."

"I've got a secret to tell you, other than the story I'm going to sell to *The Sun*, when Natalie dies," said Ethel to Beverley.

"Oh, what secret is that?"

"It's something Hortense, Maguire's wife, told Natalie and which Natalie told me."

"Yes?"

"When Maguire proposed to Hortense, he went down on one knee promised he would become Prime Minister, "My face shall appear on the banknotes, and my profile shall appear on the coins," he told her.

The most important thing is that Maguire was able to keep his promise."

"What was Natalie like when she was young?" asked Beverley. There was a pause.

"They say she was a good-looking woman. She ran a funeral business with her partner, Charles Elliott, to whom she was devoted. Also, she liked to have her initials engraved on everything – N.K., N.K., N.K., N.K., on everything she owned. She even had her initials painted on her drains."

"What else can you tell me about her – oh, except that thing you're not supposed to speak to me about?" said Beverley.

Ethel answered at considerable length:-

"Natalie absolutely doted on her elder brother, Gomer. He was five years older than she and was a well-known writer. Some say her love for him was incestuous. During her early teens, she washed and ironed his shirts, darned his socks, sewed on buttons for him, made his bed, changed his sheets and even put the toothpaste on his toothbrush for him.

"When Natalie was fifteen years old, Gomer got married. Natalie completely broke down. She had wanted to elope with Gomer, with a view to marrying him. She couldn't sleep, couldn't eat and neglected her studies. She was supposed to be doing her O'levels and had to take them a year later. Ethel continued,

"Gomer had a son who looked exactly like him. His name was Julian. Natalie adored Julian and spoiled him rotten. When he was small, she took him on outings, all over London and showered him with expensive gifts. However, unlike in Gomer's case, Natalie didn't love Julian in an incestuous way. Her love for Julian was totally unselfish and protective. Her love intensified when she was taking him for a walk along the Brighton sea front once. He was eight years old at the time. They came to a shop which sold sea-shells.

"Aren't they lovely?" said the boy.

"Yes. If you like, I can take you into the shop and buy some for you."

"Oh, no, don't do that," he said. "I'd like you to leave them where they are, so that everyone can see them."

Ethel continued.

"Eventually, Maguire replaced Gomer in her Natalie's affections."

"You've told me an awful lot," said Beverley, adding, "What happened to Gomer, his wife, Julian, Natalie's parents and Charles Elliott, in the end?"

"They all died of natural causes. The only survivor of the Klein family is Natalie."

"What did Maguire die of?" asked Beverley.

"Lung cancer. Didn't you know that?"

"How old was he?"

"Fifty seven, I think."

"What about Hortense?"

"She died of old age."

"Can you tell me anything else about Natalie?" asked Beverley.

"I'll tell you everything I know over the brown pill break at eleven o'clock, that is everything except for her secret," said Ethel.

The two warders managed to find a table in the crowded staff canteen. They stirred drugged, caffeinated capsules into mugs of hot water. A drug called Laropepinine* was in the capsules. That was why there was always such a rush to the canteen.

"Cannee nay tell me Natalie's secret? I'll not tell a wee soul," pleaded Beverley, once she had become high on the Laropepinine.

"You know perfectly well, I've been sworn to secrecy!" replied Ethel angrily.

"Tell me more about Gomer then, and his relationship with Natalie."

---

* Laropepinine: – A powerful, non-addictive, euphoria-inducing drug, which
   was combined with opiates and a neutralizing chemical compound. It was
   the chemical compound which caused the drug to leave no hangover and
   no withdrawal symptoms in its wake. Natalie thrived on the drug, which
   accounted for her permanent state of well-being. Ethel provided her with it.

"Natalie was profoundly jealous of Gomer's wife, Anne, and indeed of any woman he fancied."

"Was Gomer nice to Natalie?"

"Why, yes. He was very affectionate towards her. He phoned her every day to find out how she was. He addressed her as "my little sister". Before she became a funeral director, she wrote a pornographic novel. He helped her with it and encouraged her to make it more outrageous than it was already. He once said to her, "Carry on writing, little sister. One day, you and I will be as famous as the Brontë sisters.""

"When I listened through the slit of the door leading to her cell, I heard Natalie say, "I was called a coward, in the days of old, first by my beloved brother and then by my evil lover." Why is she so preoccupied with having been called a coward?" asked Beverley.

"Oh, that's something I left out," began Ethel. "When Natalie was seven years old, the Klein family were holidaying in Switzerland. There was snow on the ground. Gomer, aged five years her senior, rented a toboggan and led Natalie by the hand to the top of a steep slope. He said, "I'm going to give you the best ride of your life, little sister. Hold onto me.""

"During the ride, Natalie dug her heels into the snow and slowed the toboggan down. Gomer was furious. "I don't play games with cowards!" he shouted.

"That's why Natalie is so preoccupied with having been called a coward."

"She said her 'evil lover' had also called her a coward," said Beverley.

"I can't really go into that, without telling you Natalie's secret – or at any rate, what led up to her secret," said Ethel irritably.

The two women continued to stir and sip their drugged water. Eventually, Ethel told Beverley about some events in Natalie's early life.

* * *

When she was in her early twenties, Natalie Hester Klein was graced with a fashion model's looks. She was five foot, four inches tall and weighed nine stone. She had long, reddish blonde hair which she had worn in a plait, as a child. When she grew up, she shortened it and wore it in layers. Her hair was thick and lustrous and fell below her shoulders.

Her complexion was healthy and slightly tanned, which gave her an Indian appearance. Her nose was small and straight and her eyes were large and grey.

Her voice was loud, deep and was unvarying in pitch. Her accent, unless checked, was Welsh. It was not an accent which could be mimicked easily and yet Natalie Klein had a gift for mimicking others.

She favoured the kind of language which was used by colonels in the nineteen thirties. Often, her use of English was pompous, old-fashioned and flowery, but it could be interspersed, without warning, with the coarse language of the gutter, if she wished to shock or humiliate others. She loved to be the centre of attention and tended to be rather a show-off.

She was sympathetic and pleasant towards friends who confided their innermost secrets to her, but she never told anyone anything about herself. Sometimes, she made mockery of the sensitivities of others, without knowing where the barrier lay, between friendly joking and unkindness. To give an example of this, she once met a rather pathetic man in a pub.

"You've got very sad eyes," she remarked in a commanding tone of voice. "Very sad eyes indeed. You'll top yourself one day. I know it in my bones."

Sure enough, the unfortunate man later committed suicide.

Occasionally, Natalie asked people personal questions in order to tease them, but she would not tolerate anyone doing the same to her. She related to men more easily than to women. She was fiercely loyal and loving towards her common-law husband, her brother, her father and her nephew. (Her mother was dead).

An example of her brutal and yet merciful behaviour can be seen in the following incident:

She was driving from London to her father's house in the country, in her silver Ford Focus. Her father was on his way to the same house but had started his journey fifteen minutes later than she had. She came across a gruesome road accident. A driver, who had not been wearing a seat belt, had been thrown through the windscreen. He was still alive.

Natalie got out of her car and went up to the injured man, who was in too much pain to scream. She put her hand near his mouth to see whether or not he was breathing. He was.

"He's not dead," she said. A ghoulish crowd surrounded the injured man. An ambulance and a police panda car arrived on the scene. Two policemen got out of their panda car. One of them gulped when he saw the injured man and held a handkerchief to his mouth. Natalie went up to the other policeman and tapped him on the shoulder.

"Hey, officer," she said, within the injured man's hearing, "get that man off the road as soon as you can! My father's due to turn up any minute now and if he sees him, he'll faint."*

This was the sort of behaviour, both savagely cruel and yet kindly and loyal which typified much of Natalie's character.

* * *

Klein and Elliott was a small but prosperous firm of Funeral Directors and Monumental Masons, near the bottom of

---

*   Natalie's father was subject to fainting attacks, whenever he saw blood.

19

Denmark Hill in Camberwell, London SE5. It was run by Natalie Klein and her partner, Charles Elliott. It had been sponsored by Natalie's father. Natalie was the daughter of Selywn Klein, a well-known figure in the world of journalism. He was the Editor of the widely read *British Echo*, as well as numerous prestigious publications. The Klein family were Welsh in origin and were extremely well-off.

Although he was a stern parent, Selwyn Klein was kindly, good humoured and was liked by all who knew him. He was also a fantastic wit. Once, Natalie had a cold and was making heavy weather of her complaint, by wrapping herself up in towels. Selwyn went into her bedroom and said, "Do you want me to send for a priest?"

On another occasion, Natalie went to dine with her father. It was a Tuesday. He offered her some wine.

"I don't drink on Tuesdays," she said.

"Wht not?"

"On Tuesdays, I give my liver the day off."

"Do you dress it up in its best clothes and send it to the seaside with a bucket and spade?" asked her father.

Selwyn's original name was "Rhys-Clynndyddwyn" but he was so bored with having to spell it out, that he changed it by deed poll to "Klein".

Natalie's elder brother and only sibling, Gomer Klein, was a famous writer. He was vain, good-looking as well as brilliant. If so much as a week passed by without one of his books being reviewed, he became depressed and bad-tempered. However, he was described by everyone who knew him as being a "gentle soul."

When Gomer was happy, he liked to stand on the balconies of a seaside villa, in the south of France. His father used to rent the villa for his family's summer holidays. Gomer liked his family's summer holidays. Gomer liked stare at naked women on the beach through his binoculars.

"Gomer, you went to America common and you came back vulgar," his father said assertively on one occasion. (Gomer had once lived in America. He had written articles for *Time* magazine.) He was prosperous as well as talented and his father's words had little, if any affect on his vanity.

Natalie was self-conscious about coming from such a successful family and was determined to be a good capitalist in her own right. She met a sympathetic, attractive and humourous man called Charles Elliott who impressed her by his wit, kindness and good looks. He was a Cornishman and was proud of it. He has a thick, Cornish accent. His hair was light brown and he had large blue eyes.

Elliott's former career was varied. He had once been a gravedigger. He was extremely conscientious and hard-working at all times. Finally, he became a boat-builder. He refurbished several Cornish luggers, all of which were more than sea-worthy. His favourite Cornish lugger was called the *Natalie K.* He sold her to a man who crossed the Atlantic on her.

Eventually, Natalie persuaded Elliott to go into partnership with her. She chose to be a funeral director, because she had a taste for the macabre. At first, her father was reluctant to sponsoring her firm, but eventually he came round to her statement that no recession could stop people dying.

* * *

Natalie's and Elliott's funeral parlour consisted of a shop on the ground floor, known as the front office, and a workshop, combined with a cellar in the basement. The rest of the premises comprised an office on the first floor, which was used by Natalie. The second and third floors were residential. There was a small, unused attic on the top floor. Natalie liked to refer to the premises as "our house".

"Natalie! Can you hear me?" Elliott was calling to her in her office upstairs.

Natalie was sitting in a darkened room, which was decorated with *momenti mori*. She had her feet on her desk, a pocket calculator in one hand and a brown paper bag, containing radishes in the other.

"What do you want, Charlie? I'm doing the accounts."

"Our Branch in Dulwich Village needs a hearse at three o'clock this afternoon. Fortunately, we've got two spares. Tomorrow, I'll be doing a job in Crystal Palace, where the boys are working on the Talbot widow,"

"She's not very good news, is she, that woman," said Natalie.

"No. She's the wailing, breast-beating type. Latin temperament, one of those. You never warned me about her. I put Diazepam in her tea on your advice."

"That's about the only advice of mine you've ever taken."

"What are you doing this afternoon?" asked Elliott.

"I'm going to the cinema. You know I often go to the cinema in the afternoons."

"You always leave all the work to me, don't you?" said Elliott irritably.

"You're right, I do. If I wish to go to the cinema, I shall do so."

"But you hardly do *anything*. You don't even talk to the bereaved any more."

"I get squeamish about facing the bereaved, so I stick to admin work. Besides, I haven't got the right manner. I get nervous. I tend to speak abruptly."

Elliott mimicked Humphrey Bogart's voice. "You can say that again," he said. He continued, "I still don't see why I have to do *everything*. Besides, we're one pallbearer short. Arthur Sprout's got flu."

"Flu? You never warned me about this? Has he been on the premises with it?"

"Don't get worked up, Natalie. He hasn't been in here and

22

you won't catch it. Don't you ever think about anything besides your health?"

"No."

"I could have built another boat and put to sea by now, instead of living with a hysterical hypochondriac," said Elliott.

"How dare you! I am not a hypochondriac."

"Let's say no more about it. A little help from you once in a while wouldn't go amiss."

"I count the dough, don't I? I fiddle the books.," said Natalie defensively.

"That's it. You do all the things you enjoy doing and you leave the duties to me."

"I suppose I'll have to forego the cinema this afternoon," said Natalie reluctantly. "I'll take the bloody hearse. Which one is it?"

"The second on the left in the garage. The keys are in the ignition and she's well tanked-up."

Natalie got into the hearse, turned the ignition on and revved up the engine. She ground the gears as she exited from the garage and drove towards the gate, leading to the street. The hearse screeched to a halt.

"Easy, now, easy, this is a hearse, not a racing car," said Elliott.

Natalie leaned out of the window and looked over her shoulder, slowly and deliberately, as if to suggest that the business she was running was no more than a sick joke.

"*Wha-fiddle-de-dee and great balls of fire*, you astonish me," she said, mimicking a Southern Belle's accent. "Until now, I could have sworn it couldn't be anything but!"

"You can be quite comical when you want to be," said Elliott.

"Aren't you going to open the gate? I can't bomb this thing over to Dulwich if you don't open it."

He looked at her, his face angry and stern but admiring.

"One doesn't *bomb* hearses anywhere, Natalie; one drives them with fucking reverence!"

"Don't swear, dear, it's common."

* * *

There was an unexpected hold-up in traffic travelling to Natalie's destination. She was about fifteen miles away from Dulwich Village. About four vehicles had stopped at a zebra crossing in front of her. A man she didn't see was walking on the pavement near the crossing, waving a half-empty bottle of whisky in the air and shouting about nothing in particular. He was approximately thirty years old, six foot tall and wore tinted glasses. He had thick, jet black hair, cut fairly short and was wearing a navy blue coat over a blue denim suit. He had already tried to open the passenger's doors of two cars but both the doors were locked.

Natalie couldn't see what was going on. All she could hear was a lot of shouting. She got out of the hearse briefly and then got back in. She took out a paperback book of Edgar Allan Poe's poems from the locker under the dashboard. The book fell open at *Ulalume*. This was her favourite poem, and she liked to read it to herself whenever she was agitated or flustered. Suddenly, she was startled by a stranger reading over her shoulder.

"A bit dour," the stranger said and removed his tinted glasses. His eyes were brown, melancholic and bloodshot. He was waving his half empty bottle of whisky in the air as he spoke. He had a strong southern Irish accent.

"Who are you and what the dickens do you think you're doing in here?" asked Natalie angrily.

"Can you take me to the nearest pub?" replied the man and Natalie feared that he would become violent if she didn't do what he wanted.

"If there is one on my route, I will drop you off there.

Your methods of getting people to do what you want are most unorthodox."

"It's the only way I can get what I want," said the man.

"In your case, I have no doubt that it is."

The first of many silences ensued. Natalie looked at the man closely and his appearance pleased her. She smiled at him. He drank some more whisky and passed the bottle to her.

"Want some?"

"I'm behind the wheel. You really are a walking proverbial dickhead."

"I've had all I want. More than I need."

"That is obvious," replied Natalie coldly. She seized the bottle from his hand and threw it out of the window. The man laughed inappropriately and went on laughing for about five minutes. His was not the laughter of a happy man.

"Why are you so sad?" asked Natalie.

"I'm very happy!" the man shouted aggressively and banged his fist on the dashboard. "I've got nothing to be sad about."

"You're lying but your sadness is not unattractive."

"Christ, you're pompous!"

"People who drive hearses *have* to be pompous, otherwise they go bust." The man looked over his right shoulder.

"Is this a hearse?" he asked, taken by surprise.

"No, it's a plane. A damned silly question gets a damned silly answer."

There was another silence. The man looked at Natalie and Natalie looked at the man.

"Natalie Klein's my name. Natalie Hester Klein, to be precise. What's your name?"

"Seamus Murphy. Just call me 'Murphy'."

"You're Irish aren't you? I can tell by your accent. It's rather pretty."

Murphy banged his fist on the dashboard a second time.

"So what!" he shouted aggressively.

"Nothing. I was just saying you've got a pretty accent."

Murphy shouted once more. "It's an accent that has kept me out of work for six years. After two, I stopped trying. I was sacked for poor timekeeping. I went to a lot of shops, but no one would sell me an alarm clock, because of what you call my pretty accent!"

Natalie began to giggle uncontrollably and turned her head away from Murphy. Murphy felt slighted by her reaction. He raised his voice in anger, yet again.

"Beneath what you see, I do have some pride left. Now that I've sunk so low, I can't sink any lower. Hence, on having nothing, I fear nothing. In that way, you are weak and I am strong. Will you give me some money?"

Natalie had never met anyone like Murphy before. She gave him a ten pound note.

"Thank you. All my family are dead but I still have a sister."

"What's your sister's name?"

"Dolores. She's older than me."

"Do you get on with her?"

"Sometimes, I do. Other times, I don't, although she's dead loyal."

There was a pause, which was broken by Natalie.

"Have you got any hobbies?" she asked.

"Reading, drinking, poker and fishing," said Murphy abruptly.

"In the first two, we are on mutual ground." Then suddenly, she asked, "Do you like Edgar Allan Poe?" in a tone of voice, suggesting that the American poet were sacred to her in some way.

"No, he is absurd, pointless," said Murphy in a flattened tone of voice.

There was another pause, which was broken by Murphy this time. "You're much more frightened of me than you were earlier, aren't you?" he said. His power to observe the frailties of others was reptilian and she read mockery in his voice.

"I am frightened of nothing and no one. I asked you if you liked Edgar Allan Poe," repeated Natalie aggressively.

"I've told you already. He is absurd, pointless."

"You're mad. How can you say such a thing?"

"All books and poems that have ever been written are about life and life is pointless. I spend my time doing the things that ordinary people enjoy doing most, reading, drinking, poker and fishing, as I said earlier. What are those things? Just escapism." said Murphy.

"You're a dismal blighter, aren't you, Murphy?" said Natalie, adding, "I like the first two things you mentioned but I don't care for fishing rods. I never have done."

"Why?"

"Because, when I was four years old, my mother took me for a walk in Hyde Park. We went to the edge of the Serpentine. I suddenly saw a man with a fish hook in his eye. My mother put her hands over my eyes. She was afraid I would see what had happened. I haven't forgotten the incident, though. I never want to see a fishing rod again, or pick one up, either."

"That's not a very interesting story. It's a boring story," commented Murphy. He sat in silence with his head in his hands.

Natalie didn't know whether to pity him or to find his melancholia attractive. She also feared him although she had denied this.

"You're a nice person underneath all this crap," he said and smiled. His was a very charming smile.

Natalie took out her mobile phone and asked Elliott to send another hearse to Dulwich Village. She said she had had a puncture. She put her foot on the clutch, extended her hand and seduced Murphy.

"Change gear!" she shouted. She sounded like a sergeant-major addressing a lance-corporal who had been late for parade.

"What?"

"Change gear, man! How many pairs of hands do you think I've got?"

"You're a peculiar woman," said Murphy.

"I'm moving into a side street. The indicator is on the left of the wheel. Push it down."

She turned left, put her foot on the clutch and the brake and brought the hearse to a halt. She put the hand brake on. Then she moved over to the passenger's seat and sat on Murphy's knee. She kissed him on the mouth, violently but with no apparent emotion. She scrambled off his knee and got out of the hearse.

"We will have to go in the back. There are blinds in the back. Get out of the hearse," she said. She had put on this commanding act to hide her fear of him which was growing.

Murphy said nothing and did nothing. "When I say, Get out of the hearse, that means, get out of the hearse. Out of the bloody hearse, man," said Natalie.

"To be sure, you invite men to despise you," remarked Murphy. Natalie was shocked and humiliated. "Bollocks!" she eventually managed to mutter.

Murphy got out of the hearse mechanically, his mind befuddled by drink, bewilderment, depression and desire. He stared at the ground.

There was a standard joke in the Klein family, about a General who had befriended a great-aunt of Natalie's. His method of getting others to do things for him was to bark staccato orders with disarming repetition, sounding like a machine-gun. He liked Worcester sauce. If the Worcester sauce was not on the table, he barked at his butler, "The Worcester, the Worcester, the Worcester, the Worcester… "

"Why are you smiling, Natalie?" asked Murphy.

"Clothes off, clothes off, clothes off, clothes off!"

"You've got a very peremptory manner."

"I'm a peremptory person. I am accustomed to saying, 'do this' and it is done."

Murphy took his clothes off and threw them onto the ground. Natalie produced a large bottle of water.

"You laundered?" she asked curtly.

"What do you mean – am I laundered?"

"Have you got any venereal disease, you slow-witted fool?"

"No," said Murphy flatly. He was too depressed to get aggressive and was strangely fascinated by Natalie's manner.

"Wash yourself first, please," she said and, because he felt so gloomy, he did so without argument.

"All right. You can get into the back of the hearse now. The hatch is open. I'll take the bier pins out, so that they won't dig into you. Lie on your back."

Although Natalie had taken the bier pins out, the rollers dug into Murphy. He was unable to complete the sex act.

She ran her fingers through his hair. This was her first gesture of affection towards him. He smiled and she returned his smile. She began to recite:

"Come up through the lair of the Lion,
With love in her luminous eyes.'"

"Fine words, those. Are they yours?"

"Aye, to be sure they are, b'fockin' Gorrah!" said Natalie, adding, "There's a motel near here. It will be a lot more comfortable than the hearse."

Murphy grabbed her by the hair.

"You'll be getting what you asked for. I'll teach you not to mimic my humble Paddy's accent."

"No! No! No!" shouted Natalie. "It's awfully sordid to talk about Ireland, just after sexual intercourse."

They found a motel nearby. This time, the sex act was more satisfactory. Murphy was profoundly unhappy afterwards, however. He stood by the bed, his eyes on the floor, looking as if he were about to mount the steps of a scaffold.

Natalie went into the bathroom and showered herself.

"To be sure, I admire your cleanliness," said Murphy.

"Get dressed, Murphy. Then get into the hearse. I'll give you a lift home."

There was a long silence which was broken by Natalie.

"You've proved yourself to be a damned good man about the hearse," she said in a stilted tone of voice, "so I wish to see you again."

Murphy failed to reply.

"Where do you live, Murphy?"

"Top floor flat, 307 Albany Road, Camberwell."

"I wish to see you in your flat on Mondays, Wednesdays and Fridays, at quarter past two. I will pay you fifty pounds every time."

"What's wrong with Tuesdays and Thursdays?"

"Those are the days I go to the cinema on."

"Can you pay me in cash?" asked Murphy.

"Yes. You'll be earning fifty pounds per session, as I said. That amounts to a hundred and fifty pounds a week, as well as your dole money."

"I don't understand why you are making this arrangement with me," said Murphy.

"Must I be reduced to spelling it out?"

"Aye."

"Can't you say, 'yes'? 'Aye' sounds damned silly," said Natalie.

"I meant, yes."

"I need what you've got to offer," said Natalie vulgarly.

"I've got nothing to offer you, except for a nihilistic view of the meaninglessness of things and the misery and uselessness of life."

"The state of your mind does not concern me," said Natalie. "I'm not interested in what you think or how you think. I am referring to the work you did for me this afternoon. Your services were satisfactory."

30

"You sound like some fockin' old colonel. Do you mean you want me to be your whore?"

"Dead people have travelled in the back of this vehicle, Murphy. In pomp. In style. In reverence. Kindly don't use language like that in here."

"I don't understand you at all. You're a raving lunatic," said Murphy.

"You're probably right but fortunately, I know I am. We've reached Camberwell. I'm going to have to bung you out now. I've got to deliver this vehicle in a spirit of dignity. Buck up. Out you get!"

"You will come to my flat next Monday at quarter past two, won't you?"

"What I say I'm going to do, I do," said Natalie assertively.

They parted company. Murphy went for a walk. He bought a can of beer from an off-licence and sucked it greedily through the hole until it was empty up. Then he wandered up Denmark Hill and noticed the offices of *Klein and Elliott*. He saw a hearse in the street with *Klein and Elliott* painted on it in gold letters, like the hearse which Natalie had been driving.

* * *

When Natalie kept her appointment and arrived at Murphy's flat the following Monday, she had driven her own car, a silver Ford Focus. Murphy told her what he had seen. "'*Klein and Elliott*' is the same firm that buried my parents," he said, adding, "Charlie Elliott is an old friend of mine."

Natalie was alarmed. There was no lift where Murphy lived. She was out of breath by the time she reached his flat. The bannisters were loose and came away in her hands as she mounted the stairs. Alcoholics, meths drinkers and junkies were sitting on the stairs, huddled in groups. The walls were covered with graffiti. There was an overpowering smell of human waste about the place.

The door leading to Murphy's flat was open. Natalie went straight in.

Murphy's room was extremely tidy. Antique-looking books had accumulated in neat piles on the floor. There was a shortage of bookshelves. Natalie was puzzled when she noticed that some titles of the books were in German. Murphy was in bed, reading a book about the philosophy of Nietzsche which was also in German.

"Do you really read German, or is this just an affectation?" she asked.

"I may be Irish but that doesn't make me uneducated. Yes, I do read German," said Murphy defensively.

"Well, I'm not Irish and I don't read German, or speak the language either. The only German I know is, '*Churchill ist ein Arschloch**', which Hitler used to say from time to time."

Murphy laughed. It was a strange, tortured laugh but a laugh nevertheless.

"You're the only person I know who keeps promises," he said.

"Then you must keep peculiar company."

"Are you going to get into bed with me?" he asked.

"Yes," said Natalie, in a stilted tone of voice, adding, "Here's fifty pounds, in cash. Keep it rough but don't knock me about."

"You don't have much respect for men, do you?" said Murphy, after the sex act.

"Apart from the man with whom I live, my father, my brother and my nephew, no."

"I'm going to the bathroom for a few minutes," Murphy said urgently.

"Buck up, then. I'm due to see a film in Leicester Square which starts at half past four. I don't want to miss the beginning of the film. There's still time for another quick fuck," said Natalie coarsely.

---

*   *Arschloch:* This vulgar word is self-explanatory

"You said you went to the cinema on Tuesdays and Thursdays. Today's Monday," said Murphy.

"I'm altering my routine a bit."

"What are you going to see?"

"*The Texas Chainsaw Massacre.*"

"I've never heard of it. Is W. C. Fields in it?"

"No, he isn't. Hurry up and do whatever you've got to do in the bathroom."

Murphy spent about ten minutes in the bathroom. Then he went back to bed and had sex with Natalie a second time.

"May I use your bathroom, please?" she asked.

Murphy had hysterics. "I don't want anyone going in there!" The violence in his voice startled her.

"Why?" she asked in an off putting manner.

"It's not very nice in there! Don't ask me any more questions."

"Very well then, I must be off."

"I think I love you," he said in a frail tone of voice, as Natalie was about to leave his flat.

"Why?"

"Because I like to be treated as a tramp and addressed by my surname. Also you don't make any emotional demands on me. I'm no more than a worthless parasite."

Natalie looked at her watch. She had plenty of time to get to Leicester Square.

"Come, come, my good man, you underestimate yourself," she said patronizingly.

"I can only take. I have never given anything to anyone in my life. That is why I hope you will never love me in return," said Murphy.

"You're a bloody good fuck but nothing will cause me to love you."

"Do you dislike me?" asked Murphy.

"I neither like you nor dislike you. You do what I want the way I want it done, so I'm not indifferent to you," said Natalie.

"You put on this cold act to hide your fear of me, and you deliberately frighten others to hide the fact that you're afraid of them as well." said Murphy, with sudden hostility in his voice. The remark jolted Natalie, but she did not take it seriously enough to brood about it.

"I've got to get on now, Murphy. I'll be back in two days' time," she said. For a reason, which she couldn't understand, she felt distressed and disturbed when she was with Murphy.

She arrived at the cinema just in time to see *The Texas Chainsaw Massacre.** Its grisly contents cheered her far more than the events of that afternoon. That evening, Elliott took her out to dinner, having asked her where she had been, before she had gone to the cinema.

* * *

For three weeks, Natalie's arrangement with Murphy worked out satisfactorily. She continued to be pleased with his services and had now become virtually dependent on them, even though she felt profoundly distressed after each session. When he failed to answer his door bell one day, she was shocked, because she realized that she had fallen in love with him. The heavy, two-inch thich door was unlatched, however. She threw her weight against it. Murphy was asleep with his book about Nietzsche's philosophy open in his hand.

"I'm not surprised it sent you to sleep!" said Natalie, her mouth an inch away from his ear. He turned over but still did not wake up. She noticed a large empty space, where bricks in the wall above his head had been. In the space, wrapped in polythene, was something which she thought was washing powder at first. It was heroin. Natalie was irritated because Murphy had been

---

*   The Texas Chainsaw Massacre. A macabre film encompassing, grave rohhing, necrophilia, cannibalisim, murder and kidnapping.

34

asleep when she had arrived. She remembered his vehement request that she was not to go into the bathroom.

"Wake up, you idle bugger! I'm going into your bathroom now!" she shouted.

She went in. The bathroom consisted of a bath, with chipped enamel in it, a dusty wash basin and a lavatory. There was a toothbrush in a dirty glass, some toothpaste, some soap and a razor. Lying across the drain in the wash basin was a small syringe, half full of blood.

Some white powder had been spilled onto the floor. Natalie told herself it was Vim. She knelt down and tasted it. The taste was unfamiliar but she had some idea what it was and how thriftily it had been saved up with the regular income of its slave. She deliberately broke the glass in which Murphy kept his toothbrush and toothpaste. She crushed the glass on the floor with her foot, and crushed it again with her hand. The pain of the broken glass in the palm of her hand made her less aware of her tears.

Murphy had started to sneeze and sweat. He staggered into the bathroom in a semi-stupor, unaware of the time. He knew that he needed another heroin injection.

"What's the matter?" he asked, in a frail tone of voice, which was deceptively gentle. "You can tell me. I won't tell anyone."

Natalie composed herself.

"I won't be coming back any more, Murphy," she said in a steady, unfaltering tone of voice, "I've found out that you use heroin and I don't want to watch you dying."

* * *

Murphy held his stomach to lessen his cramps. He tried to stand up straight, as he watched Natalie removing all his heroin from the space in the brick wall, and putting it into a carrier bag. She rushed downstairs, carrying the bag.

Murphy ran after her in a fit of rage. His need for the drug and his knowledge that she had robbed him, gave him enough strength to beat her up, if necessary.

"Hey, stop, will you, you fockin' bitch! I need that!" He heard the door of his flat slamming behind him, and realized that he would not be able to get back into his dingy rooms. His fury reached a climax, and as he lumbered down the stairs, he fell and sprained his ankle. This caused him so much pain that the cramps in his stomach appeared minimal in comparison.

Natalie had almost reached the ground floor of the building. Her path had been temporarily blocked by the dossers, who were swaying backwards and forwards, singing a tuneless old song:

> *"I don't want to join the Army. I don't want to go to war.*
> *I'd rather hang around Piccadilly Underground,*
> *Living on the earnings of a wh...'*
> *Oops – igh born lady."*

"Watch it, Tom," said one of the dossers, the only one who wasn't singing, "It's 'er that goes up there."

He and the others divided like the Red Sea to make a path for Natalie.

* * *

Traffic conditions had caused Natalie to take longer than usual to get home. It was about three thirty. She felt ill and disgusted and was about to enter the house, go upstairs and lie down. She heard two male voices in the front office. She listened to their conversation from the street, before she unlocked the door.

"I know it's not the first time I've asked you, but I've got to have some money," said a voice with a familiar Irish accent. It was Murphy's voice.

"You've had two hundred pounds from me recently," shouted Elliott, "I'm not giving you any more."

"Then use the firm's funds! I've got to have the stuff."

"You should never have got onto it in the first place. My partner watches the accounts like a hawk. The answer is "no". She'll find out and I know better than to cross a woman's path. It's no good your kneeling down, licking my hands. I'm not giving you anything. Go to hospital and come off the stuff."

Natalie unlocked the door to the front office.

"Why didn't you tell me you'd given two hundred pounds to this man, and why is he licking your hands?" she asked.

"I… well, he and I have an agreement," said Elliott nervously.

"An agreement to do what?"

"I've never been educated properly and he's known me for some time. He helps me with my English," said Elliott.

"Your English? What are you talking about? You *are* English."

"He has often taught me things about Shakespeare," said Elliott defensively.

"I find that an odd reason for him to be licking your hands. Are you batting for the other side?"

"If that's what you imply, I'll bugger off now. This man is a junky. He is also an old friend of mine. I've tried to persuade him to go to hospital and withdraw from heroin but he won't go, so I've been giving him my own money. His name's Seamus Murphy."

"I know. I've met him before."

"Oh? Where was that?"

"He was hitchhiking once and I gave him a lift," said Natalie, adding cautiously, "He asked me for money so I gave him ten pounds."

"Did you know at the time that he was a heroin addict?" asked Elliott.

"No, but I knew there was something very odd about him," replied Natalie mildly.

She had to shout because Murphy was lying on the floor in the front office, screaming. Natalie showed no outward emotion, about the horrible spectacle of degradation before her eyes and kept her private grief to herself. She was terrified of Murphy telling Elliott about their affair, because she suspected that he would leave her.

* * *

Johnny Rucelli, a thirty-five year old, husky-voiced New Yorker of Italian descent, was banging frantically on the door, leading to *Klein and Elliott*'s front office. He was surprised to find it closed on a weekday. His exceptionally loud, Bronxy voice was attracting almost as much attention as Murphy's screams.

"Don't waste any time," said Natalie, adding, "Take him down to the cellar. The chains I used in my sadomasochistic days, to pay back gambling debts, are still down there. Shackle him. Keep him on whisky and *Diazepam* until his cramps wear off. It's cruel but there's no alternative, and there's a fucking man banging on the door."

"But that's sadistic! We can't! We… "

"Shut up, Charlie! Take Murphy down to the cellar and I'll softsoap the man outside."

"I won't have any part in torturing him. We ought to call an ambulance," said Elliott.

"An ambulance! An ambulance! We can't have an ambulance coming to a place like this. We'd be the laughing stock of the neighbourhood. It would mean getting the police out, as well. I'm not having some junky interfering with my trade. Take him down to the cellar. I asked you to do this earlier."

"No, I won't!" persisted Elliott.

"What? I can't hear you with all this bloody screaming going on."

"I'm not taking him down to the cellar. It's not heated down there."

"That's the last thing a junky would notice. Do you think he would be conscious of room temperatures?"

Rucelli could hear a lot of noise coming from the front office, even from the street. He hammered on the door repeatedly. In the meantime, Elliott carried Murphy out of the front office in a fireman's lift and took him downstairs.

Natalie opened the front door and greeted Rucelli with a benign, artificially understanding smile.

"Say, are you guys closed all the year round?" demanded Rucelli. "Don't people die no more in Britain?" The Italian lilt in his voice, combined with his expensively tailored clothing, gave Natalie the impression that either he or his family might have had Mafia connections, sometime in the past and that money was no object to him. She made a mental note to charge him more than the customary price, if he wanted to arrange for a funeral to take place.

"I'm so sorry you were kept waiting like that. Would you care to come in and sit down, while I check that the phone is manned," said Natalie.

Elliott realized that she was right about Murphy. "I've taken him down to the cellar," he said. "You deal with the client and don't be too abrupt with him. Remember, he's not your lover."

"Please make yourself comfortable," said Natalie graciously, "I apologize most sincerely for the delay. It must have been deeply distressing for you."

"Yeah, it was. You seem a pretty laid-back, spaced-out bunch of guys. Maybe, folk don't die so much no more in Britain, huh?" repeated Rucelli.

"I apologize once more for keeping you waiting. What can we do for you?"

Rucelli continued to raise his voice in anger.

"I guess I chose to come to London to bury Sammy, because I'm pretty wound up right now, about da goddam American way of death. There's only one thing worse than that and that's da goddam American way of life. I want a simple fooneral and I know the British are able to throw a downmarket, low-key, low-profile type of fooneral." Rucelli continued,

"Back home in the States, you can't back out in no style, no goddam more, without a fleet of fat flash morticians and a flash casket, carried like it was some lousy bag of groceries.

"Sammy had heart trouble and knew that he was gonna die, man. Just before he died, he said: "Blossom, dear, I either gotta have me a British fooneral, or else I don't get buried at all.""

"Your name is Mr Blossom, sir?" said Natalie.

"Nah. That's what Sammy called me. Johnny Rucelli's my name and Sammy and me was making it just fine."

"I am sure we shall be able to do exactly as you wish, the way you want it done, Mr Rucelli," said Natalie obsequiously.

"Yeah. I chose you guys because a fella I met at some races you folks call the 'Durby', said you didn't charge as much as da other goddam parlours in this town."

"The gentleman was indeed right, sir. We try to exploit sorrow as little as we can. Our consciences force us to charge less than our rivals and to keep things nice and simple," said Natalie, who was struggling to keep a straight face. Her nerves were shattered.

"My Sammy wanted a simple job, so I guess I came to da right tomfool joint."

"You have indeed, sir. We believe in religious values, not in profits, but we do insist on our clients paying in cash. It is not that we doubt your honesty. It's just our rule."

40

"I guess that's fine by me, Lady. I've got a hell of a lot of dough with me, right now. Just make da job simple and dignified, huh?"

Natalie gave Rucelli a charming smile.

"Your wish is our command, sir. We charge four thousand pounds, inclusive of VAT for the simple burial you ask for. Other mercenary firms, such as *Crumblebottom and Bongwit*, up the road, charge far more, because to them, profits come before people."

Klein and Elliott's standard overall price for a simple burial was three thousand pounds, inclusive of VAT. *Crumblebottom and Bongwit's* was two thousand, five hundred pounds, inclusive of VAT.

"Sounds fine by me," repeated Rucelli. He handed Natalie a bundle of fifty pound notes, which he took from a monogrammed, crocodile hide wallet. He had given her ten thousand pounds without his knowledge.

"With respect, sir, I must ask you to let me count your payment, just to make quite sure you haven't overpaid me. I didn't see you counting your money. I wouldn't want you to be dealt with dishonourably," said Natalie, with her tongue pressing against her cheek.

Natalie counted the money and kept the ten thousand pounds which Rucelli had given her. She was aware of the fact that she had taken a vast sum of money from him on false pretences.

"You haven't overpaid me, sir," she said. "You have given me exactly four thousand pounds. Now, forgive me for intruding on the more painful side – your Sammy, would you mind telling me how tall he was?"

"Four foot three inches."

"A child – your son? How very tragic for you, sir!"

"Nah. A goddam dwarf. Him and me was hittin' it off real cool. I met him at a gay joint patronized by freaks in L.A. and

I guess it was love at first sight. Pa'd already made his roll in prohibition and he passed all his dough on to me, so I gave Sammy a home. We lived together till he died."

"I am truly very sorry, sir," said Natalie. "Have you got any particular preferences, any special floral formations, any personal touches?"

"May I see your casket catalogue?" asked Rucelli.

Natalie nearly laughed out loud but controlled herself. "Certainly, Mr Rucelli", she replied. "Here are our patterns. The section at the back of the catalogue relates to loved ones shorter in stature."

The items listed in the catalogue varied from the very conventional to the ridiculous. Rucelli chose a coffin with a *Vuitton* cover.

"I will see to it that your Sammy is buried in a coffin with a *Vuitton* cover, sir. Would you kindly excuse me for a moment," said Natalie.

"Yeah, I got all day, now that I've found da right guys." Rucelli sat with his arms folded, chewing gum. When the gum got stale, he spat it out and slapped it under his chair.

Natalie went down to the cellar to tell Elliott to shut Murphy up. His withdrawal symptoms were at their worst and he clawed at Elliott, when he gave him glasses of whisky, mixed with *Diazepam*.

"Undo the fockin' chains!"

"No! She's the captain of this ship and I must do what she tells me to do."

"Captain of this ship? Captain of this ship?"

"Tell Murphy to shut the fuck up!" shouted Natalie.

Murphy swore and continued to swear, until he reached an orgasm of pain and rage.

Natalie came upstairs to the front office and joined Rucelli. The American had witnessed many revolting murders, even as a boy, during his father's Mafia days and was fairly unruffled by what he had overheard, although he found the commotion irritating.

"Say, lady, wouldja mind tellin' me, – what the hell's all that shoutin'?"

"Shouting?"

"Yeah, I can hear two fellas downstairs, screamin' and shoutin', like they was bustin' each other to pieces, man. What's da big idea, huh?"

"Oh, that. You must excuse me," said Natalie. "I'm most embarrassed and I can't apologize enough. My nephew's mother won't allow him to watch television at home, so he comes over here to pester me in the afternoons. He's watching a video downstairs. I've told him to lower the volume but he keeps turning it up".

"What sort of movies does your nephew like watchin', for Christ's sake? Snuff movies?"

"What sort of bitch is the captain of your ship?" screamed Murphy, more loudly than before.

"My nephew's watching *Mutiny on the Bounty* at the moment. Please accept my apologies. Some tea?"

"Nah. Don't wanna abide by no British customs except da foonerals."

"I hope everything will be to your satisfaction, sir. Just one moment, please, that horrible boy has turned the volume up again."

"Take a look at him. We'll have to get him to hospital," said Elliott, when Natalie appeared in the cellar once more.

"No! Knock him on the head with something. I've got a batty American upstairs complaining about the noise. I've just taken ten thousand pounds off him. I only asked him for four thousand pounds."

"In other words, you've swindled him."

"Not in other words; those are the perfect ones, Charlie! I was raised on the work ethic. I wouldn't have any self-respect if I wasn't a good capitalist. The American upstairs is absolutely bonkers. He wants us to do a four-foot three-inch dwarf in a *Vuitton*."

"A *Vuitton*?" exclaimed Elliott.

"Yes, a bloody *Vuitton!*"

"We've got one *Vuitton* left and I've kept it as a relic. It's only four feet long, so what are we going to do about the remaining three inches?" asked Elliott.

"Cut its feet off, you dickhead! Use your head. But stop that noise, or the fruitcake in the front office will ask for his money back, and will take his custom to *Crumblebottom and Bongwit*," shouted Natalie.

"I'm so sorry abut that, sir," she said as she came back to the front office." I can assure you this won't happen next time we meet. Which hospital did your poor friend die in?"

"Da goddam London Clinic, surrounded by a bunch of good-for-nothin' Ay-rabs."

"How shocking! Is he in the mortuary there, now?"

"Sure thing, man."

"Then I will have him collected immediately. All you have to do now is leave everything else to us."

"You promise there won't be no fuckin' noise? Hell, I want this thing to be done with some goddam reverence, man!"

"I can assure you that that boy will never be coming here again. He is most selfish but there again, he is extremely deaf."

Rucelli was softened by Natalie's remark. He smiled for the first time he had met her and shook her warmly by the hand.

"Thanks a lot, lady. Sorry I got hostle."

"Indeed, you were not hostile. It gives us pleasure to take the sting out of death and to relieve what we know to be an unendurable sorrow. Here is our business card. If there's anything else you wish to discuss, please feel free to ring us up at any time of the day or night."

Natalie and Elliott waited until the American had left. She

reached out for a palmful of *Laropiprant.*[*] After about twenty minutes, the drug kicked in. She began to shout, in a manic manner about the difference between French funerals and British Funerals.

"The French haven't the faintest idea how to throw a decent funeral," she began. "French hearses are the pits. Their numberplates are invariably covered with mud. Their bier racks are unpolished. Their priests rant likr the blood Gestapo and their pallbearers are appalingly badly dressed and wear fucking baseball caps!"

"You should see how impeccably dressed British pallbearers are in comparison."

"All right, Natalie. I'm going downstairs to see how Murphy's getting on," said Elliott quietly.

* * *

It took Murphy about three weeks to get accustomed to the absence of heroin. The physical craving was replaced by his usual melancholia. Natalie refused to go near him, so he confided his misery to Elliott. He said at exhaustive length:

"As there's nothing I can do to make someone happy, I'd like to be able to make them unhappy. Every time I hurt someone, I delight in hurting myself more. By hurting myself, I am hurting the memory of my parents, who brought me into this stinking world. When others have interests and motives for living, I despise them. The only thing that fulfills me in life, is finding someone's weakness and humiliating that person."

"What you need is a doctor. I can't help you," said Elliott patiently.

---

[*] *Laropiprant:* This eurphoriant drug was available, even when Natalie was a hundred and one years old. See early part of book.

Later, Murphy asked to be shown round the house.

"So, this is your bedroom, is it?" he asked.

"That's right."

"Are you not well? You've sure have got an awful lot of medicines in here."

"None of them is mine. The bottles of pills are Natalie's."

"Is she ill?"

"No, there's nothing wrong with her. She's got a morbid, pathological fear of illness, germs, anything like that. I know how silly it may seem to you. I've had to live with it for years. She actually believes that if she doesn't take all these pills every day, she will become ill." Elliott continued, "She lives in permanent fear. She won't even go into a chemist's shop because she's so frightened of germs. She's got this chemist, a crooked chinaman, called Oscar Wong, who owns a chemist's shop, in Bayswater. He delivers a crate of vitamin pills, antibiotics and sleeping pills to this address once a week. He comes here because she pays him so generously."

The sly expression on Murphy's face baffled Elliott. When their eyes met, Murphy looked away.

"I thought she wasn't afraid of anything," he said.

"That's what I thought when I first met her," replied Elliott, "but illness is the only thing that she has an irrational and unnatural fear of. She is also afraid of being called a coward, for some reason."

"Why?"

"This all goes back to her childhood. She's got an older brother called Gomer, whom she looks up to and adores. He called her a coward once.

"She had regarded Gomer as a god and was mortified. I think her love for him was incestuous. Ever since, she has desperately tried to prove that she is not a coward. She has always been very close to Gomer, as I said. In her teens, she dressed in men's clothes, in order to emulate him."

Elliott continued, "Let's not talk about it any more. It depresses me. I don't know where she's gone but I'll buy you a drink anyway."

Murphy agreed, and within a month, he returned to his old flat in Albany Road.

Natalie wanted to forget him, but a sense of recklessness within her, prompted by her memory of his primitive technique as a lover, drove her to his flat one afternoon, when she had walked out, of a film which had bored her, after about half an hour. Her feeling of lust had overcome her vindictiveness towards Murphy for having used her.

"Hullo, may I come in?"

"I thought you were never coming back," he said.

"You thought wrongly, didn't you?"

"I want to ask a favour of you," he stated.

"What do you want?"

"Can you see this small piece of paper on the bed?"

"Yes."

"It's a prescription for some medicine. The only good chemist's shop is John Bell and Croyden's which is in Wigmore Street."

"It would be easier if I used my friendly chemist. John Bell and Croyden's is a very long way away."

"They're the only people who have the medicine I need. They're holding it until it's picked up. Won't you do this, just for me?" pleaded Murphy.

"What's the medicine called? John Bell and Croyden's is really very inconvenient."

"It's some medicine to help me to overcome the psychological effects of heroin withdrawal. Please do this, just for me," said Murphy in a pathetic tone of voice.

Natalie softened on seeing his charming smile, not knowing the extent to which he hated her, for having had him shackled in her cellar, and for having stolen his supply of heroin.

"All right, Murphy, I'll get it for you. I'm very pleased you've stopped using heroin," she said.

John Bell and Croyden's was more crowded than usual that day. All sorts of exhibits from weighing machines, weight-losing machines and skeletons stared at Natalie from the windows of the chemist's.

She tried to bribe passers-by to enter the building on her behalf, and said that she had had a row with the manager. She was dismissed as a crank by everyone she approached.

She did not know that Murphy had followed her, using the London Underground, and that he had got out at Bond Street, the closest stop to the chemist's.

He followed her into John Bell and Croyden's and watched her as she went to a counter where disinfectant was sold. She bought a bottle of Dettol and poured the foul-smelling liquid onto her hands, before covering her face with it. Murphy continued to watch her, as she looked for the prescriptions counter.

She saw an anaemic-looking man with a harrowingly loud cough, who was sitting precariously on one of the chairs used by the collectors of medicines. He looked at least seventy years old. A woman, about the same age as he, was sitting next to him. She was wiping the sweat from his forehead and had loosened his tie for him.

The man was resting his head on the back of his chair, and was holding a handkerchief in front of his mouth. When Natalie looked at him again, she saw that it was covered with blood.

"It's lucky they can cure tuberculosis with antibiotics these days, isn't it, our Pete?" said the woman sitting next to him, in a heavy Yorkshire brogue.

Natalie poured Dettol onto her hands and covered her face with it once more. She went pale and trembled all over with fear, a fear so violent, that if she had been faced with the chance of dying at that moment, she would have taken it. Murphy was standing just behind her.

"You lied to me when you said you weren't afraid of anything, didn't you?" His shouts reverberated round the chemist's. "I even believed you. You're scared of illness, aren't you? Look at you, you gutless, cowardly bitch, you're scared to death."

"I am not scared!"

"Why are your hands shaking like that? You're a bloody coward."

"You came here to torture me, when I've never wronged you," said Natalie.

"I came here to prove that I could see through you. You only work with the dead, because the dead can't turn round and tell you that you are a coward and a hypochondriac." He gripped her tightly by the arm. She slapped his face and he slapped her back. He gripped her by the arm once more.

"I am not a coward! I am not a coward!"

"Prove to me that you're not a coward, then. Go up to that man with the handkerchief, sitting over there. Go and ask him if he wants a glass of water."

"No! I'm getting out of here."

"Not so fast, daughter! You had me taken down to your cellar, where you told Charlie to chain me up, didn't you?"

The heads of the many occupants of the queue, in front of the prescriptions counter, not unlike the queues of those waiting for food in Soviet Russia, turned unanimously towards the stormy couple.

"Let me go!" Natalie bit Murphy hard on the hand. He let out a sharp scream.

"Excuse me, sir and madam, is this noise really necessary?" asked a man in a white coat, who claimed to be the manager of John Bell and Croyden's. He appeared more concerned about the noise, than about the length of the unattended queue in front of the prescriptions counter.

"I thought I told you to ask that man with the cough, if he

49

wanted a glass of water," shouted Murphy, after the manager had disappeared. Also, I'll tell Charlie about our affair if you refuse to do as I say."

Natalie scratched Murphy's face. They fought at a distance of about twenty yards from the man with the cough.

"Watch it, you bastard! You're bullying me," she shouted, adding, "Hey mister, you over there, do you want a glass of water?"

"Go up to him and ask him nicely, otherwise I'll tell Charlie about our affair, as I said."

"No! No! Help! Rape!"

The manager suddenly re-appeared. "I'm sorry, sir and madam," he said, "I must insist that you leave the premises at once. There are some very sick people in here and this kind of behaviour is totally unacceptable. If you don't both leave, I will have to call the police."

"Don't blame me," replied Murphy, "I didn't want to come here in the first place. It was her fault. She was afraid of coming here alone, because she's a hypochondriac, as well as a coward, do you hear? Also, she had me chained up in her cellar, as if I were a common masochist."

The manager cleared his throat.

"Lower your voice, sir, for mercy's sake!" he said eventually.

Natalie rushed out into the street and hailed a taxi. She was in floods of tears. The taxi driver was a Negro with gold-plated teeth and a flashy smile.

"Denmark Hill, Camberwell, please." She wound down the window, as the taxi moved away, and called to Murphy who had tried to follow her.

"You'll pay for this the hardest way you've ever paid for anything in your life, Seamus Murphy! No one hurts, insults or blackmails Natalie Klein, without being punished."

The taxi driver was pleasant and sympathetic.

"Hey, I don't mean to butt in on you, ma'am," he said, "but

people insult me each day of the week, and if I cried every time someone insulted me, the streets of London would be flooded with my tears and everybody would be swimming to work, not walking."

After hearing the taxi driver's kind words, Natalie's weeping became more intense. She gave him a handsome tip.

* * *

Elliott was typing invoices with one finger when Natalie stormed into the front office.

"Hand over the typewriter and two sheets of paper. This is an emergency."

Elliott was as kind and as good-natured as he always was. He noticed her tear-stained face and did as he was asked to do.

"What's the matter, Natalie?"

"I can't say. I'll tell you one day but not now. I'm taking the typewriter and paper upstairs."

It took Natalie two hours to destroy Murphy's soul. Her letter to him was three hundred words long. Its tone was vitriolic, vicious and deadly but redeemingly articulate. Her gift for the written word, turned what might have been a string of fishwife's abuse, into a scholarly missile of death.

When either Natalie or someone dear to her had been shabbily treated or slighted, she pursued the guilty party with obsessive and inveterate hatred. Her punishment was one stage more severe than the act which had provoked her.

"An eye for a tooth and a limb for an eye" was her motto. No form of persuasion, however logical or reasonable, could intercept her missiles, or prevent her from launching an additional fleet of missiles in their wake, regardless of the subsequent psychological state of her target. Only when her victim grovelled at her feet, would she relent and bring her vicious vendetta to a standstill.

The words, 'I will write them a letter' were not infrequently on her lips. Her letters to 'offenders' were legion and their tone, varying from moderate criticism to cruelty, was dependent on the severity of the slight caused to her. When she wished to injure someone, she preferred ink to the spoken word. She had the power to turn ink into cyanide.

When she had finished writing her letter to Murphy, she noticed that she had torn shreds of skin from her fingers. After she had sealed the letter, she felt as if a heavy weight had been lifted from her.

"What have you done to your fingers, Natalie?" asked Elliott sympathetically.

"Bind them, Charlie."

"What have you done to your fingers?" he repeated.

"I've just said, bind them. Murphy insulted me. I don't want him in here again."

The phone rang after Natalie had posted the letter. She answered it.

"I rang to say how sorry I am I hurt you," said Murphy. "I didn't mean to hurt you. I wanted to hurt myself, because I'm a mean little man with no respect for people who've got something to live for."

Natalie opened her mouth on instructions from her heart, to explain the contents of her letter and to tell Murphy not to open it, but her tongue rebelled like a militant picket. She hung up.

For two days, her guilt about the crushing wording of her letter to Murphy, conflicted with her recurrent fury about his behaviour in John Bell and Croyden's. She appreciated his decency to apologize but was unable to forgive him.

Part of her wanted to reconcile with him, but the greater part of her felt that no words could undo the humiliation that she had had to suffer in a public place. She had been called a coward and that was unforgivable. She tried to feel compassionately towards

Murphy. Every time she did so, her compassion was drowned by a surge of hatred.

Elliott sensed her distress. Eventually, she told him about the incident in John Bell and Croyden's, leaving out Murphy's threat to blackmail her. Elliott offered to take her to a Russian restaurant in the west end of London, where Russian folk songs were played and sung. Natalie loved Russian folk songs.

The restaurant was crowded. A woman with a loud, clear voice was singing a well-known Russian folk song called "Katyooshka". Her colleague was playing a balalaika. Natalie clapped happily in time to the music, which started slowly and gradually gathered speed.

Elliott was bored. He disliked the song but Natalie was excited and elated. She continued to clap in time to the singing and laughed with joy.

"Excuse me, madam," said the head waiter who was carrying a silver saucer with a telegram on it.

"I ordered another double gin and tonic. Is it coming?" asked Natalie.

"Is your name Miss Natalie Klein?" asked the head waiter.

"Yes. What's the matter?"

"This arrived five minutes ago. Someone working for you delivered it here."

"How strange! Will you please bring me a double gin and tonic. I've ordered it already."

"Very good, madam." Natalie read the telegram and turned white.

"What's the wrong? You're not clapping any more," remarked Elliott. He had not noticed the delivery of the telegram, nor had he seen her opening it.

Natalie rose to her feet. The telegram fell from her hand. She fainted. When Elliott bent over to see whether she was breathing, he found the telegram on the floor. It was verbose and uncommonly long for a telegram. It read:

"I LAMENT THE DEATH OF MY POOR BROTHER, SEAMUS MURPHY, WHO WAS KILLED, DRIVING A CAR INTO A TREE. HE DIED WITH A POISONOUS LETTER IN HIS HAND. IT WAS WRITTEN BY YOU.

"PLEASE GOD, HIS VICIOUS MURDER SHALL NOT GO UNAVENGED AND AS HIS SISTER, I SHALL PURSUE HIS MURDERESS UNTIL SHE IS LAID IN EARTH.

"FROM DOLORES MURPHY, EVER-LOVING SISTER OF A MOST EXCEPTIONAL AND BELOVED BROTHER.'"

Elliott glanced at the telegram and wondered whether Natalie had been sleeping with Murphy. The manager of the restaurant came over to their table.

"Do you need an ambulance, sir?"

"No," replied Elliott, "I'll take her home. She's had a shock."

That night, he kept Natalie sedated on a higher dose of her usual sedatives. His kindness gave her strength. She forced herself to work the following morning.

She sat in her office, calmed by some blue pills, which she referred to as her "comforting blue boys". They were in fact *Diazepam* and they were ten milligrams each. Elliott banged about in the basement, working on coffins.

"You're prettier than I thought you'd be, daughter." The voice was low-pitched with a southern Irish accent. "My name is Dolores Murphy."

The sepulchral huskiness of Dolores's voice made Natalie shudder. Her southern Irish accent was more pronounced than Murphy's. She was about forty years old but looked much older. Her face was sunken, like a skull's.

She was exceptionally thin and was dressed from head to foot in black lace. Her head and shoulders were covered by a matching black shawl. Natalie was struck by the fact that she had one front tooth. This, combined with a pair of small, piercing black eyes, which blazed from hollow sockets in an emaciated face, made her appearance terrifying.

Natalie bent over and took a swig of gin from a bottle on the floor by her feet. She wiped her mouth with the back of her hand and sat up to face her visitor.

"What can I do for you, madam?"

The older woman tapped the floor with her walking stick three times. "My name is Dolores Murphy, as I said. I am the sister of the late Seamus Murphy. My brother's body is in the mortuary at King's College Hospital. I wish your firm to bury his remains."

Natalie took a deep breath, and put her hands under her desk so that Dolores wouldn't see how much they were shaking.

"My name is Natalie Klein. I received your telegram. I am at a loss for words, as I have none to offer. Anger is a natural emotion to have when a person is bereaved, and even if death is caused by an accident, it is equally normal to feel the need to blame someone for it."

Dolores tapped her walking stick on the floor once more.

"You talk far too much, more than becomes you, daughter."

"Perhaps I do, but I can and must assure you that in absolutely *no* circumstances did I kill your brother," said Natalie.

Dolores got up and leaned over the desk. She was taller than Natalie and therefore more frightening. Natalie was struck by her foul breath. Dolores gripped her by the arm and did not allow her eyes to wander from her face.

"I have earned my living as a fortune-teller. I work in fairgrounds," she said, adding, "I earn very little but enough to survive. A curse has been put on you. You will never know lasting happiness for as long as you live."

Dolores paused for breath. She continued, "The day will come in a few years' time, when you will think that you have found it, but it will not last. I've already seen to that." Dolores continued, at interminable length.

"You will meet a powerful man and you will become a close friend of his and his wife's. He is very famous. That man will not know anything about you when he meets you. He will treat you like a daughter, because he will not know what you are. One day he may find out. Your fear of him finding out will torture you."

"What am I?" asked Natalie.

"Even you do not have that knowledge, yet but you will know before the day is out. The man of whom I speak, is a man who will never fully understand what you are, because that which is sick is alien to him.

"When what must be known is known by all, the man of whom I speak, will have made you proud to be his friend, so you will live in fear that even he may have to be told."

Arthur Sprout, one of the pallbearers, suddenly came into Natalie's office.

"Arthur, would you please listen to the end of this women's speech," said Natalie. She was scared stiff and rushed upstairs to the bedroom which she shared with Elliott.

To her horror, her comical words failed to humiliate her visitor. Dolores followed her upstairs and continued her tirade.

"Even he may have to be told," she repeated.

"Told what?" asked Natalie.

"What you are. Once you have got to know this man, you will live in fear that he may have access to such knowledge one day," repeated Dolores.

"Who the hell are you talking about, Miss Murphy? Also, when you speak, kindly be more concise, less verbose and less repetitive."

"When you meet him, it is unlikely that you will remember the day I first met you, or what I said either," said Dolores.

Natalie was superstitious. She went back to her office and hid her shaking hands under her desk once more.

"How do you know all this?" she asked.

The cadaverous face peered into her own.

"Some of your actions will be evil. Others will only be foolish. That is part of my curse on you, and you will not know the folly of your actions, until after you have committed them. You have crossed my path and you shall live in hell on earth. Do not think I predict fortunes with the palms of hands. I predict them with faces and your soul is damned."

"Excuse me, madam, this calls for Mr Elliott's attention," said Natalie.

"Mr Elliott is known to me. He cannot save you."

"Good morning, Miss Murphy," said Elliott, on entering Natalie's office. "I understand how painful it is to have lost a brother. I'm willing to take care of Seamus's burial free of charge, but I will not tolerate your frightening and intimidating Miss Klein." Dolores ignored him.

"Will you pick my brother's body up, yourself? He was your friend, was he not? His body is in the mortuary at King's College Hospital, as I told Miss Klein," she said.

Elliott loosened his collar. He was unnerved by Dolores's manner but not as severely as Natalie was.

"Of course, I will pick his body up. I'll do so straight away. You stay here with Miss Klein."

For two hours that seemed like several days, Natalie stayed in her office alone with Dolores. A maid came into the office when she heard the bell ring.

"You rang, madam?"

"Yes. Would you please bring us some tea."

The servant made a gesture, imitating the opening of a bottle and the emptying of its contents. Natalie nodded at her and raised one hand above her head, keeping the other hand at waistlevel, as if stretching an accordion. This was a signal that she did not simply want the tea to be drugged. She wanted it to be loaded enough to stupefy its drinker. Natalie was immune to the effects of tranquillizers, unless she took them in heavy doses, but her unwelcome guest was not.

"Will you pour the tea out, please? I'd like you to stay in my office with us," said Natalie.

"Very good, madam."

Natalie continued to hide her shaking hands. She drank three cups of the foul-tasting drugged tea. She was still fully alert ten minutes later. Dolores drank half a cup and became drowsy within a few minutes.

The powerful narcotic eventually worked on Natalie, if only very mildly. Her face clouded over with a serene, beatific smile.

The two women stared at each other, while the maid looked at them in bewilderment, wondering who was going to pass out first. Neither did. The mutual resentment had vanished, to some extent, from their faces but the loathing which they felt for each other was still alive.

"We have brought your brother to our Chapel of Rest, Miss Murphy," said Elliot formally, on entering Natalie's office once more. He had just returned after a heated argument with Douglas Buster, a half-witted mortuary attendant at King's College Hospital.

Buster had exaggerated his act of being irritatingly slow-witted, as Elliott forced himself to keep his temper with him. Buster stated that he would not allow Klein and Elliott to have anything to do with him anymore. Natalie had once slapped him in front of one of his colleagues, because he had spelt the name on a label on someone's toe incorrectly.

Elliott had told Buster that Natalie no longer worked at Klein and Elliott's.

"How is my brother got out?" Dolores asked Elliott abruptly.

"He is dressed in a dark suit and a collar and tie."

"Is he now?"

"Thank you' is the word I think you are groping for," said Natalie.

"Please forgive Miss Klein. She is not herself today," said Elliott.

"She's herself every inch of the way. You're in bad hands and will come to a bad end, if she stays with you."

58

"Your remark is out of order!" shouted Elliott.

"If you say so. What about my brother's physical state? Are his injuries bad to look at?"

"The injuries which caused his death were internal. The immediate cause was a blow to the head but his face is entirely intact," said Elliott, adding, "Please don't think that either of us is insensitive to your suffering, because neither of us is. I will take you to the Chapel of Rest and you will be able to see your brother there."

"Thank you, Mr Elliott. It is Natalie Klein who will suffer, not you."

"That was quite unnecessary, Miss Murphy."

Behind the closed door of the Chapel of Rest, next door to the front office, Dolores knelt in front of her brother's body and prayed, holding up a gold crucifix which she had been wearing round her neck.

After Elliott had taken Dolores to the Chapel of Rest, he went back to the front office where Natalie was waiting.

"That woman's scaring me to death, Charlie. How does Murphy look?" she asked.

"His face is statuesque. An artist might say that it was beautiful."

"Indeed? Perhaps it would be respectful for me to see him. I ought to. After all, it would seem to me to be the right thing to do. What do you think?" asked Natalie cautiously.

"Go and see him if you think it would be the right thing to do, but please don't do anything silly or eccentric. That's all I ask."

"No, of course not, Charlie."

Dolores came out of the Chapel of Rest. Natalie knew how horrifying it must be to lose a brother and tried to be kind to her customer. She extended her hand to support Dolores as she struggled to come down the short flight of steps.

"I'm going in, Miss Murphy," said Natalie tactfully.

"I will wait for you outside. Whatever prayers you have

to say, if you intend to say them at all, will not shake off my curse."

Elliott had overheard her words. "If you continue to be rude to Miss Klein, you will make things worse for yourself. While I grieve the loss of Seamus and recognize that it is worse for you than it is for anyone else, it does not justify bad manners on your part. It may be Miss Klein's profession not to show her feelings but that doesn't mean she hasn't got any."

"Why do you English people always have to be so fucking pompous?" said Dolores, adding, "She's not the kind that would have any feelings."

"If you say anything more, arrangements will be made for you to dispose of your brother's remains elsewhere. We, ourselves, are charging you nothing. Consider yourself warned," said Elliott assertively.

"I've naught against you, Mr Elliott."

Natalie went into the Chapel of Rest. It had once been used as a bedsit, before the building had been converted into a funeral parlour. The see-through mailbox was still on the door, but Natalie had forgotten about it.

She stared at Murphy's lifeless fully-clothed body. Her tears were not those of bereavement. They were shed because Murphy's appearance in death had moved and excited her. His was a sacred beauty that had never been apparent to her in life.

She took his face in her hands. She repeated Edgar Allan Poe's words which she had uttered before and ran her fingers through his hair.

"Come up through the lair of the Lion,
With love in her luminous eyes."

She undressed, lay on top of his body and began to touch his private parts…

She stayed with Murphy for fifteen minutes, and left him

as she had found him. She put on her clothes. She was out of breath when she left the Chapel of Rest and the colour had returned to her cheeks.

Dolores was kneeling outside the door which opened inwardly. The drug, which had been put in her tea, was still active. It caused her to lose her balance and she tumbled down the steps, outside the Chapel of Rest, like a black rubber ball. Had the circumstances been less embarrassing, Natalie would have laughed at her ludicrous appearance.

"I saw it all, daughter. I've taken a coloured photograph."

Natalie lost her head and shouted like a maniac, stabbing the air with her finger, as she hovered over her adversary's supine body.

"I don't know what you're talking about. Let me pass, you mad Irish bitch. Get to your feet!"

Dolores took the cross from round her neck and waved it in front of Natalie, as if she were auditioning for the part of Jonathan Harker.

"Is this meant to be some kind of threat?" asked Natalie, her voice raised.

Dolores was not used to being shouted at. Natalie pushed past her and rushed downstairs to Elliott's basement room. where he had started to work once more.

"Charlie, this is an emergency. We can't have this woman coming here. She's evil and dangerous. Please promise me you won't allow her to be alone with me."

"Calm down. Try to behave like an adult. Look at it from her point of view. She's just lost a brother. How would you like it if this happened to you? She can't harm you."

"Yes, she can! I don't think you realize how lethal she is. Can't we shove her on to *Crumblebottom and Bongwit?* It would teach the sons of bitches a lesson."

"Keep your voice down, Natalie."

"Those bastards are always poaching stiffs from us. They

think they own the dead. They need someone like that woman to keep them in their place!"

"For Christ's sake, calm down and stop shouting, Natalie. You've done enough harm to *Crumblebottom and Bongwit* already. Only the other day, you pasted a notice on the windscreen of one of their hearses, when they were waiting to do a job, which read, "AM DRUNK. WILL REMOVE VEHICLE WHEN SOBER."

"Mr Sprout took three quarers of an hour to scrape it off and went without lunch. All right, so Murphy's sister's a pest. The way to win against her is to bury Seamus free of charge. Once we've done that, she won't ever pester us again.'

"We've already told her that Seamus's funeral will be free of charge," said Natalie.

Elliott saw distrust in her eyes.

"Women!" he muttered under his breath. "They're enough to drive any poor bastard to put to sea."

Natalie and Elliott did all that was in their power to placate and comfort Dolores, whose brother's funeral was conducted as requested. They were both overtly polite and cordial towards her and treated her like an ambassadress. Even professional actors would have Natalie's their skill at concealing her hatred for her.

*　*　*

There were times when Natalie was irritated by Elliott's gentleness, patience and tolerance. His stoicism and failure to show his feelings after Murphy's burial, made him appear like a caricature of the English.

He and Natalie were driving away from the cemetery after Murphy's funeral, when she turned on him and berated him for being so easy-going and polite all the time.

"All my life, I've learnt to get along with people and I come from nothing. You were born with everything but you quarrel with everyone you meet," he retorted.

"Yes." She banged her fist on the dashboard. "Because no-one values me for what I am. Only for what my family do. Why else do you think I chose a trade like this? I did so to attract attention to myself by being different from other people. If I quarrel with others, it's because the majority of people I meet are shits."

"All right! All right! I'm sick of your bad temper and your persistent tantrums. Knock it off!"

* * *

Three days after Dolores's request had been granted, Elliott brought Natalie breakfast in bed. He had learned to accept the domestic role reversal which she had imposed on him.

"You were right all along about Dolores Murphy," he said. "She's raving mad."

"I am always right," said Natalie in jest.

"She wants to have her brother's body exhumed and cremated now. She's been very offensive and abusive on the phone. She says she doesn't want anyone to go near Seamus's grave," stated Elliott.

"Why?" asked Natalie.

"Ask a psychiatrist. Don't ask me. She's threatened to make our lives impossible. If she comes back, I'm going to call the police."

In her confusion, Natalie accidentally knocked a jug of milk onto the floor. She ignored the mess she had made.

"Whatever you do, don't do that! We can't have the police coming here. It's out of the question. I don't care any more. All I want is to be rid of her," said Natalie assertively.

"May I ask you a question?" said Elliott.

"Ask any question you like."

"Did you ever sleep with Seamus?"

"No." Natalie knew she was telling the truth. She had never gone to sleep in Murphy's presence.

"You've got to understand that there's no limit to what Dolores might ask us for," continued Elliott. "She's dangerously insane."

"I've been trying to tell you that all along," said Natalie.

Elliott added, "She's been in here upsetting people every day, when you've been at the cinema. She's going to bring our trade to a standstill. Seamus never complained about her but maybe he was trying to be loyal to her. He talked to me a lot about his sister but he never said she was a psycho. If we don't get the police out, she'll ruin us."

Natalie sat bolt upright. She had finished her toast and tea.

"No!" she shouted.

"Do see reason."

She got out of bed and paced up and down the room, wringing her hands. "I *am* seeing reason!" she shouted, adding, "I'm not attracting any attention to our firm. Dolores will simmer down. She'll stop coming back if we ignore her. All right, so she's mad and we'll have to placate her. We'll exhume her blasted bloody brother and cremate him. We'll do anything she asks for but we won't call the police."

"You're attracting enough attention to yourself as it is. Why must you bellow as if I were five miles away? I will not tolerate this perpetual shouting," said Elliott

"I can't help it. I'm trying to control it."

"You went to the grave, didn't you? You went there more than once. Why did you go to the grave?" demanded Elliott.

"I — I don't know."

"You know you're not allowed in after the gates of the cemetery are locked, don't you?"

"Yes. Well, I climbed over the gates, actually," confessed Natalie demurely.

"Dolores saw you in there. That's why she wants her brother's body to be exhumed and cremated."

"Well, exhume him, then! Cremate him! See if I care. I

don't want to hear any more about that fucking woman. I will not be burdened with other people's mental illnesses. All I ask is that you don't get the police out," repeated Natalie.

"You make it sound as if you've got something to hide, even from me." commented Elliott.

Natalie picked up an ashtray and threw it to the other side of the room, in a fit of rage. "You really are a proverbial dickhead!" she shouted, adding, "Even if an establishment is respectable, no-one would expect to see the police wandering round its offices. The neighbours might think we kept a disorderly house or dealt in drugs. Then all our trade would go to *Crumblebottom and Bongwit*."

Elliott wiped his forehead and showed no emotion. He looked physically and mentally exhausted. "You may be right, boss. We'll exhume the bastard; then we'll cremate him," he muttered hoarsely.

And so the remains of Seamus Murphy were removed from the earth and transported to a crematorium. Another religious service was held. Natalie did not attend it. Whatever was left of Seamus Murphy drifted through a squalid-looking chimney into a grey sky of nothingness, as befitted the man.

Dolores took possession of a silver urn containing her brother's ashes. It was a *Klein and Elliott* urn and a *Klein and Elliott* gift. Dolores made a theatrical issue about her ownership of the urn, because it was the only object she had possessed, which had both material and sentimental value. She was aware of the financial worth of the urn. Rather than keep it in her rented bedsit, she liked to be seen carrying it wherever she went, like an athlete who had won her first cup.

She was known throughout Camberwell as the "ash lady". Jokes were made about her in pubs. Even songs were invented about her and their words were bawled drunkenly on Saturday nights.

Natalie was vehemently opposed to cremation. She was

offended by the notion of someone's remains being reduced to the size of an urn. She was also upset because she was no longer able to visit Murphy's grave.

She developed an unhealthy obsession about Dolores's decision to cremate her brother's remains, which worsened over the weeks.

She and Elliott went out for an early dinner. They assumed that they had seen the last of Dolores. Elliott went to bed at half past eight and fell asleep, aided by some wine. Natalie went downstairs to bolt the door to the front office. Her ordeal had not ended. It had just begun.

Dolores waited in the street and tapped on the door with her walking stick. Natalie opened the door.

"You were very stupid to come back," Natalie began. "You've gone too far this time. Any interchanges between us will be conducted, but by my solicitors."

She refrained from looking her enemy in the eye. Her failure to meet her eyes gave her confidence.

Dolores barged through the open door. "You won't be going near any solicitors, once you've seen this, daughter."

"You'd better sit down but if you cause me any trouble, I'll fight you to the death like a man and I'll win."

"I've got something here that you want but it isn't free of charge."

"If you're blackmailing me, you'll go to jail," said Natalie, adding, "Under the Thefts Act of 1968, blackmail is a serious criminal offence, which can carry a fourteen year stretch."

Dolores put her hand in her pocket and produced a coloured photograph. She gripped it tightly, to prevent Natalie snatching it from her. She held it in front of Natalie, who looked at it briefly and who made an agonized shuddering noise. After about a minute, she composed herself.

"If you're a Catholic, please have some compassion for your enemies. I thought your philosophy was all about that sort of thing. I'm sure your priest would tell you to give the photograph me," said Natalie.

"You are a pagan. You proved that in the Chapel of Rest, so let's leave religion out of it," said Dolores.

"Just hand it over and we'll forget this conversation ever took place."

"I'm going to but it's going to cost you."

Natalie thought for a while. It was a question of checkmate in a few moves, as long as she didn't make any mistakes.

"How much?" she asked.

"Twenty thousand pounds in cash," replied Dolores.

"I know that's a lot of money to you, but it's a pittance as far as I'm concerned. I will agree to meet your criminal demands, because that's the only way in which I can ensure that you won't come back and disrupt my business. We keep our safe containing our accumulated savings in the garage. If I honour your terms, will you promise me you won't come back?"

"I give you my word I won't come back. Have you got twenty thousand pounds in your safe?"

"We've got more than that," said Natalie, adding, "The extra money is for pallbearers' wages and essentials, such as hearse maintenance, etc. The key to the garage is on a hook on the wall over there. You'd better come to the garage with me. I can guarantee I won't pull a gun on you, if that will put you at your ease."

"Even if you *do* kill me, my immortal soul will hold the four aces," said Dolores, in a tone of voice that chilled Natalie and made her feel faint.

Dolores stared her in the eye. "I'm glad you weren't too hard to persuade, daughter. I thought you'd blow your cool and call the Law."

"Don't refer to the police as 'the Law'. It's common."

Dolores laughed. Hers was the hollow laugh of a ghoul.

"I'm going into the garage now. You may follow me. I've also got the key to the safe. I want this to be over as soon as possible, because I'm tired and I want to go to bed," said Natalie.

The older woman smiled, showing her one front tooth. She only smiled because she knew that her smile would make her look more frightening. She continued to carry the urn.

The part of the garage that Natalie took Dolores to was full of empty crates. She turned on the light, which had a single unshaded bulb. She guided Dolores over the crates, work stools and tool boxes which hadn't been tidied away.

"We keep our safe over there. Can you see that dark thing in the wall?" asked Natalie.

"I see it."

"Good. I'm afraid it will mean we'll have to clamber over all these things to get to it."

Natalie forced herself to trip over one of the crates. She deliberately dropped the key to the safe into the crate. She rolled on to the dusty floor and let out an artificial wail of pain.

"Are you hurt?" asked Dolores cautiously.

Natalie rustled up false but convincing tears.

"I've sprained my ankle. Will you help me up?"

Dolores wrenched Natalie to her feet. Then, the younger woman knelt down, as if she were looking for the key to the safe to look for the key to the safe. She picked up a hammer from a tool box nearby, and hit Dolores on the head with it twenty times, holding the hammer with both hands.

She was reassured that her victim was dead, when she saw part of her brain emerging from her brutally battered skull. She took the photograph from her enemy's hand and tore it up into small pieces. She noticed that Dolores did not carry a handbag and turned out her pockets. She found a five pound note, two one pound notes, some Kleenex tissues and a tattered picture of the Crucifixion, which had been removed from a prayer book. She tore that up as well.

She pulled Dolores's ultra-light body into the nearest

hearse. There were two. She opened the hatch leading to the bier compartment and dragged Dolores's body through it.

The load would have been too heavy in ordinary circumstances but the urgency of the deed gave Natalie extra physical strength, that even a healthy eighteen-year-old man might have envied. She pulled down the blinds in the bier compartment, secured Dolores's body with bier pins to stop it rolling about, and locked the hatch.

She rubbed axle grease onto the number plates at the back and front of the hearse, and sprinkled dust on top of the axle grease. Elliott had already filled the tank with petrol and had left the key in the ignition.

Natalie checked that there was no blood on the floor of the garage. She wiped the hammer clean and returned it to the tool box. She picked up the silver urn, containing Murphy's ashes and put it into the bier compartment by Dolores's body.

She swept up the tiny pieces of the photograph and put them into her mouth. When her neat, tidy mind was satisfied that there was no evidence of her action, she got into the hearse, turned on the ignition and drove it through the gate, taking care not to rev the engine. She closed the gate behind her and got back into the hearse. It was raining heavily.

Natalie looked at her watch. The time was five past nine. She decided to drive to Bodmin Moor. The hearse could reach a maximum speed of ninety miles per hour, but she knew that she would not be able to reach Bodmin Moor before about two o'clock in the morning, because of the rain.

She took six *Diazepams*, ten milligrams each. She remembered one of her doctors saying that the taking of six *Diazepams* was "really sinking the Bismarck," and laughed out loud. Within fifteen minutes, she reached the M25 motorway leading out of London. By this time, the *Diazepam* had kicked in. She felt so calm that her calmness alarmed her.

She joined the M5 motorway, which led to Exeter and took

the A30 leading to Bodmin Moor. The unlikelihood of anyone wandering onto the moor in such torrential rain, gave her confidence.

She had heard terrifying stories about lesbianism in women's prisons. She knew that she would be sentenced to life imprisonment if she were found out. She imagined with horror what it would be like to share a cell for the rest of her life with two hirsute women abusing her good looks. If she was going to be caught, she decided that she would kill herself, rather than face prison. At the same time, the possibility seemed unreal. She was not going to be caught.

Elliott had taken her to Bodmin Moor on many occasions. He had catered for her interest in romantic literature, in which heroes and heroines got lost on the moor, pursued by an adversary, be it a highwayman, an escaped convict or a hound. He had shown her some of the mineshafts, which could be approached by bumpy narrow roads, leading off the main moorland road. He had pointed out the mineshafts which were not filled in. He had taken her to Bodmin Moor most weekends and she knew her way about the moor almost as well as he did.

She turned off the main moorland road, onto a narrow, uneven road, which was blocked by sheep that did not respond to her horn. When she drove onto a grass verge to avoid the sheep, the back wheels of the hearse got stuck in a rut. If she hadn't been drugged, she would have panicked.

Instead, she remembered a film about the Battle of Waterloo, in which Napoleon, played by Rod Steiger, was shown getting stuck in mud on the battlefield. "Come on, get me out of this!" he had barked at his aides.

The memory made Natalie giggle nervously, as she got out of the hearse, to wedge the back wheels with two heavy stones, to prevent them from sliding back into the rut.

She managed to get the back wheels of the hearse off the grass verge. She reversed along the narrow, uneven road, until she reached the main road, from which she turned into another narrow road, leading to one of the mineshafts, which Elliott had shown her. It had stopped raining. The full moon illuminated the narrow road and made her task as easy as it would have been in daylight.

Natalie's reserve of mental and physical strength, caused by the *Diazepam*, made it easier for her to pull Dolores's body towards the mineshaft, about twenty yards away from the narrow road.

It took her some time to get the body as far as the edge of the mineshaft, because the ground was so bumpy, the mud so slippery and the vegetation so coarse. Her fear of being caught made her work faster and more urgently.

She had read in the newspapers about corpses being identified by their teeth alone. The effect of the *Diazepam* was beginning to wear off, so she took six more tablets. She prized open Dolores's mouth, hoping to find that the sluttish-looking woman had never consulted a dentist. She shone the torch that was round her neck into her victim's mouth. Dolores had the one front tooth but the normal number of molars on each side of her upper jaw. There were no teeth in her lower jaw.

Natalie continued to shine the torch into Dolores's mouth. Many of the back teeth in her upper jaw had been drilled and filled. The others either had cavities or were completely decayed.

Natalie took a hammer from the hollow area under the bier compartment of the hearse and forced open the dead woman's mouth once more. She made up her mind that she would knock out the remaining teeth and throw them down the mineshaft after the body.

As she brought the hammer down, she hit her fingers hard. The pain was sharp and nauseating. Her nerve was going and her hands were shaking. She decided that she would be faced with no choice but to leave Dolores's back teeth in her mouth, although she had managed to knock out her single front tooth.

Natalie reviewed her plan to dispose of the body. By this time, the second dose of *Diazepam* had started to work. She picked up a stone and threw it down the gaping mineshaft, to see how deep it was. The thud that followed about ten seconds later, reassured her that, although the mineshaft was not as deep as she hoped it would be, it was still deep enough to hide her load.

The extra dose of *Diazepam* had given Natalie the strength to push Dolores's body into the mineshaft. She threw the urn containing Murphy's ashes in after the body. She kept the torch round her neck and threw the hammer into the mineshaft as well, as it had her fingerprints on it; she was not wearing gloves.

She staggered back to the narrow road where she had left the hearse. There was nowhere to turn, so she reversed for two miles, until she reached the main road.

Suddenly, she had a terrible shock. A motorbike behind her, overtook her and had a head-on crash with a lorry travelling the other way. The motorbike-rider was killed instantly but the lorry-driver failed to stop.

Natalie's heart skipped a beat. She wondered whether the lorry-driver had taken her number. Then she realized that she had covered the number plates of the hearse with axel grease, and had sprinkled dust on top of the axel grease. She almost sang with joy.

She headed for London. She drove along the same roads she had driven along when she had left the capital.

* * *

It was six o'clock in the morning by the time Natalie arrived in Camberwell. She burned her clothes in a dustbin which she and Elliott used as a brazier. She returned the hearse to the place where she had found it, washed it, cleaned the number plates and checked that there was no blood on the bier rack. She filled the tank with one of the spare petrol cans, which she and Elliott stored, and walked back to the house naked, carrying the keys to the garage and the house.

If Elliott had seen her, she would have said that she had been walking in her sleep. He knew that she was pretty eccentric and he would have believed her.

He was still asleep when she went upstairs to their bedroom. She showered, got into bed and fell asleep. When she woke up, two hours later, she had no recollection whatever of what she had done or where she had been.

She felt very unwell, and had a vague notion that at some time during the night, she had had a bad dream. Apart from that, she might just as well have had a lobotomy.

Her memory punished her body in the form of physical symptoms. She was worried, because she had the outward signs of a physical illness but had no idea what had caused it. She rang up her favourite doctor, Dr Sergei Festenstein at nine o'clock that morning.

Dr Sergei Festenstein, a Jewish émigré from Leipzig, Harley Street's most envied and most accomplished diagnostician. He was the Kleins' family doctor. He was a very melancholy man and was particularly attached to Natalie, because she had been born during the *Se vuol ballare* aria of *The Marriage of Figaro* at the Royal Opera House in London. He had delivered her personally. He had been invited to the Royal Opera House by her parents, and had taken more applause from the audience, for the delivery, than the tempestuous Latin in the role of Figaro. "Figaro" left the stage after the aria in a rage and his understudy took over from him.

To look at Dr Festenstein was a combination of Clark Gable and Gregory Peck. His appearance, combined with his guttural Leipzig accent, set Natalie's blood on fire. He said that there was nothing wrong with her, except nervous exhaustion.

When Natalie was sixteen years old, she had a verbal accident in Dr Festenstein's consulting rooms. She saw an unknown woman behind the reception desk. "My God, that man, Festenstein is attractive. He must come like the Volga!" Natalie said to the woman who replied furiously, "Kindly keep your opinion to yourself and wait in the waiting room, if you don't mind."

Natalie turned to Dr Festenstein's secretary and asked, "Who is that disagreeable new receptionist? Is she an agency temp?"

"No," replied the secretary. "She is Dr Festenstein's wife."

Natalie's father, Selwyn Klein, was a frequent visitor to Dr Festenstein's consulting rooms.

On one occasion, when her father was in the London Clinic, convalescing from a hip replacement operation, he had a bottle of whisky on his bedside table.

Dr Festenstein was known for his perilous temper. He seized the bottle, passed it to the Charge Nurse and gave him a thunderous slap on the ear.

"How dare you allow him this, you brainless nincompoop, when I've just saved his liver!" he shouted.

* * *

Three years passed since the murder of Dolores Murphy. Natalie continued to see her victim. Sometimes, she appeared in the street, clutching her brother's ashes. She continuously approached her and repeated the words, "My immortal soul will hold the four aces." However, the intervals between her appearances became longer. Natalie started to enjoy her work once more.

One morning, she took a phone message when Elliott was out on business. The caller said that he had had an uncle called Augustus Brown, who had died in Riverfield, a town north of Barfax City in the Midlands. Burial had been requested in the London area where the rest of the Brown family had been buried.

Natalie collected Brown's body from the mortuary in Riverfield General Hospital. She had a flat tyre on the motorway near Riverfield. She drove onto the hard shoulder. A lorry driver, motivated by morbid curiosity, changed her wheel. He dragged Augustus Brown's body out of the hearse, by tying a rope to the coffin handles and attaching the other end of the rope to the front of the lorry. He left the coffin on the hard shoulder.

He couldn't think of a way to get the coffin back into the hearse, once the wheel had been changed, however. Natalie cursed him for his lack of initiative. He drove off in a temper. She paced up and down on the hard shoulder, like an expectant father, no longer caring whether she had made a fool of herself or not.

She sat on the hard shoulder, using Augustus Brown's coffin as a seat and rocked backwards and forwards. She had her back to the upcoming traffice. Her nerves were shattered. She thought about her childhood. She tried to remember what the original underlying cause was, of her not wishing to be considered a coward.

Initially, her thoughts went to her elder brother, Gomer, whom she hero-worshipped. She remembered the time he had called her a coward, because she had dug her heels into the snow, when he and she were going down a steep hill on a toboggan.

Both the Klein children were sent to boarding school. Natalie was a compulsively vain, attention-seeking exhibitionist at the time, and her outrageous behaviour increased her popularity with the more timid children, who encouraged her and caused her behaviour to deteriorate.

She attracted attention to herself to hide the extent to which her fear of being considered a coward, tortured and shamed her. Somehow, she felt that she could hide this from other children by committing perpetual acts of mischief.

She befriended a girl called Emma Robinson. The two

became inseparable friends. Their friendship was strengthened by Emma's admiration for her apparent fearlessness.

Another reason for Natalie's exhibitionist behaviour at the strict Protestant boarding school, which she attended, was her need to be recognized as a person in her own right, rather than simply as Selwyn Klein's daughter and Gomer Klein's sister. She was devoted to her father, but ninety per cent of her misdemeanours at school were motivated by a need to stand on a pedestal of her own creation. She believed that it was better to be an exhibit in the Chamber of Horrors, than not to be remembered at all.

* * *

Emma Robinson invited Natalie to stay during the summer holidays. Emma was an only child, who lived with her parents in a seventeenth century house in Surrey. Emma's father was plagued by heart disease. The Robinsons found Natalie well brought-up but were intrigued by the anecdotes which she told them about her naughtiness at school and her impertinence towards her teachers.

Two boys, called Mark and Douglas-Cyril Oppenheimer were staying with the Robinsons. Under his laughing, stoic exterior, Mark was a sad boy whose father had just died. His mother was a friend of the Robinsons and was temporarily too overwrought to cope with her sons at home.

Mark had a cherubic face and a twinkle in his eye. He forced himself to be cheerful and not to let his father's death upset him openly, for fear of being considered "wet". Like Natalie and Emma, he was ten years old. He was slim but Douglas-Cyril, the eldest of the two brothers, was extremely stout. He was thirteen years old.

Mark was pleased by the prospect of accompanying Natalie, Emma and Douglas-Cyril to the cinema one afternoon. He was uncommonly attractive for a ten-year-old. Even though they were very young, Natalie and Emma painted their faces to compete for Mark's attention and this flattered him.

Mrs Robinson drove the four children to a cinema showing the film, *Taras Bulba*. Mark sat between the two girls, both of whom tried to impress him by making him laugh. Natalie was more interested in the film than her companions were. The hero of the film was Taras Bulba's son, who was accused of being a coward.

He was challenged by his own brethren to ride a horse over a ravine to prove that he was not a coward. The sound of the galloping horse's hooves, sometimes only just making it to the other side of the ravine, and the sight of the pieces of rock falling into the ravine, after it had been ridden over, had a hypnotic effect on Natalie. She turned to Mark. "Isn't he brave?" she said.

Mark agreed with her but did not share her zealousness. "I'd give anything to be thought of as being as brave as that," Natalie added, ignoring the woman in front of her who continuously hissed for silence.

"Would you, now?" said Mark. "I've got an idea. You'll be able to prove that you're just as brave, if not braver. Wait till the interval."

A middle-aged ice-cream vendor wearing horn-rimmed spectacles and thick face powder, stood in the aisle, during the interval, while a queue gathered in front of her. "I bet you don't dare go up to that woman and say: "There's a very good-looking boy in the cinema who'll fuck you for a shilling," said Mark.

"Don't do it, Natalie!" said Douglas-Cyril, who was stuffing popcorn into his mouth.

Emma also pleaded with Natalie not to do it, but Natalie wanted to make more of an impression on Mark than Emma had made.

"Excuse me, madam," echoed a voice which lapsed into a heavy Welsh accent.

"Wait your turn!" said the ice-cream vendor. Her unfriendly tone of voice made it easier for Natalie to be impertinent to her.

"I've come to say: "There's a very good-looking boy in the cinema who'll fuck you for a shilling.""

"One shilling! One shilling! Tell your friend he's going to have to offer me far more than just one shilling."

"I did what you told me to do, Mark, but she says her rate is far higher than just one shilling," said Natalie.

"Then go back and tell her she's only worth a shilling."

"Excuse me, madam, my friend says you're only worth a shilling."

"'Ere, get out of it! And don't be so bloomin' cheeky!'" shouted the ice-cream vendor, loudly enough for Mark to hear her, so he knew that Natalie had accepted the dare. He was surprised that she had done so, and wondered how far she was prepared to go without his being implicated.

Later that day, the four children were playing on a building site near a busy main road. Mark picked up a brick and handed it to Natalie.

"Can you see that red sports car at the lights?"

"Yes."

"I bet you don't dare throw this at it."

Emma tried to persuade Natalie not to do so; so did Douglas-Cyril. Natalie said she thought it was a bad idea but Mark reminded her of her wish to be considered brave. The sound of the galloping horse thundered in her ears, as it had when she had approached the ice-cream vendor. She held the brick in both hands and threw it as hard as she could, making a heavy dent in the sports car's paintwork.

The driver was a twenty-three-year-old antiques dealer. He was taking his girlfriend out and was trying to impress her with his new acquisition. He pulled into the side of the road, got out of his car and went straight for Douglas-Cyril, the eldest child.

"Is this little brat your sister?" Douglas-Cyril opened and closed his mouth, like a goldfish waiting to be fed.

"N- no, sir," he eventually managed to splutter.

The four children turned and fled with the driver pursuing them. If he hadn't tripped and fallen over, he would have caught them. Natalie confessed her misdeed under pressure from her parents, who were told about the incident by Mrs Robinson.

Her parents were so shocked that they asked their butler for glasses of brandy. Natalie was confined to the library and made to learn *The Charge of the Light Brigade*[*] by heart.

This was an easy, even pleasurable task, because the poem occasionally rhymed in threes. Also, Natalie could identify with the theme of misdirected courage. When she was almost word-perfect, she was asked to stand on a stool in front of her parents.

Occasionally, her brother, Gomer, prompted her through the window, by mouthing the words of the poem and winking at her. Both the Klein children had been made to learn the poem at some stage of their disciplinary education.

When Natalie had finished reciting, her mother[*], who had remained pale and shaken, as if she had actually been trampled on by the Light Brigade, said: "I'm so utterly appalled, Selwyn dear. I think we ought to teach Natalie a proper lesson and make her recite the poem to the driver of the sports car as well."

"I think that would be unjustifiably hard on the driver, taking the monotonous tone of her voice into account, and considering what he's had to go through already," Selwyn commented mildly.

* * *

Natalie laughed as she remembered the incident and paced up and down on the hard shoulder once more. Her feeling of merriment conflicted with a sense of nostalgia about her

---

[*]   Tennyson

[*]   Natalie's mother died of breast cancer when she (Natalie) was twelve years old.

childhood. She decided that she would keep the promise that she had once made to herself, namely that one day, she would prove to others that she was not a coward.

She had given up trying to flag down drivers and get them to help her and, as she grew more aware of the grotesqueness of her situation, she despaired. She had called the AA but they had not turned up. Her escapades of bravado as a child had been futile. A man, who had once meant a lot to her, was dead, having publicly called her a coward, when he had found out what she feared most.

Also, Dolores was still at large. Natalie's subconscious had censored the knowledge that she had murdered her. Dolores's appearances continued, if after long intervals. She appeared in the streets, in crowded waiting-rooms, at social gatherings and in many other places. Every visit was more painful and more vicious than the one before it.

Three hours had passed. No one showed signs of wishing to help her. She sat on top of Augustus Brown's coffin, facing away from the motorway. Still, the AA had failed to turn up. She got up and paced up and down, yet again, her mood alternating between fury and gloom. She knew no one would help her and she no longer cared.

PART TWO

JACK MAGUIRE

Jack Maguire

Jack Maguire was well-built, was graced with good looks and was born in 1950. He had been born destitute. His grandfather, once an opulent newspaper proprietor, had gambled away all his money. His name was Thomas Maguire.

His grandson, Jack Maguire, hailed from Toxteth, a slum district in Liverpool. He had three brothers and four sisters, all of whom were younger than he. His family lived in a cramped underground room, which comprised a sink, a single gas ring, some bunks, two clothes lines and a lidless lavatory.

All Maguire's siblings had died of diptheria, as did his mother, Mary Maguire.His unemployed father was so devastated by her passing that he hanged himself from a beam in the family room.

From the age of twelve onwards, Maguire was determined to better himself. He was fiercely ambitious and yearned to be rich.

At the age of about fifteen, he was almost six foot tall, had large, bright blue eyes and a shock of blond hair. A lot of people thought that his hair was dyed, but in fact, it was natural. He inherited his hair colour from his mother.

He had a small but aquiline nose and white teeth which were jagged and unequal in length, giving him rahter a ratish look.

He often recalled an incident when he was sitting cross-legged on the filthy pavement outside his family's room, eating stale bread sprinkled with sugar. He was thirteen years old. A girl, two years his senior, was walking along the pavement. She was tall and slim, had long red hair set in ringlets and was wearing an emerald green dress. Maguire thought she was beautiful. He particularly liked red hair and emerald green together.

He knew he had nothing to offer her, other than a piece of his sweetened bread.

"I don't want it," she said. "I don't associate with poor boys"

Predictably, Maguire was very upset. Her remarks intensified his determination to become wealthy.

He thought vaguely of becoming a newspaper proprietor, like his grandfather, before he had fallen on hard times.

At the age of eighteen, when Maguire was the sole survivor of his family, he began to suffer from mood swings.

He decided to leave his room and Toxteth altogether. He hitchhiked to London, making three journeys. He finally made up his mind to copy his grandfather and aimed to own a national newpaper, preferably in Fleet Street.

He was always robust and outgoing. He went to the first pub he could find in the Strand. He went up to the bar, bought half a pint of beer with the meagre amount of dole money he had managed to save and met a twenty-year-old man called Joe Ellison.

Ellison had long brown hair parted in the centre and a cockney accent. The two young men started a conversation. Ellison told Maguire he was lonely and was living in a bedsit. He offered the younger man some space in his tiny room. Maguire was happy to sleep in the same room as Ellison, on a spare mattress on the floor.

"Where do you work?" asked Maguire.

"I'm a cameraman on *The Daily Herald*."

"Are you now? I want to get a job on a national newspaper. How do I set about it?"

Ellison was struck by Maguire's heavy Liverpudlian accent. "The best thing for you to do is get a job on a provincial newspaper to start with."

"How do I do that?" asked Maguire.

"You should go to a public library and ask for a list, giving the names and addresses of every provincial newspaper in the country. Once you've found something suitable, you should apply for a job, working for the provincial newspaper of your choice.

"How can I do that? I haven't got any references or experience either."

"It sounds hard, I know. You just have to take your chances," said Ellison.

Within two weeks, Maguire managed to get a job as a cub reporter on *The Walsall Chronicle*. The Editor, who interviewed him liked his thick Liverpudlian accent and admired his sense of resolve.

During his employment at *The Walsall Chronicle*, Maguire found a bed in a Salvation Army hostel, in order to save money. He refrained from telling the authorities there, that he was earning, as the Salvation Army only provided beds for down-and-outs.

Maguire worked as a cub reporter on *The Walsall Chronicle* for two years. He was hard-working and his style of writing was dry and original, which caused him to leave the paper with a glowing reference.

He bought a new suit and boarded a train bound for London. Like his friend, Ellison, he lived in a bedsit and attended several interviews, hoping to find a job on a national newspaper.

Eventually, he found a job as a reporter on *The Daily Sketch* where he stayed for five years.

He got on well with his colleagues and drank with them in

the local pub after work. He also got on well with his Editor, Jacob Tynes.

Being a mere journalist was not enough for the ambitious Jack Maguire, however. He yearned to be a newspaper proprietor like his grandfather.

The wife of one of his colleagues introduced him to a well-known philantropist called Sir Joshua Heale. Sir Joshua listened to Maguire's life story and was impressed by what he had to say about his experiences. He told Sir Joshua that he intended to own his own a national newspaper and that he wished it to be a socialist newspaper.

Sir Joshua gave him a chance to ressurect an almost extinct newspaper called *The Eye*.

The Eye had once been a national newspaper but it had deteriorated and was limited in its output. It was only four pages long and had very few readers. Maguire was excited by the prospect of turning *The Eye* into a major national newspaper.

He worked night and day and achieved his ambition. He turned *The Eye*, into a national newspaper which he called *The British Eye*. He enabled it to become a popular national newspapers and it had offices and presses in Fleet Street.

The paper thrived so well that Maguire was able to repay Sir Joshua with interest. He has a knack for supervizing the journalists under him and began to emply correspondents in the majority of foreign cities.

He saw to it that any journalist, both at home and abroad, who was unable to provide a lively, succienct and concise account of surrounding events, was swiftly relieved of his responsibilites.

Maguire was more than just a workaholic. His attention to detail was seen by some of his employees to be pathological. He desperately tried to erase the memories of his childhood from his mind, but the more he tried to do so, the more vivid they became.

The ownership of one national newspaper was not enough for him. He was successful in buying another newspaper, a socialist paper which he called *Maguire's Voice*. Like *The British Eye*, this paper, too, had offices and presses in Fleet Street. In fact, *The British Eye* and *Maguire's Voice* were next door to each other.

By the time Maguire had worked on *Maguire's Voice* for four years, he was still not satisfied with being a mere newspaper proprietor. His mood swings became even more frequent.

Although he had become well-off, he began to identify with the underdog, rather than with himself and his riches.

He was still fiercely ambitious and he felt that he would never be happy, unless he went into politics as well as journalism. His fantasies reched dizzying heights. After lying awake for nights on end, he realized that he was destined to become Prime Minister of Britain. He did not harbour exceptionally left wing views, but saw himself as a moderate socialist.

He was exhausted by his work and lack of sleep and decided to go to Paris for the weekend. He had never sampled the city's night-life before so he hailed a taxi and travelled to a night club on the *rive droite*.

He danced with a black-haired, gypsy-like beauty called Hortense Gautier who had escaped from her upper class home for the evening.

Hortense hailed from a wealthy family based in St Cloud on the outskirts of Paris. Maguire told her about his two newspapers and his ambition to become Prime Minister. He also told her about his impoverished childhood in Liverpool.

Hortense admired his single-mindedness, his achievements, and his rise from rags to riches.

She was bored by the superficial upper-class snobbery, prevalent in the circles which she had been forced by her superiors to mix in.

She found relief in the company of this blond, moody, young

man who spoke his mind and who appeared to be intolerant of fools.

Because of his thick blond hair, he struck her as being something of a teddy-boy, a trait which she failed to recognize in the aristocratic young men, to whom she had been introduced previously.

Maguire saw in Hortense the qualities which he had seen in his mother, whom he had not known since he was a child. He also loved her on account of her purity, seldom seen in French women. He stayed in the *Hôtel Vendome* in opulent Paris with Hortense for about a week, having decided that he would postpone his return journey to London. She, in turn, rang her father up and told him she would not be coming home as she had met a glamourous, rich Englishman, whom she wished to spend the rest of her life with. Her father, a wealthy banker called Jean-Alphase Gautier, told her he would be cutting her out of his will.

It was in the *Hôtel Vendome* that Maguire proposed to Hortense and promised her she would be the wife of a British Prime Minister one day. He made a further promise, regarding his attainment of power,

"My face shall appear on the bank notes,
And my profile shall appear on the coins."

Hortense associated Brahms's *Hungarian Dance Number Five* with Maguire, because it was his favourite piece of music. Another thing he liked about this music, was its permanent swing from massive energy to moodiness. Maguire continued to be a manic depressive, on account of his wretched childhood. Hortense found this characteristic attractive.

As well as being the proprietor of *Maguire's Voice* and *The British Eye*, Maguire managed to become the Labour MP in a constituency in south-east England, called Barfax East.

It was a period when the Lunatic Left were becoming over-influential within the Labour Party, so he set up his own

Party, which he called "Maguire's Party". This was a superior replacement of the Social Democrat Party which had ceased to exist.

Maguire's constituency, Barfax East, which had consisted of a group of southern Midland counties. Maguire had already become popular, which was largely due to the successful sales of *Maguire's Voice* which had become the most popular newspaper in Britain. During General Election campaigns, the words, "*My face shall appear on the banknotes and my profile shall appear on the coins,*" were splashed across the top of the front page of *Maguire's Voice*.

Some people resented Maguire. If they were upper class, their resentment was due to their envy of a man who had started with less than they and got further. If they were working class, they hated him because they were envious of his riches.

Jealousy of Maguire's success increased. Printers on *Maguire's Voice* staged a long-drawn-out strike. The printers had demanded the "right" to write the paper's editorials themselves. Maguire was tough to the end.

The strikers knew they would get no-where with this hot-blooded Liverpudlian from the slums of Toxteth. They returned to work.

* * *

It was during an Election campaign that Maguire, predictably, was canvassing for his own Party. He had just finished campaigning in Riverfield which was also in his constituency. There were two other candidates, one Labour and one Tory, both of whom were unpopular.

Maguire was travelling in a vehicle, called the "Maguire Mobile". He was standing in the back with his head protruding through the roof. He had employed a driver, called Harold Munn. Munn had worked for him for about fifteen years.

The Maguire-Mobile was similar to a Landrover and had

been painted purple and white, like a twenty-pound note. Maguire's blown-up photograph replaced that of the Queen. His chosen slogan covered one side of the Maguire-Mobile in prominent black letters,

"My face shall appear on the bank notes,
And my profile shall appear on the coins."

Maguire recited these words over a loud-hailer in built-up areas.

Munn followed the signs to the motorway. Maguire began to dictate "condolence letters" to his personal assistant and henchman, Miss Jane Bechtold. Miss Bechtold was neatly-dressed, bossy and efficient. She was a tall brunette. She was wearing a pale blue linen suit and spoke with a trace of an American accent.

She had worked for Maguire for ten years. She was sitting in the front of the Maguire-Mobile, taking instructions from her boss.

There had been an accident on the motorway and traffic, in all three lanes, had come to a standstill. Soon, it picked up again.

"Mrs Emily Davies has just lost her husband who had cancer. Send her a standard letter from File number 43," said Maguire. He handed her a local newspaper, containing a short entry in the Deaths' column. He had encircled the entry.

"File number 43 would hardly be appropriate, Mr Maguire," said Miss Bechtold. "Correspondence in that file begins with the words, '"Mr Maguire and his colleagues are happy to congratulate you on the birth of a son/daughter.'"

"Never mind the number. You know the one I mean," said Maguire.

"You're referring to File number 41 – the one in which letters begin with the words, "In circumstances as tragic as yours, words are futile but…""

"That's the one," said Maguire. He threw an apple core from the open roof onto the motorway.

"Very well, Mr Maguire, but I've told you before, not to throw things over your shoulder."

"All right, all right, matron!"

"Anyone else to get a 41?" asked Miss Bechfold.

"Yes. A few." He gave her a list of names and addresses from *The Riverfield Express*. When he had finished, he crumpled the newspaper up in a ball and threw it to the front of the Maguire-Mobile. It landed on the floor, by Miss Bechfold's feet. He was in a mischievous mood and wanted to hear her ticking him off. The traffic came to a standstill once more.

Suddenly, he looked to his left with a dumbfounded expression on his face. He ordered Munn to drive onto the hard shoulder and stop.

"What the hell's that, Miss Bechtold?"

"A bizarre spectacle, Mr Maguire. Probably a joke. We must get on."

Maguire stared in disbelief at the coffin lying behind a hearse, abandoned on the hard shoulder, and a young woman in black sitting on top of it.

"We're not going on. I'm getting out to see what all this is about," he said.

"There's no point," replied Miss Bechtold. "It would only mean one vote gained, not to mention involvement in something very peculiar and best avoided."

"I deal in principles, not numbers and this is one of them. If someone needs my help, I will help them," said Maguire assertively.

He got out of the Maguire-Mobile and walked towards Natalie.

"Jesus, madam, you seem to have come to a dead end," he said.

Natalie recognized him as she had seen him repeatedly on the television. She had been impressed by his looks and greatly admired him on account of his life story. She felt humiliated by her undignified circumstances. She spoke in abrupt staccato sentences to hide her self-consciousness.

"You could say that. I've been having trouble shifting my stiff back onto my wagon."

Maguire regarded his new acquaintance, his bright blue eyes shrewd and questioning and his thick blond hair blowing behind him in the wind. He had seen a massive slice of humanity in his life but had never come across a situation quite so bizarre as this.

"Your stiff?"

"Oh, sorry, I meant dead body."

"I don't understand how it got out in the first place," he said, in a startled tone of voice.

"A wheel had to be changed. A lorry driver had to drag the coffin out of the hearse first and he was unable to put it back."

"Why?"

"Because of its weight, I suppose."

"Why couldn't he have used his common sense?" asked Maguire.

"Maybe because he had none."

"Then why didn't you tell him *how* to use his common sense?" Natalie flushed to the roots of her hair.

"If I'd seen an obvious solution to my problem, I wouldn't be here now. What do *you* suggest I do?"

"It's simple. You solve the problem in several moves." Maguire put two fingers of each hand into his mouth and wolf-whistled.

"I do wish you'd stop that whistling, Mr Maguire, every time you want to attract my attention. It's awfully common," Miss Bechtold called from the Maguire-Mobile.

Maguire looked at Natalie and smiled. She returned his smile. Then he turned to Miss Bechtold. "Get the iron rod."

"Get the iron rod, what?"

"Get the iron rod, *please.*"

"That's better; you're becoming house-trained."

Miss Bechtold took a heavy metal rod for wrenching things

open, from the back of the Maguire-Mobile and handed it to Maguire, who took off his jacket and loosened his tie. He shoved a cigar into his mouth as he did so. Miss Bechtold stood behind him.

While sorting out the problem, he spoke to Natalie like a lecturer addressing students.

"First, you get the coffin open. Then you roll the body out. Then you lift the coffin into the back of the hearse. Then you swing the body over your shoulder... "

He winced as he did so. The pain in his shoulder was like a knife with its handle rotating. He walked towards the hearse with the body over his shoulder, and was about to throw it into the coffin. Natalie gaped at him in astonishment. After a silence lasting for about two minutes, she said,

"I know you. I've seen you on the television. You're Jack Maguire, aren't you?"

"That's me. I'm Jack to my family, my friends and my relatives, and 'Mr Maguire' to my constituents. You can choose what you want to call me."

"I'll call you 'Jack', if I may," said Natalie demurely.

A bus containing brownies, stopped behind the Maguire-Mobile on the hard shoulder. The traffic on the motorway remained stationary. A girl aged about ten, with her hair in pigtails and wearing a brownie's uniform, went up to Maguire and asked him for his autograph. He had not had a chance to lay the body in the coffin but the brownie was unconcerned.

"Your autograph, please, one to keep and the other to sell," she demanded.

"Smart thinking. This sounds like an order, not a request. How much do you charge?"

"Fifty pence to sell and fifty pence to keep," said the brownie.

"A shrewd business sense, and a brownie, I see. I bet your Dad's proud of you."

The girl smiled at him precociously and handed him two autograph books, one after the other.

"Would you mind holding the books steady, please so that poor Uncle Jack can write his name for you."

"Who have you got over your shoulder?" asked the brownie.

"I'm surprised you haven't asked me earlier. That's Ben. He works for me. Sometimes he gets tired. He's fainted. I've been told to stand him on his head and in a few minutes' time. In time the blood will get to his brain and he'll be all right again," said Maguire.

Natalie broke into paroxysms of giggles and turned away from Maguire. The girl accepted his explanation and ran off, when she had got what she wanted. She got back into the bus. Maguire felt as if he had been sprayed with shrapnel and the pain radiated to his waist.

He threw the earthly remains of Augustus Brown into the coffin. The head made a strange, hollow sound on impact and Maguire swore under his breath.

"I am so grateful to you for doing what you did. You're very kind. Is there anything I can do for you in return?" Natalie asked stiltedly.

"What are your politics?" Maguire asked hoarsely, after recovering his breath.

"I am an anarchist."

"Is there an anarchist candidate in your constituency?"

"No."

"Who the hell do you vote for, then?"

"For Guilda Mount*, of course. She's the closest thing to anarchy that you can get!"

Maguire laughed and showed his jagged white teeth in a smile which delighted Natalie. Also, unlike Murphy, who had had black hair, Maguire's blond hair was a refreshing contrast.

---

* Guilda Mount was a well-known, tough, controversial young woman, who had modelled herself on Maggie Thatcher. She was the Tory Party leader in Natalie's constituency.

"I like that! Miss Bechtold, did you hear what she said?"

"Yes. I heard it."

"I would like to work for you," said Natalie.

"Why?"

"Because I think you are very good-looking. Also, I like the way you loosen your tie at the neck. I find it extremely attractive."

Maguire took a few minutes to reply, while nursing the pain in his shoulder. He didn't comment on the nature of her remark.

"You'd better come along with Miss Bechtold and me," he said. "Leave your gear on the hard shoulder. I'll have it collected and delivered to you, if you give me the details. We're going back to my headquarters, which are about fifteen miles away. We'll collect my own car and you can stay in my house with my wife and me, until all this rubbish is sorted out. What does a pretty girl like you want to do this kind of work for, anyway?"

"I have a feeling for the dead," said Natalie spontaneously. She noticed that Maguire was eyeing her strangely so she added, "There's always money in death. No recession can stop people dying."

Maguire felt ill. He loosened his tie further. The gesture set Natalie's blood on fire.

"I liked your second explanation more than your first," he said. "What's your name?"

"Natalie Klein."

"All right, Natalie, come along with Miss Bechtold, my driver, Mr Munn and me. We'll go to my Party headquarters and then we'll go to my house, as I said. I know my wife will like you and so will my children, some of whom are about the same age as you."

The traffic on the motorway started to move slowly. The Maguire-Mobile arrived at the Maguire Party headquarters where a lilac-coloured Daimler, with mauve-tinted windows was parked. Maguire got out of the Maguire-Mobile, clutching his shoulder. He opened the driver's door of the Daimler and eased himself behind the steering wheel.

"Come on, Natalie and Miss Bechtold, in you both get," he said, adding, "Drive the Maguire-Mobile to my house, Mr Munn. Follow us."

"Where are we going?" asked Natalie she was sitting in the passenger's seat of the Daimler. Miss Bechtold was sitting in the back. She resented being expected to sit in the back.

"To my house in the country. It's about an hour's drive away. It's near a village called Radley-on-Hill. My house is called Radley Hall."

Maguire turned on the ignition and drove off.

"Got any overnight stuff with you, Natalie?" he asked abruptly.

"Of course not. I wasn't to know any of this would happen," replied Natalie.

"Someone in Radley Hall will give you what you need. Next time you go out on business, see to it that you are better prepared, in case you run into this kind of trouble again. Yours was not exactly the predicament that an ordinary, well-wishing motorist would wish to get involved with," said Maguire mildly.

His tone of voice gave Natalie no indication whether he was joking, or berating her, so she continued to shield herself with the defensive abruptness, which she often used as armour.

"These things happen. That's all there is to it." Her staccato tone of voice had deteriorated to a military bark. He recognized the tone of anger in her voice and could not decide whether she was appallingly bad-mannered, or admirably bold. He did not comment but continued to look at the unfolding, country road, through the eyes of a jaded emperor, whose ministers had interrupted his siesta.

For the next few minutes, neither Natalie nor Maguire spoke. Miss Bechtold dozed off. Maguire's silence was due to exhaustion and low spirits which were exacerbated by his aching shoulder. Natalie was silent because she was not a small-talk conversationalist and only spoke, if she had something specific to say. However, she had been brought up to be polite in return for help, so she forced herself to start a conversation with Maguire.

"Have you got plenty of painkillers in the house we're going to?" she ventured.

"I suppose so," Maguire replied in a depressed tone of voice. A silence of ten minutes ensued while he tried to ignore the pain in his shoulder. Suddenly, Natalie said: "I've just thought of something you'll find funny. A man was travelling in a car with Sir Winston Churchill late at night. The man said to Sir Winston: "'It's very dark, isn't it?'" Sir Winston replied: "'It usually is at night.'"

"It's possible Sir Winston may have had a point," said Maguire, but had he been feeling less tired and depressed, he would have laughed. There was another long silence, which he broke.

"Do you speak French, Natalie?" he asked.

"Yes, I do. Why do you ask?"

"Because my wife's French. Although she speaks impeccable English, she likes to speak her own language sometimes."

"I'll speak French to her, then."

"Do you speak any other languages besides French?"

"Russian," replied Natalie tersely.

Maguire smiled. His mood transformed straight away. He loved the Russian language and spoke it fluently. He asked Natalie some questions in Russian. Her answers were even more abrupt and staccato than her remarks in English. Somehow, they sounded more amusing in Russian.

"Where the hell did you learn to speak Russian like that?" asked Maguire (in English).

"I taught myself."

"You mean you had no lessons?"

"No. My parents wanted my third language to be Italian. They wouldn't let me have Russian lessons."

"Your accent — it's Siberian. It's excellent and I'm very impressed by it, but wherever did you pick it up? It sounds so strange."

"By listening to Russian folk songs."

"No, seriously, Natalie. You can't pick Russian up, just by listening to Russian folk songs."

"I listened to tapes as well."

"Have you ever been to Russia?"

"Yes, once."

"Who did you go with?"

"No one. I went by myself."

"You mean you went alone?"

"Yes. My parents said I couldn't go to Russia, so I went there, without telling them I was going there. I told them I was going to stay with friends in Cornwall."

Maguire was astounded. "You really have got guts," he said.

Natalie suddenly thought of Murphy's cruel words to her in John Bell and Croyden's. She didn't say anything and stared vacantly ahead.

Her host eventually drove through some wrought iron gates. He followed a sinuous drive, which was flanked on each side by evergreens and flower beds.

At the end of the drive, stood a large, Bath stone house near a tennis court. There was a flight of steps leading to a garden, which was framed by more flower beds. There was a swimming pool, in the centre of the garden.

A black Labrador bounded from the garden to greet Maguire. A maid, wearing a light green uniform, her dark hair coiled on top of her head, arrived on the scene, just in time to prevent the dog from scratching the Daimler.

"Good evening, sir," said the woman, who was in her fifties.

"Evening, Minda! I've got a visitor with me as you can see. Miss Klein's the name. Natalie, this is Minda, who's put up with us for years on end, God help her. I hope you like the house. You have got a permanent invitation to it."

Natalie was still not entirely at ease with Maguire but her attraction to him outweighed her discomfort.

"Thank you, Jack, This is a beautiful house. You are so kind."

"I'm not kind!" said Maguire irratibly. She closed the door of the Daimler very gently, afraid that her instinct would be to kick it, in the way she had shut the doors of her hearses, after getting out of them.

"No," said Maguire quietly.

"No?"

He chewed his unlit cigar. "You have not closed the door properly," he said. "Try again."

They entered the house and Maguire went to a wash-basin in a cloakroom, near the front door, where he washed his hands thoroughly. Miss Bechtold went to her office. Natalie waited for Maguire in the same way that Murphy had waited, when she was showering herself on the first day they met.

"To be sure, I admire your cleanliness," she said, instinctively mimicking Murphy's Irish accent. She did not know that she had spoken, until Maguire fixed her with a curious stare. He said nothing but studied her with his bright blue eyes piercing, his facial expression fox-like and his blond hair dishevelled, expecting anything.

The house, like its owner, was clean, neat and tidy. A bright red carpet covered the hall which led to a flight of stairs. These divided the left to right at the top, beneath a copied painting of Napoleon rearing on a white horse.

Beyond the hall, was an oak-panelled drawing room, whose walls were stacked with classical books. The room overlooked the garden. In one corner of the room, was a giant, nineteenth-century globe. Nearby, on a polished table, was a silver-framed photograph of Maguire, Mrs Maguire and their children.

Chess sets, some with wooden pieces, some with bronze pieces and others with marble pieces, lay on a few occasional tables. This room was as tidy as a museum. There was a large table near the window, on which lay a pile of books, mainly about journalism, together with a bust of Maguire which was sculpted out of clay and which made him look older than his years. A jumbo-sized egg-timer dwarfed the bust and the combination of the two had an odd effect on the eye. There was also a porcelain bust of Maguire nearby.

"Want anything to eat or drink?" asked Maguire, who had seated himself near the giant globe.

"I only want tea and nothing else." Maguire liked Natalie, although he thought she was a bit strange. He also found her original, unconventional and feisty. He spat out his unlit cigar and wolf-whistled, putting both hands in his mouth, as he had done on the motorway. She laughed spontaneously.

"What the hell's so funny?" he asked.

"I like the way you whistle." Minda, the maid, came into the room and asked Maguire what he wanted.

"A full, cold chicken, a bottle of beer, tea for Miss Klein and nothing else," he said.

"Missus say not good for you to eat so much in one go."

"To hell with what Missus said! Get me what I want. I won't be ordered about by a bunch of hens!"

Minda returned with the things she'd been asked to bring, and gave Natalie a cup of unsweetened tea. Maguire wolfed the whole chicken in the same amount of time that it would have taken most people to eat a sausage. He ate with his fingers, having pushed the knife and fork provided for him, to one side. He took a long gulp of beer from the pint-sized bottle and looked contented.

"Tea all right?" he asked.

"No. It's not all right. I can't drink it without sugar," replied Natalie peremptorily.

Maguire whistled again and told Minda to bring some lumps of sugar in her fingers. She brought a silver container in which were several lumps. Natalie put four lumps into her tea, which she stirred thoroughly, afraid of leaving any sugar untasted.

"Keep your wits about you," said Maguire to Minda. "Miss Klein's got a very sweet tooth." As he said this, he took his shoes off and threw them into a corner. He rested his feet on one of the side tables, chewing another unlit cigar, which he had taken from a silver case.

"You've had a long day, so take off your shoes," he commanded.

"I don't really think I can do that in here," said Natalie.

"Do you think you're in a convent? You're tired. Take them off."

"No."

"Do you want to become a nun? You've been sitting around for a long time, so when I say take off your shoes, I mean take them off!"

Natalie did as she was told and imitated Maguire's action. She threw her high-heeled shoes to another corner of the room. One of her shoes accidentally hit the pedestal of a table supporting chess pieces, knocking a marble bishop onto its side and bringing a castle over as well.

"A bishop and a castle in one move!" said Maguire, laughing. "You really have got guts. By God, I've never seen such guts!"

Natalie was reminded of Murphy's cruel references to her cowardice once more, and of his sister's words of venom to the same effect. Even in her sleep, the words of the two siblings haunted her and caused her to wake up, shaking.

"You only work with the dead, because the dead can't turn round and tell you that you are a coward," one of the siblings had said to her.

Now, these words were being contradicted. The unmotivated and uncalled-for kindness, shrouded though it may have been, by a layer of primitive brashness, touched Natalie and moved her to tears. She bent over to give Maguire the impression that she was picking something up from the floor. She turned towards the window, wiped her cheek with the palm of her hand and forced herself to cough discreetly.

"Jesus, woman!" shrieked Maguire, banging his fist on one of the tables, and causing the chess pieces to shake, "What the hell's the matter? We Maguires don't stand for this sort of thing. We Maguires are tough!"

"No one has ever said anything like that to me before. You are so very… kind…"

"I do wish you'd stop telling me that I'm very kind! This is the third bloody time you've said I'm very kind since we met on the motorway."

Maguire's angry, frustrated words were more helpful in Natalie's circumstances, than words of gentleness or compassion. Her urge to cry had been obliterated. To be seen sobbing in his presence would have been the cruellest indignity of all.

"Can you play chess, Natalie?" asked Maguire.

"Only if my opponent allows me to cheat with my Knights."

Maguire laughed uproariously. Natalie was flattered by the fact that he had laughed at one of her jokes.

When he had finished his beer, he excused himself, and said that he had things to do. He asked Natalie to help herself to any drinks that she wanted. She went to the drinks cabinet, poured herself a large gin and tonic and studied the room more carefully. She looked at the paintings on the walls. The first picture to make an impression on her was that of a lady, in her forties. She had flowing black hair and was dressed in pale pink silk. She had striking blue eyes, which were wide and oval and which occupied much of her face. Her eyes were the same colour as Maguire's.

Next to each other on another wall, were portraits of two girls, aged about seventeen. They were identical twins. The only difference between them was that one had wild, fearless eyes, whereas the eyes of the other girl were brooding, histrionic and even sad. The two girls looked more like Maguire than the other lady. Both had long platinum blonde hair.

The black Labrador barked as a car's engine was heard coming down the drive. Maguire entered the drawing room unexpectedly.

"That will be my wife," he said. "I see you've been looking at my twins. I bet you can't tell the difference between them. Even I can't always tell the difference, except when they speak."

"How old are they now?"

"They will be twenty-two in a months time."

An elegantly dressed lady, carrying a black patent bag entered the room. Natalie recognized her from her portrait. Her classical, vivid beauty had not been romantically exaggerated by the artist, and she looked even more remarkable in reality. She was wearing a tailored yellow suit, black and gold ear-rings and black patent leather shoes.

"You're late again, Ma," said Maguire. "I'd like you to meet Natalie Klein, who's said she'll help us on our campaign. Natalie, this is my wife, Hortense."

The women shook hands. Natalie took an instant liking to Hortense, and continued to pump her hand up and down, absurdly longer than was necessary, as if it were a handle that needed oiling. Maguire eased her hand away from his wife's. His facial expression gave no indication whether he was puzzled, amused or irritated.

"You are simply incorrigible, Papa!" Hortense exclaimed in a shrill tone of voice, showing a strong French accent. "Taking your shoes off in a drawing room and throwing them into a corner. Even the children knew better than that when they were small."

"Sorry, Ma, I was tired," said Maguire quietly.

"Have you offered Natalie some tea?" Hortense asked, and looked in disgust at the chessmen lying on their sides. She put them back in their original places. Maguire looked at Natalie and winked at her.

Hortense muttered the word 'barbarian' under her breath and kissed her husband on the forehead.

"Natalie's had tea, Ma and she likes a hell of a lot of sugar. Maybe, she'd like some more."

"I would like some more," said their guest, smiling shyly. "Please," she added hastily.

"Would you please bring a proper tray of tea, a jug of milk and a bowl of sugar," Hortense said to Minda when she came into the room. She added, "Mr Maguire has thrown chicken legs onto the carpet, I see. I did tell you he wasn't to be given chicken in here. He won't use a knife and fork, unless he is seated properly at the dining room table."

Minda came back, carrying a heavy tray, on which was a tea set, comprising a silver teapot, a silver jug of milk and a large silver sugar container with a lid on it, on which the words, *Je t'aime, Jacques'* were engraved in minute italic writing.

"It's very nice of you to help us, Natalie," said Hortense. "Jacques has told me a lot about you already. He says you speak Russian."

"Not only does she speak it like a native; she also taught herself the language and went to Russia alone, without telling her parents where she was going."

Natalie could not understand why Maguire had told his wife this. She also could not understand what was so extraordinary about teaching herself Russian. She had found it an easier language to pick up than French and German and it had only taken her six months to learn it.

Maguire left the room to attend a press conference which was held in an office, in another part of the house. Natalie looked at Hortense. She was about to speak to her.

Dolores Murphy had come back. Natalie failed to understand how this woman had been able to triumph over the powerful and overwhelming aura of positive energy, which surrounded Maguire, and which had remained in the drawing room, even during his absence. She was convinced that the intruder was real but tried to tell herself that this was a hallucination.

Hortense could not see Murphy's sister, but Natalie was so certain that she was in the room, that she was not afraid of asking Hortense to order her to leave.

Dolores's face was whiter, even than it had been in life. Her eyes were just as sunken and as menacing. Her body was covered with black lace, and a matching black shawl was draped over her shoulders. She did not appear to be put off by Hortense's presence and walked closer to Natalie, who withdrew, as far as she could, until she touched the window.

"Please don't come to this house. Anywhere but this house," she said; her voice was scarcely above a whisper.

"I've brought my brother with me, today," answered the intruder, with the husky voice of the undead. "You like it when I bring my brother, don't you?" Her soft Irish voice was more frightening than a louder, harsher voice would have been.

"Please, I don't want to see your brother."

Natalie clutched Hortense by the arm. She was thankful that Maguire was not there to see that she was capable of fear, which in her eyes would have been more worthy of reproach than prostitution.

"Please make her go! Get her out!"

"Who?" asked Hortense.

"It's the sister again — the sister with the urn — she's back!"

"Whose sister?"

Natalie gripped Hortense by the arm more tightly than before. "She's in the room with us and you've got to make her go!"

"But there is no one here. *Je ne comprends rien du tout!*" Hortense always instinctively lapsed into French when she was in a situation beyond her control.

"The urn lies on the tray. It waits for you," said the soft Irish voice. "I put it there before the tray came by."

Natalie behaved as if Maguire were in the room. She tried to ignore the Murphy sister. As she poured out tea and milk, her hand shook so violently that she spilled more than she poured.

"Are you having sugar?" Hortense acted as if nothing had happened, but suspected that there was something seriously wrong with her guest's mind.

Natalie could no longer read the words, *"Je t'aime, Jacques"*. She seemed repelled by the silver container offered to her.

"Papa says what a sweet tooth you have," said Hortense, smiling, "and now you won't touch the sugar. Surely, you can't suddenly have decided to diet?" The older woman continued to hold the sugar container in front of Natalie, partly out of kindness and partly because she was proud of the engraving, which she had had put on the container herself, and which she feared Natalie might not have seen.

"Come to hell with us, daughter. There is no place for you in the land of the living."

"Get out of this house, you ridiculous Irish bitch!"

"Who are you talking to, Natalie?" asked Hortense.

"My brother's waiting for you, daughter. We both know what you did to his body."

Natalie grabbed hold of Hortense's arm in another vice-like grip.

"That isn't sugar! There's no sugar, not in there, there isn't! It's something else. For God's sake, make her go!" She screamed these words with increasing ferocity until she fainted.

* * *

The press conference held by Maguire was rowdy. The reporters had become over-excited, while interviewing this eccentric with a thick Liverpudlian accent, who had put on a tweed workman's cap, incongruously combined with a white flannel suit.

"How's your Daimler, comrade?" called out a *Daily Worker* reporter, wearing a black rubber mackintosh.

"My Daimler's going like a bomb, thanks, comrade," retorted Maguire. "I bet your boyfriend likes your charming mackintosh."

Laughter ensued. When it died down, an unshaven *Guardian* reporter, wearing an ill-fitting brown suit and black-rimmed glasses, got up, rattling a ream of paper in the air, until he found the right place. Maguire was reminded of an allegedly comic scene near the beginning of *Henry the Fifth* and waited with patient disdain.

"How do you reconcile your wealth with your egalitarian values?" asked the *Guardian* reporter, adding "You founded the socialist paper, *Maguire's Voice* didn't you?"

"That's a silly question," replied Maguire, his voice raised in anger and frustration. "Through my financial actions, I've been able to give thousands of jobs to people who would otherwise be on the dole."

The *Guardian* reporter flapped through his papers, letting some of them fall to the floor. He continued, "You've been described as a gold-obsessed bastard who… "

"By an idiot, yes," interrupted Maguire. "I don't need what you call gold, now. I'd made all the money I needed to last me for the rest of my life by the time I was thirty."

"So, what makes you tick?"

"I like people and I like helping them. Without my self-made capital, I wouldn't have been able to help anyone. My sympathies have always been with the underdog."

The *Guardian* reporter was in a vicious mood that day, because he had gone home the night before and had found his wife in bed with his chauffeur, who was a smarter and better-looking man than he. He could not confess his misery to anyone, without having to admit that he employed a chauffeur.

As he was a militant Left-winger, this would have been intensely embarrassing. He couldn't bring himself to hit his wife or to sack his chauffeur. His grievance had reached a climax and was intensified by the fact that his chauffeur had blond hair and looked rather similar to Maguire.

"How come you live in a luxurious house as well as running the *Maguire's Voice?*" asked the *Guardian* man.

"Perhaps you should learn to talk less and listen more. I've just told you I can and I've also told you why," said Maguire patiently.

"What you have said hasn't made me any the wiser," said the *Guardian* man.

"The wiser, I dare say not. Only better informed." Maguire got a standing ovation.

The *Guardian* reporter had been educated at Eton, although he had put down an invented comprehensive school on his many job application forms. He had taken his comfortable boyhood days for granted. He was totally preoccupied with himself, his career and his wife's infidelity.

He then asked Maguire a personal question. Maguire was about to explode in a fit of rage, when he was startled by Hortense's hurried entrance to the scene. She was looking baffled and worried. She whispered something in her husband's ear, gesticulating violently as she did so. He listened without interrupting her, with his arms folded.

"Christ, Ma!" he shouted, when she had finished speaking. He looked equally as surprised as she. He turned to the reporters.

"You'll have to excuse me, ladies and gentlemen," he said. "Something's gone wrong in my house."

"An excess of fancy chess sets and not enough room to accommodate them?" said *The Daily Worker* reporter in the black rubber mackintosh.

"No," said Maguire, smiling, "just an excess of chipped queens."

Hortense had not explained what had happened coherently, because there were so many reporters around. Her description of Natalie's behaviour gave her husband the confused impression that their guest was suffering from epilepsy.

When he returned to the drawing-room, he loosened his tie and took Natalie upstairs, carrying her in a purposeful manner, devoid of emotion. A photographer, seeking an opportunity to catch him in a Rhett Butler pose, was held back by Hortense.

She followed her husband as he mounted the stairs. "But Papa," she said, wringing her hands, "she kept turning round and looking at something. It was so odd. What do you think she was looking at?"

"How the fucking hell should I know?" snapped Maguire. He had become short-tempered because of the pain in his shoulder.

"Then there was all that extraordinary business about the sugar. What does it all mean?"

"Bugger the bloody sugar! I'm going to the room upstairs on the left. Get the doctor."

Maguire took Natalie into a dark room and left her lying on a bed. She was beginning to regain consciousness, although she was not yet fully orientated.

"She has gone now, has she not?" she asked. She was unaware of the fact that she was speaking to Maguire.

"Yes, she's gone to get a doctor. You had some kind of turn."

"She won't bring the ashes back. You won't let her bring them back, will you?"

"Don't shout. I've thrown the cigar away. I'm sorry if it bothered you."

"You don't understand. Please don't let her bring the ashes back. Anything but the ashes."

"We Maguires don't smoke, although I sometimes smoke cigars. Keep your voice down. There are reporters downstairs who might think I was seducing you."

"I'm talking about the other ashes," said Natalie.

"What ashes, for Christ's sake?"

"The ones that dreadful woman brings."

"If you're referring to my wife, you're being bloody impertinent."

"No! I'm referring to the *other* woman, the one who's always in black and who was here earlier."

Crises had a calming effect on Maguire.

"Epileptic turns are often precipitated by unpleasant hallucinations," he said. "If you've got epilepsy, the doctor will sort all this crap out. It's essential that you take the medicine he gives you, or you will end up swallowing your tongue."

Maguire continued, "It's a physical condition, not a mental one, and it is a physical ailment, not a mental one and it is easily treated. I'm going to draw the curtains. You are to rest until the doctor comes."

"Will you stay until he does? I don't want her to come back when you're not here."

"No one will come in here, except Hortense, the doctor and me."

"I want you to stay!"

Maguire flew into a rage. "Will I, fuck! I've got a press conference still going on, which I've had to interrupt because of this incident. I'm not sitting up here, talking a lot of rubbish about ashes. Jesus, woman, I'm trying to win a General Election, not run the bloody Y.W.C.A.!"

"Please stay," persisted Natalie, undaunted by Maguire's quick temper.

"There's no need for me to stay, Natalie. Nothing's going to happen to you here. I've got to go," he said.

A reporter from *The Sun* lobbied Maguire as he walked downstairs.

"Rather a noisy household you've got here, Mr Maguire. Do you keep a spare woman upstairs like Mr Rochester?" he asked.

"My daughter fell. She may have broken her leg. We're waiting for the doctor."

"Your daughter's very attractive. May I please go up and speak to her?"

Maguire loosened his tie again. A stray lock of blond hair fell over his forehead, giving him the appearance of a harassed Romany gypsy, who'd just been asked to move his wagons.

"Fuck off, guv," he said quietly.

* * *

Dr Alistair Mutton was a long-winded, mild-mannered man with a flushed face but a friendly smile. He had a full grey beard. To look at, he was a cross between Tolstoy and Karl Marx. It was for his gentleness and his sensitivity that he was most noted, but his inability to stop talking, once he had started to speak, particularly on telephones, exasperated anyone who had dealings with him.

He had been the Maguires' family doctor, since the birth of their eldest son, Timothy, then aged twenty-five. Maguire and his family were healthy, they rarely visited Dr Mutton, except during flu epidemics.

Natalie was reassured by the fact that Dr Mutton had never met any of the doctors whom she had consulted in the past, all of whom had described her as being a 'pathological hypochondriac'. The only exception to this rule was Dr Sergei Festenstein, who pandered to her every whim, and who always found something wrong with her, even if there was very little wrong with her.

"So you've had a fit?" said Dr Mutton quietly.

"Something like that."

"Is there a history of epilepsy in your family?"

"No."

"Have you got a GP?"

"Not really."

"Either yes, or no. Who is your doctor?"

Natalie's subconscious told her that it might not be wise to mention Dr Festenstein, so she said she didn't have a doctor at all and was most assertive about the false information given. She added in passing that, a doctor whom she had once consulted some years ago, had died, without her being able to remember his name.

Dr Mutton changed the subject. "Do you have a profession?" he asked.

"Yes. I am a funeral director." Dr Mutton cleared his throat.

"Have you had similar attacks before?" he asked.

"Often. Sometimes, once or twice a week. Sometimes, not more than once a month."

"Have you had these attacks all your life?"

"No," said Natalie spontaneously.

"Have you had any head injuries – any motor accidents?"

"No."

"When did the attacks start?"

"A few years ago."

"Are you taking any drugs?"

"Yes, a hell of a lot of stuff, to keep me alive."

"Who prescribes you all these drugs if you have no doctor?"

"I get them on the black market."

Dr Mutton looked puzzled. "What are you taking?" he asked.

Natalie listed about twenty different names, none of which struck Dr Mutton as being harmful or likely to cause epilepsy. He said he thought all her pills were unnecessary.

"Why do you feel the need to take all these pills?" he asked.

"I'd be afraid to go about my daily business, if I didn't take them. I need to make sure I won't get ill. I'm never secure, unless I can be sure that I won't become ill."

"You've got a deep-rooted fear of illness, haven't you?" said Dr Mutton mildly.

"Who wouldn't fear it?"

"Your fear of it has reached obsessive dimensions."

"There's nothing obsessive about looking after one's health."

Dr Mutton knew that he had an extreme case of hypochondria on his hands, but his instincts told him that the condition was more deep-rooted. Whatever the trouble was, it was psychological in origin and if the attacks were to stop, it had to be unmasked.

"What happened a few years ago?" he asked suddenly.

Natalie wiped imaginary blood away from her fingers. She opened her mouth to speak but her tongue froze.

"What happened?" repeated Dr Mutton patiently.

"A man who hated me, and whom I hated, died on the road." Natalie was speaking in fits and starts. "He had the letter in his hand. I'd written him an abusive letter."

"Did he commit suicide?"

"No. If he'd meant to do so, he wouldn't have got it right. He was Irish."

"Did you hate him because he was Irish?"

"No."

"Why, then?"

"I don't want to tell you."

"Recovery is never brought about without pain. We must all be prepared to climb over the barbed wire fence, if we are to reach the field where the green grass grows," said Dr Mutton, his trembling voice an octive lower than usual.

"I'd like to be able to answer your question, but I can't," said Natalie.

Dr Mutton leant forward in his chair. His voice was scarcely above a whisper. "Why did you hate this man?" he asked.

"Because he called me a 'coward'," Natalie replied in a frail tone of voice. Her speech had temporarily changed. It appeared that she had partly abandoned her loud, low-pitched voice.

"What did the letter you wrote to him say?" asked Dr Mutton. He began to stroke his beard. Natlie found his gesture repulsive.

She couldn't handle his question and changed the subject abruptly.

"His — his sister's a Catholic!" she shouted.

"So what!" he exclaimed. Dr Mutton continued to stroke his beard.

Natalie began to speak rapidly. Her voice sounded like a machine gun.

"His sister put him in the earth. She hates me. She had him exhumed, so that I couldn't visit his grave. Then she had him cremated."

"The expression on your face suggests that this horrified you. Why does it upset you so much?"

Natalie failed to answer.

"You can't help yourself, unless you tell me the whole truth," said Dr Mutton, adding, "I suspect that you are holding something back." Natalie took a deep breath.

"His name was Seamus Murphy. His sister's name is Dolores. I touched Seamus after he died, which is why she had him cremated."

"What do you mean?" asked Dr Mutton.

"I had no choice but to touch him, after he had died, because I knew he couldn't push me away." Natalie's answer was gabbled and manic once more.

"You speak like a child, " commented Dr Mutton. He took his handkerchief out of his pocket and wiped his forehead with it.

"His sister bears an unnatural grudge against me," said Natalie.

"Unnatural behaviour sometimes provokes a natural grudge in the next of kin," commented Dr Mutton mildly.

"I can't see things from your point of view. This woman has stopped at nothing to persecute me. She follows me wherever I go, making sinister and terrifying threats. She always carries the urn containing her brother's ashes under her arm. Sometimes, she wakes me up at night and shovels them down my throat, until I wake up choking…"

"Go on," said Dr Mutton.

"She told me that her brother was right to think I was a coward. I wouldn't mind so much if she attacked me when I was alone. She doesn't. She does it in front of other people now. She even got into this house today and started to insult me. Mrs Maguire saw her."

"That is where you are wrong, Natalie. Mrs Maguire did not see her. That's why I was sent for."

"My word has never been doubted in my life. I don't understand why you should be an exception to this rule," said Natalie angrily.

"How did she get into this house?" asked Dr Mutton.

"She can come and go any time she wants. She's not like you or me, you see," ventured Natalie.

"I do not see," said Dr Mutton. "What are you trying to tell me about this woman?"

Natalie didn't answer. There was a silence of about five minutes.

"In what way is this woman not like you or me?" asked Dr Mutton patiently.

"She's dead. I killed her. I hit her repeatedly on the head with a hammer. I took her body to Bodmin Moor and put it down a mineshaft."

"Were there accomplices?"

"No."

"Did your action strike you as being morally wrong?"

"Of course not," replied Natalie. "The woman might have told the truth, if I'd taken her to court on grounds of harassment, so I had to do her in," she confessed finally.

"Don't you feel any guilt at all?"

"No."

"Have you no conscience?"

"Of course, I have a conscience. I wouldn't hurt anyone who hadn't hurt me or mine. I wouldn't rob an individual, only an organization. I am loyal to my family and my partner. I am compassionate towards those who suffer and I am kind to animals and children."

"What about your victim's relatives? They may not have done you any harm but they are suffering from a bereavement caused by you," said Dr Mutton.

"I understand what you are saying. Dolores Murphy had no relatives. No father, no mother, no children, nothing. She and her brother were the only survivors of the Murphy family."

"The fear that you might one day be found out couldn't be very pleasant for you." said Dr Mutton.

"I won't be found out."

Dr Mutton paced up and down thoughtfully for a few minutes, with his hands clasped behind him. Then he said, "I'm not morally obliged to repeat what you've told me, because a doctor is not supposed to speak to anyone about his patients. "When you "see" Dolores Murphy, all you really see is what little there is of your conscience, taking on a visual form. No one else here saw this woman. Only you. Your subconscious is trying to tell you that you've committed a serious crime, namely murder."

"It wasn't really serious. A French court would have called it a 'crime of passion'. Dolores knew that I had got carried away with her brother's body. You won't tell Maguire, will you?"

"*Mister* Maguire to you."

"I don't mind about the killing. It's the other thing I wouldn't

116

want him to know about, the... er... interference with Dolores's brother's body. It's just that I don't think he'd consider it to be a terribly conventional thing to do," said Natalie mildly.

"What you have told me is in confidence."

"Good. So when Maguire asks you what's wrong with me, you will say 'epilepsy' won't you?"

"Do stop calling him 'Maguire'. Since you're staying in his house, it's damnably discourteous of you. No, I won't say anything to him about your association with the brother and sister. I know you want him to continue to be your friend. He likes you and I think you like him very much, which is why you need another chance."

"Thank you, Doctor. Will Dolores Murphy come back?"

"She will. However, the frequency of her visits will depend on how active your conscience is. It would be an understatement to say that your scruples are fairly relaxed. Hence, I don't think she will pester you very often. Her visits will become increasingly fewer and further between," replied Dr Mutton.

"Doc!" Maguire's voice reverberated from the hall. He came upstairs and went into Natalie's room.

Dr Mutton picked up his bag.

"A word with you, Doc," said Maguire.

"Yes, Mr Maguire?"

"What the hell's wrong with Natalie?"

"At this stage, it's hard to say. It might be a complex condition, but I wouldn't go so far as to totally exclude a diagnosis of epilepsy, or a variant thereof."

"Can we cut out the medical jargon? You're talking to a layman," Maguire said, almost rudely.

"It may be epilepsy. However it's something else, as well, I feel. There are two things wrong with Natalie," said Dr Mutton.

"What are they?"

"There are two things wrong, with her as I said. First, she's a clinical hypochondriac, who is so obsessively preoccupied with her health, that she feels the need to take hundreds of pills a day."

"How many?"

"She didn't say. A hypochondriac does not know he is harming himself by tipping explosive cocktails of pills down his throat. He is convinced that he is doing himself good and his condition is hard to treat. In Natalie's case, it's possible that her fits are precipitated by the excessive doses of pills."

"Christ, what a bloody load of rubbish! You said there were two things wrong with her. I've heard the first thing. Now, let's hear the second thing," said Maguire impatiently.

"Natalie had an unfortunate experience some years ago. She had a nasty shock. I don't know the exact details but she feels that she is, for some reason, a coward. Perhaps, someone called her a coward once. I'm not sure. Also, I don't think she's really suited to the kind of work she does. She's a funeral director, as you are no doubt aware. This probably causes her anxiety and that alone can cause fainting attacks."

"And the screaming when she recovers consciousness? What about that?" asked Maguire.

"When one faints in unfamiliar surroundings, one is often terrified before becoming orientated. The brain is not fully primed and the sufferer may shout strange things that others can't understand."

"Is that it?" asked Maguire.

"Yes, that's about it." said Dr Mutton.

"Well, Missy," said Maguire, after Dr Mutton had left the house, "There's nothing wrong with you, except that you are apparently taking far too many pills, all of which are unnecessary. Also, you lack self-confidence, because someone called you a coward once. I could tell from talking to you earlier that you are not a coward, but you must prove that to yourself and not to me. Will you agree to work for me full-time during my campaign? Will you take the opportunity of proving that you are not a coward?"

"I will take it."

Maguire shook Natalie by the hand. His handshake was almost strong enough to break her bones. "I congratulate you," he said, as if a million pounds were at stake. "You've made the right decision. But if you do canvass for me, you're going to have to mend some of your ways. First, I don't want to hear any dotty talk about ashes. Second, you are not to bark at any of my constituents, unless they give you cause to do so."

"I'll do everything you say," said Natalie.

"I'm sure you will. This is an important day for both of us. We are helping each other. You are helping me to win this Election and hopefully to become Prime Minister, and I am helping you to realize that you are stronger than you know. You had a traumatic experience a few years ago. I don't know what happened exactly, but whatever happened, you're going to get over it."

Natalie's mobile phone rang. Elliott was on the line. "Natalie, where the hell are you? Are you all right?" he asked.

"Don't worry, Charlie. I'm perfectly all right. I had a puncture on the motorway, and I had a lot of trouble with Augustus Brown's coffin. I met Jack Maguire, who's campaigning to be Prime Minister. Mr Maguire's sorted Augustus Brown out."

"The hearse with his coffin in it, was delivered to the shop. What worried me was the fact that there was no sign of you," said Elliott.

"As I've just said, Mr Maguire's sorted Augustus Brown out."

"What the hell do you mean, he's sorted him out?"

"It's a long story. I'm giving up funeral direction and I've agreed to work for Mr Maguire full-time. I'll come back after the Election."

"Have you been to bed with him?" asked Elliott urgently.

"Certainly not! He's got a wife and children."

"Who's going to help me in the shop?" asked Elliott.

"Mr Sprout will take over from me. I haven't deserted you. I will be coming home at weekends. I'll be back after the General Election, as I said," replied Natalie.

"You can't leave me alone with Arthur Sprout. He's only a bloody pallbearer."

"That doesn't matter. He's got a good head for figures and he knows how to handle the bereaved."

The line went dead. Natalie continued her conversation with Maguire.

"Will I ever get better?" she asked.

"It's not a question of whether or not you'll get better There's nothing wrong with you."

"You've given me a lot of reassurance. You talk to me like an equal," said Natalie humbly.

"You *are* my bloody equal!" said Maguire assertively. His aquamarine eyes, which were sometimes intensely piercing, were gentle and friendly.

"Is there anything I can give you in return for your kindness — something that has material value?" asked Natalie.

"Yes, there is. A hammer."

Natalie suddenly remembered something about a hammer. She wondered whether she had used one to kill Dolores. She shuddered.

"A hammer. Whatever for?" she asked.

"To knock the last nail into your coffin of no self-confidence," said Maguire. "We dine at eight. Hortense will give you some things, if you want a shower or a bath first. Don't be late."

* * *

As was his habit after his rounds, Dr Mutton dined alone in a pub . That evening, he dined in a pub near Radley Hall, about three miles away from the Maguires' house. There was no Mrs Mutton. Dr Mutton batted for the other side. He thought at length about his strange new patient during his meal. He ordered gammon steak and peas, which he found unappetizing. He washed his food down with tepid beer.

Although he had promised Natalie that he would treat her confession in confidence, he changed his mind while he was having dinner. He felt that a soul is better off, if it is punished by imprisonment on earth, than by hell fire after death.

This view was clearly not held by his patient but Dr Mutton thought afterwards that his need to save her soul outweighed his obligation to keep his promise. He became depressed and confused. He decided to act on impulse. That way, he could satisfy his conscience, he told himself. He decided to tell Maguire that his new friend was a murderess, as well as a necrophiliac.

He parked his maroon Mini Clubman Estate outside a public phone box. (He had lost his mobile phone). He did not intend to call the police, but to ring Maguire up and see how things went from there. It was only nine fifteen, according to his watch and he assumed that this would not be too late to make his phone call.

* * *

Natalie was sitting next to Hortense on a dark brown velvet sofa, while the older woman told her about the research, which she had been doing while completing her PhD in French Literary Studies. She spoke at length about the *Théâtre de L'Absurde*, its nihilistic themes, its propensity to startle and shock and its dominant flavour of black comedy.

Hortense's knowledge was boundless and Natalie, who had opened the conversation by expressing an interest in black humour, felt honoured to be listening to these revelations free of charge.

After speaking about the *Théâtre de L'Absurde*, Hortense moved on to *Crime and Punishment*,* of which she had recently seen a theatrical production. She asked Natalie if she had seen it.

* Dostoensky

121

"Yes, I saw it, but why did they have to employ such an elderly man for the part of Raskolnikov? I thought his charm lay in his youth as well as his nihilism," said Natalie.

Her remark reminded her of Murphy. She felt an impulse to confess her crime and the circumstances leading to it but checked herself.

"I didn't know that nihilism was charming in any way," said Hortense.

"It is in my opinion. A young man's tortured thoughts are attractive to a lot of women. When I read that book, I have a burning urge to take Raskolnikov from the printed page and drag him into bed with me."

"I don't agree with you," said Hortense. "A man who has little to live for is a bore." This further reminder of Murphy, and the manner in which Maguire contrasted with him so refreshingly, delighted Natalie and made her laugh out loud. It was not a natural laugh. It was a strange cackle that an obscure private joke can sometimes provoke.

"For Christ's sake, shut up!' shouted Maguire from the other end of the room. He was wearing braces and shirt sleeves and was watching *Match of the Day*, chewing an unlit cigar He had a passion for football and was mesmerized by the match. West Germany were playing England.

"Of course," Natalie continued, speaking quietly, "I could not live with a man like that for twenty-four hours a day. The negative mood might become infectious after too long. I am only speaking about one-night stands."

Hortense laughed out loud.

"Shut up, the pair of you!" shouted Maguire once more. "You're both being mean. I want to watch my game."

"I view *Crime and Punishment* in a different way," Hortense continued her voice lowered. "Dostoevsky was a black humorist in his own right. It doesn't matter whether Raskolnikov was physically attractive or not. It's the whole tone of the book that is comic. She added, " I feel we must all try to find Napoleon within ourselves. Take Raskolnikov for instance, he committed two murders, just to see if he dared to do so. This brings us back fo finding Napoleon within ourselves. He committed two murders to prove that he was as strong in his world, as Napoleon was in his world. Here was a man who sought Napoleon, within himself, but who ended up going to prison. Now, that is true black comedy."

Natalie admired and respected Hortense, however she couldn't understand why the older woman kept referring to Napolean. Her strangely woven path though it may have been in lies and murder, had met fleetingly with that of Hortense. She had found that she was almost on the same wavelength as her hostess.

Hortense had implied that she had been amused by the theme of a book, about a young man who had committed two murders, in order to find Napoleon within himself. Somehow, her approach towards the book, made the notion of murder less serious in Natalie's eyes and greatly relieved.

Although Hortense was only speaking about fiction, Natalie realized that she needed to find an inner strength within herself. Only when she had done so, would she have been able to shake off the visits from Murphy's sister.

She thought briefly about Hortense's reference to Napoleon. She, herself, did not revere him. She regarded him, in her own words, as having been a "revolting, pint-sized megalomaniac". She refrained from giving Hortense her opinion, because the older woman was French, and there was a possibility that she would have been offended by her words.

"There's one thing you must remember, Natalie," said Hortense, interrupting her thoughts. "You shouldn't really identify with the main protagonist in *Crime and Punishment*. Raskolnikov was a coward and I know *you* are not a coward."

"You are not a coward." The words echoed, and repeated

themselves until Natalie felt hypnotized by them. She thought of appropriate lines from her favourite poem, by Edgar Allan Poe, *Ulalume* which she though of in times of adversity or extreme excitement. She leant forward, as if in prayer and spoke them to herself:

> *"'And I said: "She is warmer than Dian;*
> *She rolls through an ether of sighs -*
> *She revels in a region of sighs.*
> *She has seen that the tears are not dry on*
> *These cheeks, where the worm never dies…"'*

"Are you all right?" Hortense asked suddenly.

Their conversation had been in French. Natalie would have found it peculiar and taxing to express intimate thoughts in English. She regarded English as a language in which only discreet and guarded sentiments could be expressed, which is why she kept herself to herself as much as she could.

The two women had been speaking for about an hour. Natalie felt freer, but her tongue was unused to the unnatural movements that the speaking of French imposed on it. It felt very stiff and her mouth was dry as a result.

"Are you all right, Natalie?"

"I'm all right," she replied, this time in English. "I'm going to get a gin and tonic, if I may."

"Feel free; the house is yours."

Maguire was still watching *Match of the Day*. It was a close game and the only form of entertainment, apart from the opera, that could hold his attention. Natalie walked past him on her way to the drinks cabinet.

An English full-back was hovering near the goal and was jumping up and down. The camera showed his foot kicking the ball, but Natalie could not see where the ball had gone.

"Was that a goal?" she asked Maguire, not because she was

interested in football, but because she wanted to flatter him by identifying with one of his interests.

"I'm afraid not. It hit the post."

The phone rang. Hortense answered it.

"It's for you, Papa."

"Who the hell is it?"

Hortense covered the mouthpiece. "It's Dr Mutton."

"Christ, Ma, not him, again! I've spent most of the afternoon with the bloody man. What does he want, now?"

"Mr Maguire's got someone with him," said Hortense. "I can take a message."

"I need to speak to him about a very urgent matter."

"He needs to speak to you about a very urgent matter," repeated Hortense.

"Does it concern an illness, relating to someone in the family?" asked Maguire with a strong rasp in his voice.

Hortense repeated his question to Dr Mutton.

"No, but I *must* speak to him."

"He says he *must* speak to you," repeated Hortense.

Maguire lurched over to the phone, looking over his shoulder, as another English full back tried to get a goal. His telephone manner had never been his forte. The idea of having to speak to someone as long-winded and as verbose as Dr Mutton, caused him to fly into a rage.

"Yes?" he snapped, taking the wind out of the doctor's sails.

"I've just had a somewhat unappetizing meal," began Dr Mutton with his slow, intonation. "I've been reading the Gospel according to St Mark over my gammon steak. It is so enlightening. You should mention religious themes in your speeches. They are a great vote-catcher. He continued to speak, before Maguire could interrupt him.

"I had to wait for ten minutes before I could use this phone box. The woman before me was talking about the many different ways there are of cooking scrambled eggs. I never thought there were so many."

Maguire was exasperated by Dr Mutton's flow of unsolicited information. He sighed heavily into the receiver which supported his chin. Natalie wondered what Dr Mutton was saying. She went to the drinks cabinet, a second time and refilled her glass.

Dr Mutton suddenly realized that he had forgotten to identify himself. He became confused, embarrassed and flustered.

"Oh, by the way, it's Mutton here," he ventured.

"B-a-a-a-a-h!" shouted Maguire.

Dr Mutton felt deflated. He forgot what he had planned to say and hung up. He satisfied his conscience by telling himself that at least he had tried to expose Natalie's guilt. As far as he was concerned, trying was as good as succeeding for some reason. He decided not to think about the matter anymore.

"What did Dr Mutton want, Papa?" asked Hortense, as she watched the glass shaking in Natalie's hand.

"That man, Mutton, is a Jesus glutton," said Maguire irritably and went back to his game.

"Did he say anything important?" Natalie forced herself to ask.

Maguire failed to answer her. He began to chant a strange, melancholic dirge, grossly out of tune. To Natalie, it somehow didn't sound like a song. She suspected it might be a funeral march. or a tune of bad omen.

It was in fact *God Save the Queen*.

"It's not possible!" Maguire shouted suddenly, banging his fist on the occasional table in front of him. "It's just not possible!"

The glass containing gin and tonic fell from Natalie's hand. It smashed as it hit the floor.

"What isn't possible?" she asked, as the bile rose to her mouth.

'Our bloody goalkeeper's been knocked unconscious!'

* * *

The Maguires had left by the time Natalie had come down to breakfast. She had a hangover. They had gone to their constituency headquarters. The newspapers were on the kitchen table. The popular press had given more coverage to Maguire's press conference, than the quality papers. *The Daily Stretch's* front page headline read as follows:

MAGUIRE DRAMATICALLY LEAVES PRESS CONFERENCE DUE TO DOMESTIC CRISIS

The headline was followed in smaller print by the words, *"Mystery Shouting Heard."*

The Sun was the crudest of them all. The story covered the whole of their front page. The headline read:

SINISTER SHOUTING AT MAGUIRE'S HOUSE –
"F--- OFF, GUV' IS HIS EXPLANATION.

* * *

In the short time that she had known the Maguires, Natalie had been a hindrance to their campaign. She decided to atone for the trouble she had caused them. She made up her mind that she would dedicate herself to making Maguire Prime Minister and thought intensively about the methods she would use to achieve this end.

She had already made a plan, but she knew that Maguire would not have apporved of her methods. She told herself she would not mention her plans, either to Maguire or Hortense.

The Maguires came back to Radley Hall while Natalie was getting ready to leave the house. She thanked them and promised them she would be coming back to help them, as soon as her domestic affairs were settled. Maguire gave her three hundred pounds in twenty pound notes.

"You're to have this. Buy yourself a slap-up tea and a few drinks at the Ritz. To work for me, you're going to need all the energy you've got," he said.

"Why, thank you, Jack! That's ever so generous of you."

"Goodbye, Natalie," said Hortense. "Remember, you'll always be welcome here and I want you to have all the friendship that I can give you."

"Oh, thank you, Hortense! One day, I'll pay you back."

Maguire followed Natalie out of the house and onto the drive. He noticed the hearse, which had been parked there by his driver, Mr Munn, who had collected it from *Klein and Elliott's*.

Natalie pointed at the hearse which looked like a glossy carrion bird, with its elm-surfaced bier-rack freshly waxed and its silver bier pins gleaming. "You'll find this useful," she said, "I'll be able to drive at least ten of your supporters to the polls in it at a time."

Maguire frowned. It was the first time Natalie had seen him looking worried.

"It's your vehicle I'm not too confident about," he said mildly.

"I don't understand. It's exceptionally reliable," replied Natalie. "Why aren't you confident about it?"

Maguire stared at the ground.

"Because I want to become Prime Minister," he said quietly.

* * *

When she arrived at *Klein and Elliott's*, Natalie told Elliott that it would be in their mutual interests for her to work on Maguire's campaign. The opinion polls were varied. The Tories stood no chance of winning. Maguire's Party was in the lead, with the Labour Party only fractionally behind it. Natalie feared that a Labour victory would lead to the nationalisation of the funeral business.

Elliott was swayed by Natalie's opinion and promised to manage *Klein and Elliott* in her absence. Although the business officially belonged to her, she was beginning to get bored with it. The only side of the business which interested her was fiddling the books and counting the money.

She had said she would return to what she called the "house" at weekends, and he had come to accept Sprout's new role in the firm.

* * *

Natalie took up Maguire's offer and ordered tea at the Ritz in Piccadilly. She drank the two "white ladies", a pot of tea and caviar sandwiches. She drank the two hurriedly and she felt a sense of well-being. She didn't realize how intoxicating the drinks were. She started to pour out the tea but the pot fell from her hand.

Murphy's sister was back.

"You thought you were safe," said the hideous woman dressed in black lace. The part of Natalie's mind operating at that moment, was the part which had no idea that Dolores was dead. When she had spoken to Dr Mutton, she knew at least that she had killed Dolores and her only fear was of being found out.

"You've punished me enough, haven't you?" said Natalie, her voice raised. The tea-room where she had been eating and drinking was crowded, mostly with a group of American tourists, some of whom were quite drunk. They stared at Natalie, fascinated by this pretty but strange young woman, who was talking to the air with her quaint English accent.

Among the people staring at her was Harley Street's wealthiest and most disreputable psychiatrist, Dr Humphrey Buttercrow.

He had been consulted by Hank Donleavy Jnr, a flashily-dressed, middle-aged American, who owned four five-star brothels in Texas and three casinos in Los Angeles. Like many Americans, Donleavy felt insecure in Europe, and was noted for his habit of hiring a psychiatrist in every European city he visited.

Dr Buttercrow was his London man, who had been prepared to see him over tea at the Ritz at his patient's request, rather than in his austere Harley Street consulting room. This agreement had been made, provided Donleavy paid treble the consultation fee and the bill for the tea and alcohol as well.

When he heard Natalie shouting, Donleavy had already become bored with confessing the inadequacies he felt when he was visiting what he referred to as "sophisticated joints". He stared at Natalie, in whom he had developed a voyeuristic interest.

"Say, lady, is something bothering you?" he called out.

Natalie didn't know he was joking and accepted what she thought was his genuine offer of help.

"What's your name, lady?"

"Natalie Klein."

"You've got to help me! It's the woman who's trying to shovel her brother's ashes down my throat!" she shouted obscurely.

"Ashes! Nuts! I can't see no one doin' that to ya, lady," said Donleavy.

"You *must* be able to see her. For Christ's sake get her out of here!" Donleavy laughed. Dr Buttercrow looked passively amused. He had heard Natalie giving her name.

Dolores pushed Natalie to the floor and sat astride her. She prized open her mouth, and shovelled her brother's ashes down her throat once more. Natalie found it difficult to breathe. She screamed and sobbed hysterically.

Donleavy suddenly felt guilty about having teased Natalie.

"Hey, I didn't mean to joke about that dame, Doc," he told Dr Buttercrow. "I feel real bad about it. I want you to give her whatever treatment you consider to be necessary." He handed Dr Buttercrow ten thousand pounds in fifty pound notes. Dr Buttercrow was astounded. "I'd do anything for that sum of money," he said banally and shook Donleavy's hand firmly.

"Please don't mention it, sir. I'm due to go to the Bahamas for two months in a few days' time. Obviously, I can't have Natalie followed up as an out-patient, so I'll admit her to my clinic in the west country. She can't come to any harm there."

"Tell me about your clinic?" said Donleavy, if only to make conversation.

It was in Dr Buttercrow's interests to lie to his patient.

"It's a beautiful place. It's like a five-star hotel, surrounded by glorious countryside," he said sentimentally and waved his arms in the air. "It's such a lovely place that our only problem is persuading our patients to leave it, once they're better."

"Well, am I proud!" Donleavy exclaimed, slapping Dr Buttercrow on the back. "I feel I've done someone a good turn and that sure is nice therapy for a disreputable brothel-keeper!"

Dr Buttercrow made a mobile phone call.

A private ambulance, connected to both Dr Buttercrow's Harley Street rooms, and his west country clinic, turned up outside the Ritz. The lying psychatrist knelt over Natalie, through morbid curiosity, combined with greed. He fondled the bank notes which Donleavy had pressed into his hand. A nurse in Dr Buttercrow's employ pushed a hypodermic syringe into Natalie's arm and knocked her out.

* * *

Dr Buttercrow was very slim. He was approximately, six foot, five inches tall and had thinning grey hair. His eyes were pale blue, like an albino's. He was nicknamed "Buttock Row," because of his penchant for sodomy, as well as heterosexual sex. His sexual style was unsatisfactory. He invariably finished before he started.

He had founded his clinic, on the proceeds of the soaring consultation fees which he had extracted from his Arab clientele. Ironically, the clinic was situated on Bodmin Moor, where Natalie had hidden her worst enemy's body.

It was a mental institution for women, and the majority of its inmates were the adulterous wives of Arab sheikhs. Their sadistic husbands had paid dishonest psychiatrists, such as Dr Humphrey Buttercrow, to punish them.

The clinic was a granite-walled building with small, high-up, barred windows and a slate roof. It was, indeed, as Dr Buttercrow had said, surrounded by beautiful countryside, the charm of which lay in its wild and desolate appearance. Obviously, the patients could not see the countryside from their cells because of the high-up windows.

Dr Buttercrow occupied a lavish office in the clinic. There was a sumptuously decorated dining-room with stained glass windows, in a wing which was sealed off from the patients. The patients were confined to padded cells and were fed on gruel, twice a day through a hatch.

When Dr Buttercrow was not in the clinic, he saw other patients in his Harley Street consulting room. The clinic on Bodmin Moor was manned during his absence by two sexually frustrated, powerfully-built matrons, aged about forty-five, both of whom were karate black belts. They were from Yorkshire and were known by their surnames, which were Blarmey and Sikes. Sikes was the tougher of the two. She had staring eyes and closely cropped greying hair.

Blarmey had a menacingly large, hawk-like nose, which caused her appearance to be particularly frightening. Neither Blarmey nor Sikes had had heterosexual relations since they had started to work at the clinic fifteen years earlier.

Both women were sex-crazed and when the going got tough, which was nearly all the time, they used each other's bodies with bestial urgency on the floor of the room which they shared.

Sometimes they stood against the wall. They wore stiff khaki overalls and wide, black leather belts. They never bothered to remove their uniforms when they were satisfying their sexual needs. These were so overpowering that they simply didn't have time.

When Natalie regained consciousness, she found herself in a cell which was ten foot square and which had padded walls. There was a mattress on the floor but no bedding.

She could not move her arms. She had no idea that strait-jackets were used any more, and was afraid of moving her fingers, in case she found out that her arms had been amputated.

During her confinement, in the Bodmin clinic she screamed in terror. Then, either Blarmey or Sikes beat her with a leather belt and injected her with intravenous depressants. She grew to fear the two women and cowered whenever one of them entered her cell. They frightened her even more than Murphy's sister had.

Dr Buttercrow visited her cell, just before he was due to fly to the Bahamas. His consulting rooms in Harley Street were topped with a helipad. There was also a helipad outside his West Country clinic.

Natalie hated his oily voice and his pale blue eyes.

"We are all here to help you," he said patronizingly.

"You're not trying to help anyone. You get kicks out of gaping at people like me, in the same way as the ghouls who stared at nuts in Bedlam!"

Dr Buttercrow enjoyed her outburst. One of his greatest pleasures, apart from skiing and frequenting his luxurious villa in the Bahamas, was watching Blarmey and Sikes beating his patients with their leather belts.

"Like a jolly good glass of port, what!" he exclaimed, as he watched a luckless patient being savagely beaten.

Natalie tried to remember her visit to the Rirz, before she had been admitted to the clinic. She had not seen Dr Buttercrow's Harley Street consulting room, whose walls were covered by Van Goghs and a Matisse, which he had splashed up and signed himself.

When he met patients in his Harley Street consulting room for the first time, Dr Buttercrow treated them like fools. He humoured them by telling them about his treacherous lack of ethics, because he was proud of his ingeniously dishonest methods of accumulating his vast fortune. He was unafraid of being disciplined by the General Medical Council because he thought he was above them.

He boasted to his Harley Street patients about wealthy Arabs, whom he had befriended, but he refrained from telling them that he had given their unfaithful wives depressants, instead of antidepressants. Thus, he hoped that they would commit suicide, not knowing what he had been doing, and with luck, leave handsome sums to him in their wills.

The Harley Street patients, to whom he bragged about his behaviour, could prove nothing, if they ever got round to reporting him to the General Medical Council. It was their word against his and he was famous and well-respected.

Some of Dr Buttercrow's Harley Street patients found him repellent and only consulted him once. However, these patients were outnumbered by patients who found him twistedly attractive.

Natalie loathed his refined, genteel mannerisms and his simpering, namby-pamby voice.

"Why were you shouting in the tea-room at the Ritz?" he asked gently, on entering her cell.

"I had a fit, an epileptic fit."

"It was not an epileptic fit. I know because I saw it."

"Epileptic fits are precipitated by horrifying hallucinations," said Natalie, subconsciously repeating Maguire's words. "I've had them before."

"You did not lose consciousness, as one does when having an epileptic fit. You saw a vision and you heard a voice."

Although Natalie had no idea at the time that she had killed Dolores, her instincts told her to stick to the cover of epilepsy.

"I saw no one and I heard nothing," she said assertively.

"On the contrary, you saw a woman carrying her brother's ashes, and you thought she was pouring them down your throat."

Natalie could not remember what she had shouted in Dr Buttercrow's hearing and his revelation terrified her.

"I said, I saw no one and I heard nothing," she repeated vehemently.

Suddenly, Dr Buttercrow pressed a button on the wall of her padded cell. He summoned Blarmey and Sikes. The three sadists forced her to come to Dr Buttercrow's lavishly decorated office in the clinic.

"Did you kill the person whose ashes were being thrust down your throat?" Dr Buttercrow asked eventually.

"No!"

"But you *did* kill the woman whom you saw, did you not? Had you not done so, she would not have become manifest."

"I saw nothing and I killed no-one," insisted Natalie.

Dr Buttercrow told Blarmey and Sikes to leave his office. There was a long silence. Natalie observed a vulgar-looking gold clock on the mantelpiece, which had just struck one fifteen. Plump-legged, winged cherubs were clinging to a marble rock, serving as the clock's base. The whole thing was contained within a glass dome. It chimed at fifteen-minute intervals.

"A charming clock, isn't it?" said Dr Buttercrow.

Natalie was silent.

"An Arab, with a recurrent depressive illness and too much money, killed himself and left it to me in his will. It's worth over five thousand pounds," said Dr Buttercrow.

"Why couldn't you have cured the Arab? That complaint is very easily catered for," said Natalie aggressively.

"I could have cured him easily, my dear. Lithium carbonate can cure depression within about five days."

"Why didn't you give it to him, then?"

"I'm not a fool. A patient cured is a patient lost, and a patient lost means I have to travel economy, when I fly to the Bahamas, as often as I do."

"A patient in your filthy, stinking hands is as good as dead," shouted Natalie. She uttered a stream of obscene abuse.

Dr Buttercrow drummed his fingers on his leather-topped desk. He listened until she had finished shouting. His face was serene and unruffled and his pale blue eyes were complacent.

"Why do you feel the need to use such words?" he asked quietly.

"Because you're detaining me against my will, when you've got no right, either legal or moral, to do so. There's nothing wrong with me, except epilepsy."

"It is not epilepsy. It is something entirely different and it is a condition which I intend to treat," said Dr Buttercrow.

"Let's hear your diagnosis, then, you stinking gutter quack. What do you think is wrong with me?" asked Natalie, her voice raised.

"In layman's terms, it's a form of madness. We, in our profession, call it 'schizophrenia'."

Schizophrenia. The only knowledge that Natalie had about schizophrenia had been gained from her seeing the film, *Psycho*. She remembered a ferret-like, very nervous man, dressing up as his elderly mother and attacking women with a carving knife. Schizophrenia. The word was definitely offensive, whatever it meant.

"I haven't got schizophrenia and your keeping me here is unlawful. Maguire is expecting me and I promised him I'd work for him."

"Who's hell's Maguire?" asked Dr Buttercrow.

"If you haven't heard of Maguire, you're the one who suffers from schizophrenia," replied Natalie.

"Who's he?" repeated Dr Buttercrow.

"He's your future Prime Minister, and he'll soon put a stop to your carryings on."

"Do you mean *the* Jack Maguire?"

"That's who I mean, and that's who I'll be working for," stated Natalie proudly.

Dr Buttercrow would not only be letting down his friend, Hank Donleavy Jnr, were he to release Natalie. He also knew that the future of his west country clinic would be in danger under Maguire's leadership. He tried to shake his patient's loyalty.

"Are you British?" he ventured eventually.

"Yes. Why do you ask?"

"Are you a patriot?"

"Why should I be? I don't ask myself what I can do for this country, in the way sex-crazed JFK did. Rather, I ask what thsi country can do for me.

My loyalty goes to my family and my closest friends. My roots lie in this country, and so do all my social and family ties. I am not particularly patriotic. I leave ethics to the law courts. I mind my own business."

"Do you realize Mrs Maguire is a foreigner? She's French isn't she?" asked Dr Buttercrow.

"What's wrong with that?" There is a pause.

Natalie thought about Hortense, of her love of life and her allegiance to the spirit of French culture, on which she had been raised and her sense of friendship.

"You! You live off the suffering of others! Who are you to complain about foreigners? What about all your bloody Arabs?" shouted Natalie.

It was not usual for someone to kick Dr Buttercrow's Achilles' heel and he was taken aback. He changed the subject.

"What do you think of my gold clock?" He lifted it from the mantelpiece, as an automatic reflex, in the way he did, whenever he showed it to sympathetic visitors. He foolishly handed it to Natalie. He was so preoccupied with her accusation that he failed to take the consequences of his action into account.

She held the clock in the air and looked at him with a hate so vicious that a spurned alley-cat might have had trouble competing with it.

"Ro-co-co and a bottle of scum!" she bellowed.

She threw the clock at him, despite its weight. A shard of glass cut him above one of his eyes. He overbalanced and fell, spraining his right wrist and he was right-handed.

His reactions were poor. He took a few seconds to recover his senses, before he pushed a button once more and summoned Blarmey and Sikes. After that, four men in white coats swared into his consulting room. He told two of the men to hold his patient down, before inserting the needle which would switch her off at the mains. She was returned to her cell.

Dr Buttercrow needed the signature of a second psychiatrist, so that Natalie could be sectioned officially. Two psychiatrists needed to sign an appropriate form.

There wasn't another psychiatrist in the Bodmin Moor Clinic. Dr Buttercrow sat behind his consulting desk, his mind busy. He realized that the only way he could contact another psychiatrist would be to fly by helicopter to his Harley Street address. He was able to take advantage of the helipad above both buildings.

He phoned his secretary in Harley Street on his mobile. Her name was Elma and she was a timid, twenty-two year-old Caribbean.

Dr Buttercrow's behaviour towards his employees lacked the obsequiousness which he used to beguile Arab patients. He found it a refreshing contrast to treat some of his subordinates as lackeys.

"Ring Dr Morganton-Bradshaw and ask him to call me

back," he barked at Elma. He wished to be phoned back in order to save money, although he didn't need it.

He had deliberately hired Elma on a temporary-come-permanent basis, which meant that she could never take sick leave, and could be fired at five minutes' notice, although she had been working for him for six years.

The Health Service cuts had prevented her from getting a more secure post in a National Health hospital and it was through necessity, not choice, that she worked for Dr Buttercrow.

Naturally, she was content at first with the high wages that a temporary medical secretary earned. She worked a forty-two hour week in order to support her sick mother in Birmingham.

She needed to finance her journeys to and from Birmingham twice a week. Elma was depressed and was worried about her mother's illness, and her thoughts had wandered. (Her mother had cancer of the pancreas, which was by far the most difficult form of cancer to treat.)

"Is there something the matter with your hearing?" asked Dr Buttercrow rudely.

"No, sir."

"Then ring him up and ask him to phone me. I've told you this already. With the amount you're being paid, I don't expect to have to tell you twice."

"Yes, sir."

Dr Morganton-Bradshaw, a well-known Harley Street psychiatrist, was only fractionally less unethical than Dr Buttercrow. He had cancelled his afternoon patients and was sipping brandy in the dining-room, adjoining his consulting room. He had been lunching with Professor Bollard, who was completing his two hundred thousand word, illustrated thesis on tertiary syphilis, and Dr Bumble, a specialist in sexual deviation.

The three doctors were all blind drunk by the time they had finished eating, but before alcohol had taken its toll on the merry trio, the doctors had been talking shop. They managed to get to their feet and staggered into Dr Morganton-Bradshaw's consulting room.

"There is a popular, but unsubstantiated theory that syphilis originated from Arabs having sexual intercourse with sheep," remarked Professor Bollard, his speech markedly slurred.

Dr Bumble interrupted him. "No, no, my dear fellow, according to an article which I read in last month's *Lancet*..." He hiccupped and couldn't complete his sentence. "According to..."

"Do get on with it," muttered Professor Bollard impatiently. He, too, was plastered.

"Well, according to an article I read in last month's *Lancet*..." began Dr Bumble once more.

He stopped speaking. He bent over and was sick on the carpet, while Professor Bollard and Dr Morganton-Bradshaw laughed convulsively, like educationally subnormal children.

"I say, chaps," suggested Dr Morganton-Bradshaw after a short interval, "how would you boys like a bit of music?"

"Jolly good show, what!" said Professor Bollard.

The three drunks sat on Dr Morganton-Bradshaw's consulting couch. Then, the latter went over to the record player which he kept in his consulting room. He eased Rachmaninov's second piano concerto in C minor from its sleeve and put it on the turntable. The pure, mysterious, silver notes wafted through the room, like an antidote to the pollution therein.

"My cleaner's off sick. Uterus gone for a burton, blast it!" said Dr Morganton-Bradshaw. "Would you boys mind giving me a hand, piling up these plates in the dining room?"

"All right, old chap," said Professor Bollard. "Jump to it, Bumble! It's Stackers, Harry Stackers!"

"That's right," boomed Dr Morganton-Bradshaw, "It's Harry Stackers and Sergei Rackers!"

It was after the plates had been washed and the guests had departed than the phone rang. Dr Morganton-Bradshaw was lying in a semi-stupor on the couch his patients used. Although he thought its overall structure was disorganized and rather untidy, he loved the concerto so much, that he played it a second time. He picked the receiver up, and held it close to his ear. Heavy drinking sometimes made him deaf.

"Who is it?"

"William, old boy. I need your help and it's damned urgent," Dr Buttercrow pleaded. "Would you mind ringing me back on my mobile?"

"I suppose so, old boy." Dr Morganton-Bradshaw reluctantly returned the call.

"What's going on?" he asked.

"This is an emergency. Can you come over to see me right away? I'm at number 82."

"82 Harley Street?"

"No! 82 Oxford Street, you fucking fool! What the hell did you think I meant?"

"Not a chance, Humphrey, old man. I'm so damned drunk, I'd never be able to bomb my Ferrari round the block."

"You're only one block away from me. Come on foot, man!"

"A psychiatrist in my position couldn't afford to be seen bowling along Harley Street, holding onto the bloody railings."

"What the fucking hell are you doing?" asked Dr Buttercrow. in desperation.

"Having an absolutely spiffing time, lying on my consulting couch, listening to rollicking old Rackers."

"Do you mean Rachmaninov?" barked Dr Buttercrow.

"Yarse, and I'll tell you another thing, old boy. Something damned funny. Do you know that this was Bright Button Beriwinkle's[*] favourite piece of music? I always like to refer to good old Beria as "bright button Beriwinkle." Before raping little girls, he used to put them at their ease, by taking them on his knee,

---

[*]   Lavrenti Beria: Stalin's right-hand man and head of his secret police.

and telling them that the music made him cry, if he listened to it alone."

"I couldn't give a bugger what blasted bloody Beria did!" bellowed Dr Buttercrow. "I've got a schizophrenic woman in my West Country Clinic. She's just smashed my clock. All I need is your signature along a dotted line, at the bottom of a document, saying you've seen her, and that you consider her to be dangerously insane. That way, I can keep her in my clinic in the west country on a permanent basis."

"Why don't you slope over here, old boy? Lot easier, what! I'm prepared to sign a document saying I've seen this patient, but I'm not moving now because I can't stand up. I'm too bloody drunk," said Dr Morganton-Bradshaw.

He sang tunelessly in time to the music.

"Turn the bloody music down!" shouted Dr Buttercrow, "and stop that damned silly singing. I'm trying to talk to you."

"Do calm down, old chap," said Dr Morganton-Bradshaw," adding, "In what are thought to be his memories, Bria describes his reaction when one of his junior victims starts to scream during the sex act. He says, "I was *obliged* to put my hand over her mouth." It had to be, 'I *obliged* to put my hand over her mouth'."

"So what?" shuted Dr Buttercrow.

"Don't you think that's bloody hilarious?" said Dr Morganton-Bradshaw

"For mercy's sake, knock it off, you old fool!" said Dr Buttercrow, adding, "You've simply *got* to come to my rooms. My patient's violent."

"Is the patient male or female?"

"Female," said Dr Buttercrow.

"What's your problem, then?"

"You don't understand. She's an absolute menace."

"Why can't you just let her go? Is she armed?" asked Morganton-Bradshaw.

"No."

"Then all she can do is wander about through the countryside. No harm done. Not to herself. Not to anyone," said Dr Morganton-Bradshaw.

"She's a danger to us both," said Dr Buttercrow assertively.

"Why to us?"

"She's dangerous because she's a friend and a supporter of Jack Maguire. She won't hear a word against him or his wife. Now, she's broken my beautiful clock."

Dr Morganton-Bradshaw thought for a few seconds and sat bolt upright. A wave of nausea and dizziness suddenly went through him.

"Maguire? Maguire? No!" he shouted.

"I'm afraid so," said Dr Buttercrow. He added, "Do you know what that's going to mean to people like us? It's bad enough for you with your controversial clinic ticking over in Jersey. You're reasonably safe because it's so far away. My clinic's on Bodmin Moor. Someone like Maguire could put a stop to my livelihood and possibly even to yours."

"Your clinic sounds more seriously threatened than mine. I don't think the problem concerns me at all," said Dr Morganton-Bradshaw selfishly.

"You owe me a favour as an old colleague," commented Dr Buttercrow unpleasantly.

"We're not freemasons and I owe you nothing. Jack Maguire won't interfere with Jersey. I'm drunk and I'm not going to help you. Solve your own problems!"

"For God's sake, man, we're friends, aren't we? I've received a few letters from you which are on my files. May I forge your signature on one of them? Dash it all, old man, I can't let a schizophrenic patient loose, after what I've told you about her association with Jack Maguire. I'm due to fly to the Bahamas again the day after tomorrow. May I forge your signature, *please*?"

"I suppose so," said Dr Morganton-Bradshaw reluctantly

and hung up. His liver couldn't take the strain he had imposed on it. He needed to get to the bathroom fast.

* * *

It was five o'clock on a Friday afternoon. Elma, Dr Buttercrow's Harley Street secretary, was leaving her office carrying her suitcase. She had just received a phone call from a hospital and was told that her mother's condition had deteriorated and become critical. There was onl hald an hour in which to catch the next train to Birmingham. Elma had not bought her ticket.

Dr Buttercrow heard the door of Elma's office closing behind her and caught up with her in the corridor.

"Sorry to disappoint you, young lady. I know how much you enjoy your jolly jaunts to Birmingham. This evening, you're doing overtime because, in the past, I've paid you falsely for hours which you said you'd worked, when in fact you'd been absent from the office, for most of the day."

"A message has just come through to say that my mother is critically ill," said Elma.

"I thought you'd been told not to receive personal phone calls?"

"My mother is *dying*. If I don't leave now, I may never see her alive." Elma began weeping.

"Don't burden me with your problems," said Dr Buttercrow, "unless you're prepared to pay a hundred guineas, for me to listen to them."

Elma's first instinct was to slap Dr Buttercrow across the face but another wiser idea suddenly occurred to her.

"Have you no charity?" she asked.

"I do not invest in charity. Either you go back to your office and do as you're told, or your jaunts to Birmingham will be financed by what you earn on the streets."

It was not in her nature to take a vicious stand against

injustice, not because she lacked vindictiveness, but because she lacked courage. She returned to her office, unlocked her drawer and took out a notebook and biro.

Dr Buttercrow produced a file and showed her a letter addressed to him, which had been signed by Dr Morganton-Bradshaw. His signature was easy to read. His handwriting was italicized and the Es were Greek. The person holding the pen had either been to a grammar school or a public school.

"Have you seen one of these before?" asked Dr Buttercrow. He handed her a fountain pen with an italic nib. The pen had been filled with ink.

"No, sir."

"I thought not. I bet you've never used anything, other than a biro in your life. Try to write with the fountain pen."

As Elma did so, the ink got onto her hands and onto her notebook. She was unable to hold the pen correctly.

"You're holding the pen at the wrong angle. Try again," commanded Dr Buttercrow.

Elma wrote her name.

"That's better. Now write Dr Morganton-Bradshaw's name, just as he has written it."

"Why?"

"It is not your place to ask why."

"I'm not forging his signature. It's against the law," stated Elma.

"If you're not prepared to bend the law in this instance, you will be earning your living as a tart, starting from Monday," said Dr Buttercrow.

"I will do it, then, sir, if I must." After practising Dr Morganton-Bradshaw's signature for about half an hour, Elma got it right. The forgery was perfect. She transcribed it onto the document which would have Natalie Klein "legally" committed to a mental institution, for an indefinite period of time.

"Good," said Dr Buttercrow. "Now, you can go and see your

mother. It is more likely than not that she will last until the small hours of the morning, because that is when a patient's blood pressure is at its lowest."

The lift wasn't working. She began to walk down the stairs. He followed her. He leant over the banisters to add a sadistic amendment, to his repertoire of abject cruelty. "Do have a nice weekend," he said.

Elma suddenly became bolder. She left her suitcase where it was and walked up to where Dr Buttercrow was standing, as if to shake his hand. In so doing, she gave it a violent wrench, as she had the physical strength of a lion. The pain was so intense that he fainted.

Elma had left the building by the time he regained consciousness. He did not know that she was carrying a tape, recording Dr Buttercrow's conversation with Dr Morganton-Bradshaw, as well as a tape recording her conversation with Dr Buttercrow, about the forgery of the other psychiatrist's signature. Also, the sadistic doctor did not know that she was an active supporter of Jack Maguire.

There would have been little likelihood of her finding her mother alive. However, on her last visit, her mother had told her that she would only rest in peace, if she, were to help Maguire become Prime Minister. Elma's mind was at rest and her conscience was clear. She would find another job on Monday morning and hand the tapes into the police. She did not need such a high salary anymore. Her visits to Birmingham would no longer be necessary, as her mother had died, just before she managed to get to the hospital.

* * *

Dr Buttercrow's Harley Street consulting rooms were on the second floor of a four-storeyed building. His address was 82 Harley Street. Mr Fergus McKenzie, a consultant gynaecologist, used the rooms on the ground floor of the building. He was a respectable, clean-living Scotsman who neither drank nor smoked. He worked for three days a week in the Middlesex Hospital which was a National Health hospital. He saw private patients in 82 Harley Street on Monday and Wednesday afternoons.

He knew nothing about Dr Buttercrow's corrupt practices, and the only connection between the two consultants was the austere, oak- panelled waiting-room, which their patients shared. It was also on the ground floor.

Mercedes Caja was a regular and unwelcome patient of Mr McKenzie's. She was born in Madrid and she had lived in London for most of her adult life. She was noisy, aggressive and hysterical. To atone for her defiance of the staunch Catholicism on which she had been raised, she ordered Mr McKenzie to fit a contraceptive coil without an anaesthetic.

He had to put ear-plugs into his ears, so as not to be deafened by her screams. He told her not to indulge in sexual activity for at least a week.

"What about this evening? I'm meeting my boyfriend this evening. I won't mind the pain," said Mercedes.

"No," replied Mr McKenzie emphatically. "I've just told you you should abstain for at least a week."

"Oh, dear!"

"Let me give you a wee word of advice," he added, in a conspiratorial tone of voice. "If your front entrance is indisposed, you need feel no qualms about using the tradesman's entrance, but be sure to grease your partner's member, if you've just passed a motion."

The consultant began to insert the contraceptive device. Mercedes started to scream.

The door leading to Mr McKenzie's consulting room was suddenly thrown open, so violently that it knocked over a side table, on which seven textbooks, written by the gynaecologist himself stood in a row, with his name printed on their front covers. Maguire had forced his way into the room. They fell over like a pack of cards. Mr McKenzie abandoned what he was doing and stared at Maguire in astonishment.

"Is your name Dr Buttercrow?" asked Maguire. His loud voice startled Mr McKenzie.

"You might have waited and given the door a wee knock before you came blustering in," the gynaecologist stammered.

Maguire clutched McKenzie by the arm. "Don't think I'm deceived by the sound of a woman's screams. I know what you're doing."

Another shout was heard from the other end of the room.

"Help me! You've just left me here! Who is this man? It's neither in nor out!"

"What is neither in nor out?" asked Maguire. He walked noisily over to the other end of the room, where the consulting couch was. He ripped down the curtain dividing him from Mr McKenzie's patient. Her legs were in stirrups. She was throwing her head from side to side, screaming.

Maguire was unfamiliar with gynaecological matters. He assumed that Mercedes was being held against her will and tortured. Her pain was so extreme that she screwed up her eyes and lashed her arms in the air, hoping to grab Mr McKenzie by the hand.

"There you are! Where have you been? Who were you talking to, just now?" she shouted.

Maguire became acutely embarrassed. It suddenly dawned on him that McKenzie was a specialist in women's matters. He stared at the floor in bewilderment and then looked at McKenzie.

"Please take it out!" she pleaded.

"Jesus, madam! I haven't got the right kind of authority. I came here by mistake. I apologize."

Mr McKenzie attended to Mercedes and inserted the coil

properly, while Maguire turned away, waiting for her ordeal to be over.

"Where are Dr Buttercrow's rooms?" he asked Mr McKenzie.

"A few wee manners would be the very making of you, mon. They happen to be on the second floor. I think he's away at the moment."

"Where is he?"

"I don't know. I hardly ever see him. He doesn't tell me his business. He's a psychiatrist and I'm a gynaecologist. Our paths don't meet."

"A gynaecologist? In that case I really, apologize sincerely for what happened. I wasn't to know," said Maguire.

"If you'd had a wee look, instead of stampeding about, you'd have kenned that, as soon as you stormed into my consulting room."

"I've already apologized, sir. Perhaps you would be good enough to give me that lady's name and address. I ought to send her some flowers."

"Leave them with me and I will have them sent to her flat."

"Good. So you know nothing about Dr Buttercrow's whereabouts? This is important," insisted Maguire.

"Now that you mention it, the husband of one of his patients, an Arab gentleman, was in the waiting-room last week. He was talking to another Arab gentlemen, about a mental hospital somewhere on the Bodmin Moor, in which Dr Buttercrow had incarcerated his wife. She had been unfaithful to him. That's all I know."

"Thanks, guv, and once more, I'm sorry."

* * *

Natalie had lost track of the time. She was still at the clinic on the Bodmin Moor. All she knew was the fact that she had been flown there in a helicopter. Because of the beatings administered regularly by Blarmey and Sikes, she had forced herself to behave submissively. The intravenous drugs had weakened her so much that she had temporarily lost the use of her legs. Sikes had asked Blarmey to remove her strait-jacket. Her hands were tied behind her with bandages.

One morning, Natalie was woken from a drugged stupor by workmen repairing the slate roof above her cell. Some slates had been blown off by the moorland winds. The acoustics of the building were such that noises from the roof could sometimes by the people occupying the cells and vice versa.

Blarmey and Sikes had taken this into consideration and had drugged the inmates more heavily, to ensure that their cries of misery would not be heard by the workmen.

Natalie could hardly remember anything about the period before her confinement. Sometimes, she was comforted by dreams about a couple, who had met her and who had been kind to her.

One of the workmen on the roof was whistling. Whatever the tune was, Natalie associated it with something pleasant. As the workman continued to whistle, the grey sky in her mind, miraculously cleared and was replaced by an almost Mediterranean sun, which radiated a feeling of hope within her.

Her first suspicion was that she had been injected with a different drug. She had received a depressent injection five hours earlier, but she thought that, for some reason, it was the workman's whistling which was responsible for her sudden change of mood. Her spirits had risen as soon as the whistling had started.

She tried to work out what tune the workman was whistling. She forced herself to remember when she had heard it before. It was a tune definitely attached to a song. She had heard the song being sung in a pub, when she had gone to Ireland, but she could not understand why it gave her hope.

The whistling continued. Suddenly, Natalie remembered a song called *Make Way for the Molly Maguires*…

She asked herself why the song reminded her of chess sets? She wondered why it had made her feel happy and self-confident.

Suddenly, she recalled a recurrent dream, which she had had about a couple called Mr and Mrs Maguire, who had gone out of their way to befriend her. She remembered how exceptionally attractive Jack Maguire was with his aquamarine blue eyes and flowing blond hair.

A familiar, voice, raised in anger, reverberated down the narrow corridor, leading to her cell. She thought this was an auditory hallucination.

> *"… the lavas that restlessly roll*
> *Their sulphurous currents down Yaanek*
> *In the ultimate climes of the Pole"*

She was pleased with herself because she had been able to remember poetry by Edgar Allan Poe. It eased her confusion and it was the only substitute for liquor that she was familiar with.

* * *

Blarmey and Sikes had been doing administrative work in their office, a room with a glass-paned wall, which served as a double-glazed, bullet-proof window, covered by horizontal and vertical bars. From it, the two women could see everyone who entered and left the clinic. They were expecting a new senior consultant, to whom Dr Buttercrow was planning to show the layout of the clinic. Dr Buttercrow was hoping that the new consultant would be able to work at the clinic during his absence, and serve as a partner.

This would enable him to spend more time in Harley Street and in the Bahamas. The man he was waiting for had just been disinherited by his wealthy father, and would have sunk even to selling heroin, to maintain an acceptable life style. He had no sense of ethics and was ideal for Dr Buttercrow's purposes.

A chauffeur-driven Daimler swerved towards the entrance of the clinic, churning up the gravel in the drive. Its passenger was leaning forward, asking the driver to go faster. He seemed angry and impatient.

As the white-flannel-suited passenger got out of the Daimler, he carried with him an aura of authority which impressed and excited Blarmey and Sikes. They were both convinced that he was the new consultant. Sikes was powerfully attracted to his thick blond hair and stared at him through a pair of binoculars.

"Never seen such a nice piece of work in my life," she said. "I hope he's a dab hand with the whip."

"Give over!" said Blarmey, as she snatched the binoculars from her colleague. "I hope he's for the taking. It would give us a change from each other."

"If he's for the taking, I'll have him first, because I'm senior to you," exclaimed Sikes. She was about to operate an electronic device which opened the outside grid and the inner grid three feet away from it. The newcomer did not come to the front entrance, however. He walked briskly towards the back entrance and went straight to the cloakroom.

Dr Buttercrow was using one of the urinals when Maguire entered the room. He was in a heartier mood than usual that day, because he had just witnessed a particularly sadistic beating.

He did not look into the mirror in front of him. Nor did he look at the newcomer, but he noticed through the corner of his eye that the man was smoking a cigar and was wearing a white flannel suit.

The newcomer's air of self-confidence impressed him. He was obviously the new consultant, who seemed to have an air of authority. Dr Buttercrow went out of his way to impress him.

"Take a tip from me, old chap," he said, slapping his thigh with a swagger stick and filling the air with a whiff of stale brandy. "Here's what I say to 'em, the first time I meet 'em, to put the damned blighters at their ease, if I think they're clinic meat.

"I swan into my consulting room where they're lying on the couch, waiting for me and I say, 'Absolutely strapping stuff, sex, hey what!' Do you want to know what I do just afterwards? I bung my stinking carcass out of bed, wipe the spunk off my Hampton, crash into a bath and go for a spiffing good run round the block.

"Then I bugger up to the kitchen, where I make four socking great crumpets, all of them absolutely *squelching* with butter. Then I bowl upstairs to the bedroom and I start all over again, what!"

Maguire dropped his cigar into the urinal. He concluded that his companion was a patient and decided to be as kind to him as possible. "Jesus, guv, some like it hot," he muttered.

Dr Buttercrow thought he recognized the newcomer's voice. He looked in the mirror and was staggered by the sight of someone who was undoubtedly Jack Maguire.

He wondered how Maguire had found out about his clinic's existence. His reactions were slow. Instead of pressing a button to summon Blarmey and Sikes, he stared transfixed at his deathly pale reflection in the mirror, and stood still for at least five minutes. Maguire left the cloakroom, went outside and into the building.

* * *

Dr Buttercrow went outside and walked to the main entrance of the clinic. He went into the building when Sikes had opened the electronic grids. She and Blarmey had buttoned up their khaki uniforms, straightened their hair and tightened their studded belts. Blarmey was so excited by the appearance of the visitor, that she inadvertently put her hand on Sikes's bosom.

The gesture enraged and revolted Maguire, who stormed up to Blarmey and pinned her against a wall. Blarmey had always had sado-masochistic tendencies. She hoped he would drag her into a corner and rape her, after roughing her up first.

"Natalie Klein," said Maguire peremptorily.

Blarmey stared vacantly ahead. Part of her wanted him to hit her. The other part was afraid of him.

"Take me to Natalie Klein who is incarcerated here," commanded Maguire.

Sikes handed a bunch of jangling keys to Blarmey, who showed Maguire to a tiny room at the end of a long corridor. It took Blarmey some time to find the right key to the door of the room. Maguire lost patience by the time she had tried seven different keys. Although the door was six inches thick, he heaved his weight against it, until it gave way.

It was only then that Blarmey realized that he was not the new consultant.

"Watch it, Sikes, he's an imposter!" she shouted.

Natalie was sitting on the floor in the corner of the room when Maguire broke in. She was exhausted by the drugs she had been injected with, and was so engrossed in chanting about the "*sulphurous currents down Yaneek*" that she didn't recognize him straight away..

"What the hell are you doing in here, you fucking idiot?" It took Natalie a few seconds to come to her senses, and his sharp words gave her courage.

"They put me under. Then they brought me here."

"Who did?"

"I don't know. I think his name's Buttercunt."

Maguire laughed. "You must mean 'Buttercrow'."

"That's right. He had me knocked under."

"Had you had one of your funny turns?"

"Yes."

"Where were you?"

"The Ritz."

"Were you conscious when Buttercunt approached you?"

"Yes, but I was injected with a strong sedative, I think."

"When someone comes up to you with a syringe in his hand, with intent to inject something, you automatically put up a fight, if you are a friend of the Maguires. We Maguires are tough!"

"I did put up a fight but I was held down. The next thing I knew, was that I was here. The man called 'Buttercunt' brought me here."

"Have you got a doctor of your own in London?"

"Yes."

"Does he know about your funny turns?"

Natalie said she wasn't sure. Then she contradicted herself and said her doctor knew about her.

"The sooner you get all this rubbish sorted out, the better," said Maguire assertively.

"I'm going to London, as soon as I get out of here. Then I'll ask my doctor to arrange for some tests to be done. Once I get the results, I'll know what to do next."

"Good."

Maguire took a knife from his pocket and cut the bindings off Natalie's wrists. "Come on, get up. We've very little time," he said.

"It's the injections. I don't think I can move."

Maguire ignored Natalie. She tried to get up. He didn't help her, so that she could regain confidence from getting up alone. She clawed at the white padded wall and somehow got to her feet.

"Good girl. Come with me."

Her legs gave way and he gripped her tightly under the arm.

"Your eyes are out of focus, so look down. That way we'll seem like old friends visiting."

While he was walking away from her cell, with her, she wondered whether he had ever been afraid of anything. Natalie believed, in her confused state, that he could walk on water and feed five thousand people on a loaf and two fish.

"Yea, though I walk through the valley of the shadow of death, I will fear no evil, for thou art with me, and thy rod and thy staff comfort me," she said out loud, remembering lines which she had learned in childhood.

"Shut up, Natalie! I don't want to hear a load of crap from the scriptures. I get enough of that from bloody Mutton!"

Blarmey, Sikes and Dr Buttercrow were standing at the reception desk.

"Excuse me, sir," said Dr Buttercrow to Maguire, "that's my patient you've got with you. You are not lawfully entitled to take her off the premises."

"She's was never officially certified. You brought her here under false pretences."

"I've got a document with me with two signatures on it. The document confirms that she's a schizophrenic" rasped Dr Buttercrow.

"Bollocks! Only one of those signatures is *bona fide*. The other's a forgery." said Maguire. "A secretary, called Elma, has surrendered a tape, giving the evidence that she had been bullied into forging another psychiatrist's signature. I have a copy of the tape in my car. The other doctor's name is Morganton-Bradshaw."

Dr Buttercrow produced a Colt. 38, which had been given to him by Hank Donleavy for his birthday. He pointed it at Maguire, who kicked it from his hand and unloaded it before handing it back to its owner.

Dr Buttercrow tried to strike him but missed. Maguire knocked him down. He picked up a golf club from behind the reception desk. He was about to hit Maguire on the head with it but his opponent kicked him in the stomach, winding him.

Blarmey and Sikes fled the scene and were about as useful as Ferdinand the Bull.

Natalie had been sitting on the floor, staring adoringly at Maguire.

He wrenched her to her feet. "Come on, Missy, we're getting out of here." He took her outside to the Daimler, the doors of which were held open by his driver, a very fat man, ironically called Mr "Tonky", which is the Russian word for thin.

The moors were misty and Tonky drove slowly. Maguire's previous chauffeur Mr Munn had lost his licence, dut to drink driving.

"Drive faster, will you," ordered Maguire impatiently, "otherwise we'll be in the same place this time tomorrow."

Tonky continued to drive at ten miles an hour across the foggy moor. Maguire hit him on the ear with a rolled-up copy of *Maguire's Voice* but regretted his action. He explained that he was swatting a wasp which was about to sting Tonky.

Natalie laughed hysterically while Maguire called the police from the phone in the Daimler. He exposed the illegal behaviour of the staff in the clinic on Bodmin Moor, and revealed Dr Buttercrow's identity.

He also stated that he possessed a tape to prove that another similar clinic existed in Jersey. (This was the tape which had been recorded by Dr Buttercrow's secretary, Elma.)

The inmates of the two clinics were discharged under police supervision. A long trial took place at the Old Bailey, London. Dr Buttercrow, Dr Morganton-Bradshaw, Blarmey and Sikes were branded as neo-Nazis and were jailed for life. Not all the inmates of the clinics were British nationals but those who were, were entitled to vote. The press had a field day. The British inmates of the two clinics, voted for Maguire.

His involvement in the unmasking of the two perverted psychiatrists, gained him a substantial number of votes, that would otherwise have gone to Labour.

* * *

Hortense was waiting in the hall, when Maguire, Natalie and Tonky arrived at the house. Maguire got out of the Daimler hurriedly and went into the house first, with Natalie followed him.

"I'm afraid Natalie's been very naughty, Ma!" he said.

"How, Papa?"

"She allowed herself to be binned without putting up a fight."

"But I *did* put up a fight!" protested Natalie.

"Putting up a fight, without winning is not good enough. When we Maguires fight, we win!"

"I'm sorry, Jack," muttered Natalie.

"So am I."

Hortense embraced Natalie, as if she had been her own daughter, and ordered tea to be brought into the drawing room. Hortense made a point of asking the Filipino maid, not to bring the big silver container into the room, and requested that the sugar be brought in a saucer.

"I'll have mine upstairs," said Maguire, who was in rather a bad mood. "I'm washed out I've had to deal with a bunch of bloody felons!"

"Stop it, Papa," said Hortense. "The more you talk, the less you'll sleep tonight."

Later that evening, Hortense played the first movement of the *Moonlight Sonata*. She asked Natalie whether she knew how to play it.

"I can play it but not nearly as well as you can. I'll play it if you like but I can't guarantee you'll be very impressed by my playing," said Natalie modestly.

She played about ten bars and played far too fast.

"That was much too fast, Natalie," said Hortense.

The younger woman stopped playing for a moment and thought to herself. She was sufferig from post traumatic stress. Her memories of her incarceration in Dr Buttercrow's clinic were beginning to hit her.

She knew her pills were in London and she only felt secure if they were within her reach. She hadn't had access to them for a considerable time and felt the withdrawal symptoms.

She decided to go back to London as soon as possible to pack her suitcases, one containing her pills and the other containing her clothes. She planned to return to Maguires' house after that. She started playing once more. She ignored Hortense's words and continued to play at an absurdly galloping pace.

"I told you already, that's much too fast! I should imagine Beethoven is turning in his grave! You look so worried. You're not in the clinic any more. You're safe. I've got something to show you that might cheer you up. Do you remember our black Labradors, Rosamund and Rex?"

"Yes, I remember them well."

"Rosamund's had some puppies while you were locked up. They're in the kitchen. I'll show them to you. Would you like that?"

"Yes, I'd love to see them, Hortense."

A wooden partition with family photographs clipped to it, divided the kitchen between the cooking area and the eating area. There was a television on a shelf, and a round table.

A phone lay on a side table. Nearby, was a small, enclosed area between two doors, overlooking the lawn. Six puppies, small enough to sleep in a man's shoe, played on a rug inside a basket. Hortense picked one of them up.

"Here's a present for you," she said.

Natalie was touched by the offer and thanked her hostess,

using confused, exaggerated, rather antiquated language which, although intentionally sincere, sounded unnatural.

"Don't you want him? We've got five others," said Hortense.

"I wouldn't be able to look after him. What's his name?"

"We call him "Ballie" because he is always rolling."

Natalie gripped Hortense by the arm. The gesture was so impulsive that it startled the older woman. "You are such a very *worthy* lady!" said Natalie in an obscure, ponderous tone of voice, which to her companion sounded totally incomprehensible.

An eight-year-old girl interrupted the two women. She ran through the kitchen and out on to the lawn. She had Maguire's looks, the same blonde hair and high cheekbones. She was wearing blue jeans and a white T-shirt, with the words, *"My face shall appear on the banknotes"* painted on it in small letters. Her hair was arranged in a plait.

"Arianne!" Hortense called. "Arianne, come back here at once."

Arianne had run off.

"She's our youngest," Hortense explained. "She's very naughty."

Hortense pointed to a photograph, of a girl aged about eighteen. She was the only one of the Maguire children who looked like her mother.

"That's Sarah. She's a year younger than our eldest son, Timothy," said Hortense.

Natalie examined the photograph closely. She noticed Sarah's close resemblance to Hortense.

"Sarah is more vulnerable than the other children, I feel," said Hortense. "The cruelty that she had to suffer at school haunts me to this day. There is so much evil and resentment about, particularly against Jacques.

"Petty-minded people envy him because he is rich. One

of the girls in Sarah's class told her that the daughter of a wealthy man, was incapable of understanding the suffering of others."

"How disgraceful!" exclaimed Natalie.

"Yes it was. The whole thing started during an Italian lesson. The woman in charge of the class was stating the Italian words for different cooking utensils. One of the girls put her hand up and said: 'There's no need to tell Sarah Maguire. A spiv's daughter would never need to do her own cooking'."

"How appalling! How did Sarah react?"

"She was very dignified. She smiled sadly at the girl, as if to tell her she was an idiot."

"But afterwards, didn't she *do* anything to the girl?" asked Natalie.

"She retaliated by saying, 'It is weak and cowardly to hit someone below the belt'," said Hortense.

Natalie was shocked, because that was all Sarah had said. She began to shout passionately,

"I believe in an eye for an eye and a tooth for a tooth, and more than that, an eye for a tooth and a limb for an eye! My vindictiveness would have known no boundaries, even if I'd had to go to jail."

"I know how you feel but I'm not sure you're right. We should forgive those who are cruel and callous. We shouldn't sink to their level," said Hortense.

"Why?"

"Because forgiveness deflates."

"I wish I could think like that. You must be very strong."

"No, Natalie, not necessarily strong. Suffering and being at the receiving end of cruelty teaches us subtlety."

"I have no control over my temper when I am wronged," confessed Natalie.

"I respect you for that. So would Jacques, but you must try to understand that the only way to conquer your enemies is to

161

be nice to them. I'm not referring to World War II though. I'm referring to cruelty today."

Natalie did not agree with Hortense, but thought it would be bad manners to argue with her again. Hortense suggested that she introduce herself to Arianne who was grooming her pony on the waste land behind the tennis court.

Arianne was shovelling grass into the pony's mouth after brushing it. It was white with rust-coloured markings on it.

"Hullo. Natalie Klein's my name. I'm a friend of your parents." Natalie tried not to sound too stilted, "Your name's Arianne, isn't it?"

"That's me."

An awkward silence ensued.

Natalie was afraid of patting Arianne's pony, because she thought it would kick her. The child was the first to break the silence.

"Do you like my pony?"

"Yes. I do."

There was another silence.

"I'm going back into the house now. There are some things I need to do," said Natalie self-consciously.

Arianne had taken a liking to Natalie, and followed her into the kitchen. She talked to Hortense for a while.

Maguire came into the room to have some beer and food.

Arianne on his knee. Natalie was jealous.

She told the Maguires that she was going to London, to get a medical check-up and pack her bags, before returning to their house. She had dinner with her beloved Elliott.

She visited Dr Festenstein and told him that she had been suffering from epilepsy attacks. She said the attacks had been brought on by her guilt, due to her former infidelity to Elliott.

Dr Festenstein arranged for her to have some routine tests. He also told her to ask Maguire, not to phone his surgery any more, as he had spoken to him more than five times already that day.

"How did Jack Maguire know you were my doctor?" asked Natalie.

"You must have told him, without knowing you had done so."

After her visit to Dr Festenstein, Natalie went to an all-night chemist's in Kilburn, to collect the medicines which he had prescribed. It was nine o'clock at night. She was relieved to find the chemist's was uncrowded. The woman behind the counter told her to come back in half an hour's time. Natalie was bored and was unfamiliar with her drab surroundings. She decided she might as well get drunk and went to the nearest pub.

She took a book with her, to read in the pub while waiting for her medicines. The book was Hortense's pink satin-bound copy of the Marquis de Sade's *Les 120 Journées de Sodome**, which she said she wanted back, when Natalie had finished with it, as it was part of a set.

Natalie was intrigued by the sound of loud Irish music coming from the pub. Fifes, pipes and drums accompanied noisy singing. The music had a hypnotic effect on Natalie. She approached the bar and ordered a double gin and tonic.

The pub was full. A heavily-built, grey-haired man of about fifty was rattling a tin, calling across the room for donations to help the downtrodden Catholics of Ulster. The man, an IRA cell-commander, with three men working under him, was not yet drunk but was certainly tight. He was wearing ill-fitting grey trousers and a navy blue anorak. He was with a younger man, who was equally as well-built as he, but more neatly dressed.

Natalie realized that this was an IRA pub. She sat down in a dark corner and opened *Les 120 Journées de Sodome*, pretending to be immersed in it.

A voice suddenly blasted in her ear. It was that of the tin-

---

* *120 Days of Sodom* – an extremely pornographic book.

rattler, who had been reading over her shoulder. "This man, the Marquis de Sayed, did he ever do any good for Ireland?" he shouted above the music.

"I'm afraid he spent most of his life in prison, so he didn't have a chance to go there. If he hadn't been in prison. I'm sure he would have buckled down and done his bit for the place,"replied Natalie.

The man went on rattling the tin and stood two feet away from Natalie, who was frightened of him. She went up to the bar and ordered another double gin.

"So what was he in prison for?" queried the tin-rattler.

Natalie hiccupped. "Well... he lived in the eighteenth century, when justice was even harder to come by than it is today. He was locked up because he... sort of fought for the freedom of oppressed people in general," she eventually managed to splutter.

The tin-rattler became more friendly. "Oh, did he now? He sounds as if he had the makings of a fine Catholic fellow! Your book's in French, isn't it?"

"Yes."

"I'd like to hear the sound of a foreign language, especially if it describes a freedom fighter. Let me buy you another drink," said the tin-rattler.

The music stopped and there was an uncomfortable silence. Everyone in the room had been listening to the tin-rattler. They turned towards Natalie, who asked for another drink, which she knocked back, before the tin-rattler had paid for it.

"Would you be reading part of your book aloud then, so that the boys can hear it?" said the tin-rattler.

Natalie read aloud in French for about two minutes. The passage, which she had selected at random, described a hideous sexual perversion, involving an eighty-year old man and a six-year-old boy, who were eating each other's excrement. She wasn't sure when to stop reading, and was interrupted by the tin-rattler.

"That sounds like good Catholic stuff! It's the first time in years that I've heard a foreign language. Would you care to translate it into English for the boys?"

Natalie hiccupped again. "I'll try," she said. The tin-rattler hissed for silence.

"It says… 'Man is as free as the noble beasts of the field, but his oppressors force him to walk in fetters. His feet are in fetters… Even his soul is in fetters'."

The tin-rattler had been looking over Natalie's shoulder at the text, as her finger traced along each line, simulating translation. He pointed to a word which appeared repeatedly.

"*Merde?*" he said, pronouncing the word as 'murder'. "*Merde…* does that mean fetters?" he asked.

"Yes, that's right. It means fetters," said Natalie.

"Fine Catholic stuff!" said the tin-rattler, with a glazed look in his eyes. "I'm sure the Marquis de Sayed, whoever the blessed lad was, is resting on our holy Virgin's breast, praying his guts out for Ireland."

Natalie burst out laughing, and spat a jet of gin and tonic over Hortense's book.

"I'm afraid I'm not very good at holding my liquor," she said.

"Never mind," replied the tin-rattler. Natalie had noticed that the tin had a shamrock painted on its side.

Almost everybody put donations into the tin. Natalie found a twenty-centime coin among her small change. The coin was worth about a penny in France and was worthless in England.

"Fine girl!" said the tin-rattler. "I'm sure you've heard many a tale about the evils of the Black 'n' Tans." Natalie hadn't heard of them.

"Can those be melted down and injected into a vein like heroin?" she asked.

Her question was so obscure and incomprehensible that the

tin-rattler ignored it. He turned towards the other men in the pub.

"Come on, now, everybody, let's have a song and give a thought to our beloved Erin."*

The customers stood near Natalie, who was the only woman among them. They sang a song called *The Hanging of Kevin Barry*, which had a weird, monotonous tune, alternating between very high and very low notes. The words of the song were repetitive and easy to memorize. They sounded more suited to the tune of *Clementine*.

Natalie had become so drunk that she did not fear her fellow drinkers any more. She drowned their voices and sang the song loudly to the tune of *Clementine*. Passers-by in the street could hear the famous refrain:

(Mountjoy)

"'In Mountjoy jail, one Monday morning,
High upon a gallows tree,
An Irish martyr gave his young life
For the cause of liberty.

"'Kevin Barry, do not leave me.
Kevin Barry do not die!"
Cried his broken-hearted mother,
When she saw the gibbet high.'"

"I've never heard that song sung to that tune," said tin-rattler. "I can tell by your accent that you're a Brit, but I still know when someone's soul belongs to Ireland. How about giving us your hand?"

"My hand?" Natalie extended her hand, and smiled to hide her anxiety.

* Erin: Ireland

"B'Jaysus, no! I didn't mean that. Here, take this. It's a form. Fill it in," said the tin-rattler.

Natalie looked at the piece of paper. Although her brain was befuddled with alcohol, she recognized it as an application form to join the IRA. She was terrified.

She longed to get out of the pub and go back to the chemist's to collect her pills. She let the piece of paper fall to the floor, and knelt down, clutching her stomach. The gin had made her nauseated. The tin-rattler bent over her, almost devotedly, and asked her what the matter was.

"Too much gin," she said and was sick. The tin-rattler, who was also very drunk, stared at her vacantly. He forgot that he had invited her to join the IRA, and brought her a glass of water. Then he turned towards the younger man at his side. Tipsiness impaired his discretion. He spoke in a lowered tone of voice, unintentionally within Natalie's earshot.

"You've orders to go to Belfast and be there on Christmas Day," he said. "It's a long time ahead I know. You'd better get some sleep. Where are you staying?"

"Number 60, Brondesbury Park Villas. My landlady's a black woman called Mrs Oates. I've lived in her house for a while. She's safe.I had to throw one of her saucepans away once, when I was mixing explosives in it." said the younger man, who was also drunk and who had given unsolicited information.

"You're supposed to change addresses every two or three days. You were told that on your IRA training course," said the tin-rattler sternly.

"I said, Mrs Oates is safe. She and I get on well. She doesn't recognize my Irish accent. What am I to do on Christmas Day?"

"An execution. Ruari McKearney's orders," said the tin-rattler.

"Who's Ruari McKearney?"

"Even in the Movement, there are few people who know

who he is or where he operates, except that he has an arsenal of arms. He organizes the transportation of the arms from America, as well as other countries. It's said that the offensive side of the Movement's operations would get nowhere without his organizing skills," said the tin-rattler, who was even more befuddled than Natalie. Liquor seldom got the better of him, but it had made him careless that evening.

He added, "McKearney's our best co-ordinator and even carries out his own executions, despite his high rank. He's by far our best marksman."

"Where do I come in?" asked the younger man.

"Ruari McKearney will be carrying out the execution of Jack Maguire, who appears to support the British presence," said the tin-rattler, adding, "It will be carried out on his exit from a Belfast orphanage on Christmas Day.

"Your job is to create a diversion. You will stand by in the Churchill Hotel with the other two boys in the cell. That's where Maguire will be staying. Liam McKearney, who is almost as expert a marksman as his father, will understudy him, in case of obstacles."

"Where does Ruari McKearney get enough funds, to finance the import of arms from America and other countries?" asked the young man.

"I don't think anyone really knows. Maybe, he bets on a big scale," said the tin-rattler.

"Is it really true no-one knows where he operates?" asked the young man.

"I've just told you. I don't think anyone knows. He may use another name. He may have an underground hide-out, as well."

"So, where exactly is this orphanage?"

"An agent of Ruari McKearney will tell you half an hour before the execution. That's all I can tell you…"

* * *

When the younger man had left the pub, the tin-rattler turned to Natalie once more. He assumed she had not overheard his conversation. He was almost too drunk to stand, without leaning against a table.

"Had too much liquor, have you, daughter? How did you like the song about Kevin Barry? I liked the tune you sang it to, better than the one I know," he said, his speeched slurred.

Now that her stomach was empty, Natalie felt happier and more reckless.

"I don't know who the hell this man, Kevin Barry was, or what he did, but whoever he was, I'd like to think he was wearing tight-fitting, black leather trousers, when he mounted the steps of the scaffold, and that he had a hard-on when the noose tightened round his neck," she said in a loud, carrying tone of voice. Her words echoed round the room and were even heard by passers-by in the street.

* * *

Natalie had no recollection of what had happened. She felt the same way as she did when she had been sedated before being taken to Dr Buttercrow's clinic. The date was the first of December. She woke up in the Royal Free Hospital in Hampstead, London NW3. X-rays showed a fractured skull, caused by a single blow to the back of the head. The injury had been inflicted by a blunt instrument, probably a bottle. It wasn't serious. Her family visited her. So did Elliott and Maguire who stood by her bed for some minutes before she recognized him. Elliott disliked Maguire. He was intensely jealous of him.

"What the hell were you doing in an IRA pub?" Maguire asked.

"I was passing by. I didn't know it was an IRA pub until it was too late."

"What were you doing in Kilburn?"

"Seeing friends, I think."

"What happened? Can you remember?"

Elliott told Maguire to stop cross-examining his girlfriend. Natalie had never seen her partner looking so angry.

She ignored him and continued to answer Maguire's questions.

"There was a man of about fifty in the pub. He was rattling a tin and was asking for money to support Catholics in Ulster. Everyone sang a song called '*The Hanging of Kevin Barry*'."

Maguire was uncharacteristically patient. Because memory consists of a chain that must be worked through, link by link, he went further. "Sing it!" he commanded.

Natalie sang the song very loudly, to the same tune that she had sung it to before. A nurse interrupted her, and asked her to be quiet but she ignored the nurse.

"Then what?" asked Maguire. He was suprised when Elliott stormed furiously out of the room.

"A man asked me if I wanted to join the IRA."

"What did you say to the man?"

"I was sick."

"What do you mean, you were sick?"

"What I say. Then he gave me some water and asked me what I thought of the song."

"Yes? Yes?"

"So I said, 'I would like to think that Kevin Barry had been wearing tight black leather trousers, and that he had had a hard-on when the noose tightened round his neck.'"

Maguire swore. "Then what?"

"I don't really know what happened next. I had had a few drinks, I think I must have fainted and hit my head on something."

Maguire chewed his unlit cigar.

"Has it by any chance crossed your mind, that someone

might have found your remark offensive, and hit you on the head?" he asked.

"Why, no, not at all."

Maguire sighed heavily, bit the end off his unlit cigar, and spat it onto the floor. "Does it strike you as being a particularly sensible thing to say in an IRA man?" he asked mildly.

"I suppose not, if you are sober, that is. However, there is something else you should know, which is far more important."

"What, for Christ's sake?"

It took Natalie five minutes to repeat the conversation which she had overheard between the tin-rattler and his young accomplice, namely that the execution would be carried out on his exit from a Belfast orphanage on Christmas Day. She implored Maguire not to visit Belfast then. He looked at her in a non-commital manner.

"It's a long time ahead," he said and left the room silently.

* * *

Natalie was discharged from the Royal Free Hospital after a few days. She went straight to the Maguire Party Headquarters.

Maguire's other children were there, and were introudced to her before everyone was due to canvass.

Maguire, Hortense, Miss Bechfold and Natalie travelled in the Maguire-mobile, which was driven by Mr Tonky. Maguire's chidlren and party supporters used their own cars.

The day-to-day work in the Maguire Party Headquarters was routine. In the mornings, workers sat in rows, on either side of long rectangular tables and performed menial tasks. Natalie sat between a woman aged about seventy, and her thirty-five-year-old daughter.

Both mother and daughter were lively and giggly. The daughter's hair was dyed birght red. They were known as "Old Hilda" and "Gladys Bingo." Gladys gained her nickname, due to her *penchant* for playing bingo.

Old Hilda and Gladys Bingo talked incessantly across Natalie, who found them irritating at first, but she soon grew to like them.

The mother and daughter sang tunelessly while they worked. Other times, to ease the monotony of their work, Natalie cracked jokes which were of a predominantly sick nature, and Gladys Bingo reacted by letting out a lusty cook's laugh, which turned into a hacking smoker's cough.

The workers were suddenly startled by Maguire's voice on the tannoy.

"Shut up, Bingo!" his voice reverberated. "I can hear you cackling from my office." Then all the workers laughed and work was delayed for up to five minutes.

Busy, but menial work continued in the Maguire Party Headquarters' everyday. Canvassing took place in the afternoons and evenings.

Natalie went out with Hortense, Old Hilda and Gladys Bingo. While mother and daughter canvassed one house, Hortense and Natalie canvassed the next one, covering each side of the street on the list.

Hortense and Natalie did their work quickly. Hortense, as the candidate's wife, said more, but for Natalie, it was just a question of saying, "I'm canvassing on behalf of Jack Maguire, the candidate representing the Maguire Party. Can we count on your vote, please? Will you need transport to the polls?"

Old Hilda and Gladys Bingo were still working on the same side of one of the streets, namely Keats Street in Riverfield, but Hortense and Natalie had finished canvassing the houses on the other side of the street, and sat down on a bench to drink a flask of lemonade. They got into a heated argument about whether or not the 1787 edition of the Marquis de Sade's novel *Justine* had more or fewer merits than the 1797 edition.

Natalie argued in favour of the 1797 edition, and said that virtue does not necessarily bring about good fortune. Hortense, however, thought that the 1787 edition had more merits, because of its conclusion that good fortune is achieved, only by decent behaviour.

"That has always been Jacques's belief and mine as well," she said firmly, "and it's mine as well. He started with nothing, has led an honest life, and now he has all he wants."

Natalie was touched by Hortense's argument. "I think he's an exception to the rule. My personal opinion applies to a majority, but he is unique," she replied.

The two women continued to drink lemonade, but were interrupted by furious shouting, accompanied by the sound of a saucepan hitting the ground, followed by a woman's sobs. The trouble had been started by Gladys Bingo.

"Who did you vote for before you'd heard of Jack Maguire?" she asked, in a bullying tone of voice, while a harassed housewife was holding a heavy saucepan of burnt eggs and baked beans. She had dropped it.

"Sometimes Tory. Sometimes Labour," said the timid woman, trying to ignore the gruff complaints of a man in the background, who complained that his tea was late again.

"It depended on who picked us up, to take us to the polls first," said the woman.

"Don't you know one party from the other?" barked Gladys Bingo, sounding like a cross-examining barrister.

"One's as good as another," bleated the woman.

"So that's your attitude, is it? I think it's time I told you a thing or two about Mr Maguire!"

The woman tried to close the door, but Gladys Bingo rammed her foot in the way, before she had a chance. It was then that she had dropped the saucepan. She let out a loud cry which attracted Hortense's attention from the other side of the street.

"*Beengo!* I think you'd better come away from that house and sit in the car," Hortense ordered. She apologized to the terrified woman who asked,

"Are you really Mrs Maguire?"

"Yes, I am."

"I know about your husband. He's very attractive. My husband forces himself on me every night, and the only way I keep my sanity is to close my eyes and pretend he's Mr Maguire."

"Indeed? Can we count on your vote, as well as your kind nightly thoughts?" asked Hortense.

"I'll vote for him all right. There ain't no Liberals no more, and both the Tory Party and Labour Party are useless. Can you please send a car to pick us up on polling day? Incidentally, who was that frightening woman?"

"We'll certainly send a car to pick you up," said Hortense. Natalie, will you mark "car" on the canvassing sheet, please?"

"Thank you ever so much for calling, Mrs Maguire. I didn't know Mr Maguire had such a nice wife."

"Then perhaps you should write a letter to us, congratulating us both on our choice of partner."

The woman smiled.

The canvassing sheet applying to the whole street recorded a twenty per cent Tory preference, a forty-seven per cent Labour preference and a fifty per cent preference for Maguire's Party. On a nationwide scale, however Maguire's party and Labour were almost equal in popularity, according to the polls.

* * *

"Bingo is not to go canvassing again, Ma," said Maguire at dinner. "We'll have to keep her at headquarters on paperwork."

"Who told you about Bingo's canvassing?" asked Hortense.

"Just other canvassers. I'm not going to give names." It was Natalie who had grassed on Gladys Bingo. He turned to

Natalie. "Tomorrow, I want you to go out on your own," he said, "without Hortense standing beside you."

Natalie covered about six houses in a mainly Labour street. She said the same thing each time: "I am canvassing on behalf of Jack Maguire…" etc.

The sixth house was opened by an unshaven man in his thirties, who was wearing an imitation leather jacket.

"Inviting me to vote for a lounge lizard Lenin, are you?" asked the man.

"What the hell's wrong with that? Jack Maguire came from the slums of Liverpool," retorted Natalie.

The man lost his temper. "Maguire's policies and thos of his Party would keep me out of work indefinitely," he shouted, adding, "Do you want me to rough you up and give you a good shag?"

"I dare you to try, but I don't think you'd be able to get it up," said Natalie cheekily.

The man hit her across the face with the back of his hand. She kicked him in the private parts but bit her tongue in concentration. The blood from her tongue made her 'injury' look worse than it actually was. She made a note of the man's name and address, before returning back to Maguire's headquarters.

On entering the building, she bumped into Miss Bechtold.

"Why, you're hurt!" said Miss Bechtold sympathetically.

"It's nothing." Natalie deliberately walked with a lurch to Maguire's study.

Maguire was sitting at his desk, smoking a cigar. He looked up from his papers, his eyebrows raised. "What happened? You've been injured. I'll get a doctor," he said.

"It's not necessary," replied Natalie. "I've got his name and address. He told me he was a National Front supporter. He also said that women who canvassed for what he rudely called 'lounge lizard Lenins', were fit only to be tied up and raped. I told him his ideas were unacceptable."

"What did he say next?" asked Maguire.

"He grabbed me by the arm and said he was going to rape me."

"Christ! What did you say then?"

"I said my usual: I dare you to try, but I don't think you'd be able to get it up! Worse than that, you'd finished before you started."

Maguire looked at Natalie closely, but he did not blush because Toxeth had made him tough.

"Then he hit you?"

"Yes he did, the bastard!" said Natalie, adding, "I'm only concerned because I may have lost you a vote."

"It wasn't there to have been lost in the first place. Someone called you a coward once, didn't they?" asked Maguire.

The question startled Natalie. She didn't answer.

"Well, did they?"

"Yes."

"Has it not occurred to you that that person might have been speaking in extreme sarcasm?"

"No."

"I'm telling you they must have been. You've got more guts than anyone I've met outside my family." Maguire paused for a while, "Sometimes, I see myself in you," he muttered.

When Natalie went to bed that night, she felt a warm glow pass through her. She was so delighted by Maguire's words that she did not take her customary sleeping pills.

* * *

The Irish ghetto in Barfax East was about the size of Battersea. Its population consisted mainly of Catholics who had emigrated from Ireland, and who had married English Catholics, although some marriages were mixed. There was a small number of non-Catholics living in the Irish ghetto.

Carol Kelly was a Protestant and was married to Tom Kelly, a former navvy who had taken early retirement. Carol had a son. The boy was reared as a Protestant and left home to find work, aged fifteen. Carol's health had always been poor, and it deteriorated when her husband died at the age of fifty-two. He had prostate cancer.

She had been widowed for six years, when Jack Maguire called at her house one Friday morning. Natalie was with him. She had asked him to let her see how he advertised himself, in order to improve her own style of canvassing.

Carol opened her front door, looking tired and haggard. She was wearing a quilted dressing-gown and slippers. A scrawny-looking border-terrier followed her to the door and barked throughout Maguire's and Natalie's visit.

"Mrs Carol Kelly?" asked Maguire, smiling.

"Yes."

"Jack Maguire's my name. I'm so pleased to have met you at last. I couldn't get an answer when I called at your house before. A charming Bassett you've got there. What's his name?"

"He's a border terrier, not a Bassett and his name's Jeff."

Maguire ignored the mild snub. "I'm calling to find out whether you'd care to vote for me in the forthcoming Election.

"I'm offering a decent alternative to what the Tory Party and Labour Party have to offer. As you know, the Social Democrat Party has ceased to exist."

Maguire handed Carol some leaflets, regarding his policies. She didn't say anything because she was a little deaf. She only heard half of what he had to say.

"May I give you a day or two to think it over? If you decide you want to vote for me, I can arrange for a car to take you to the polling station."

Carol's concentration had wandered. She had not taken Maguire's identity in. Her ill-health occupied her thoughts throughout her working hours. She assumed, subconscious, that he was either a health visitor, or her doctor's new registrar doing his rounds. She associated his friendly behaviour, with her ideal of a caring doctor's bedside manner.

Suddenly, and without warning, she harangued Maguire with an intimate description of a medical condition from which she was suffering. She used disgusting language to explain herself.

Before he could interrupt her, she spoke about five operations which she had received, gave a description of what the surgeon had done, followed by what the surgeon said he was going to do next. She continued to shout in a ranting monotone for about ten minutes, while some amused neighbours pulled their lace curtains aside to listen to her.

As she brought her rambling speech to a climax, even more inhabitants of her street gave her an audience, while Natalie stood behind Maguire, convulsed with giggles.

"Then, the doctor gave me some plastic things which looked like bombs." Carol's voice rose to a startling crescendo. "I looked at them and I said to 'im as I says to you, too, "I'll be buggered if I'm going to use a suppository."

"Blimey, madam!"

"Them doctors, they're all the same. All failures, the lot of 'em."

"That's just what my party is going to stamp out, Mrs Kelly. We're going to put a stop to these doctors who don't care about their patients. We will encourage those who are wealthier to join insurance companies, to pay for private medicine, so that those, who are less fortunate, can use the National Health Service which we are going to improve.

"We shall see to it that evert National Health doctor will give patients more personal care and attention, than they do at present."

Carol was too deaf to hear everything that Maguire had said, but she assumed that he wished to help her, judging by his sympathetic manner.

His charming tone of voice had touched her and she began to sob. "I won't use them filthy things!" she shouted. "I'll do anything but that…" Her voice diminished into a tight snuffling sound.

"Maguire's yer man!" said Maguire.

"I will *not* use them! I will not!"

"You're never alone with Jack Maguire!" Then he backed away from her, smiling and waving. She wished she could see the same smile on the faces of the many bored, disinterested doctors whom she had consulted.

"Mark 'Nutcase' on the canvass sheet," Maguire told Natalie, "but make a note, so that one of our workers can come out and speak to her. There's a good chance that she could be persuaded to vote for me. Also, I think she's rather deaf."

"I'll do that, Jack."

* * *

Maguire, Miss Bechtold and Natalie went in the Maguiremobile to another street, in the Irish ghetto, about a mile away from Carol Kelly's house. Maguire was driving.

He did not like women shouting at him about medical matters. It embarrassed him and made him very bad-tempered. He was about to sound the horn, as a young man and a middle-aged woman stood in the middle of the street, arguing.

"Your hand is hovering over your horn again, Mr Maguire," said Miss Bechtold.

"Sorry, matron. I've had it rough."

"Nevertheless, it's something you've got to be reminded about."

Maguire ignored her words, and stared straight ahead with a look of composure on his face, worn as a mask to hide the frustration beneath it.

In comparison with the other houses in the street, the next

house he approached, looked as if was inhabited by someone rich. There were geraniums in pots outside the windows and the walls were covered with ivy. There were two stone lions on either side of the front door.

A woman in her mid fifties, wearing nothing but a monogrammed bath towel, was running in circles round her son, who was aged about eighteen. The woman was gabbling like an agitated hen.

This was Biddy McKearney, a nervous, bossy woman with dyed, chestnut-coloured hair. She was five foot three inches tall, young-looking for her age, and was massaging herbal nourishing cream onto her face with a cosmetic smoothing iron as she spoke.

Her son, Liam McKearney, looked as dotty as his mother. He was wearing an ill-fitting denim jacket and green corduroy trousers which were two inches too long for him. He was unshaven and had dark, shoulder-length hair. His eyes were gret, like is mother's. His nose was retroussé and his gait was unsteady because he had a hangover.

He was carrying a few plastic bags, their contents spilling out of them and was wandering onto the road in front of the traffic. As he stooped to pick something up, he dropped something else. He was continuously distracted by his mother's loud shrill voice which had a thick southern Irish brogue.

"Now, you won't be eccentric in Belfast, will you, dear?" said Mrs McKearney.

"I'm not eccentric," retorted the boy, whose Irish accent was less pronounced than his mother's.

"Yes, you *are*, dear. When a boy's eccentric, the person blamed for his eccentricity is his poor, wretched mother." His mother continued, "You're the most eccentric volunteer the Provos have ever had among their ranks.

"I want you to remember that you're going across the water to help your father in an operation on Christmas Day —an operation which is vital to the Cause."

180

"I know, Mother."

"So don't go round looking an oddity, or you'll be stopped and searched."

"I *don't* look an oddity."

"You *do* look an oddity, you *are* odd and the boys will laugh at you. You can't even pack a bag properly, let alone manage a marksman's cover. You also need to shave."

Mrs McKearney bent over and repacked her son's bundles, which were still in the middle of the road. Maguire waited patiently, hoping she would get onto move on to the pavement. Mrs McKearney found a thick, elegantly bound book in her son's luggage.

"Fine book! Is this a history of Ireland?" she asked. It was *The Lord of The Rings.*

"Tolkien!" Mrs McKearney shrieked at the top of her voice, "Tolkien!" she repeated. "What does a grown boy like you want to read Tolkien for? All he ever wrote about was pixies."

"It's to help me relax, Mother."

"You don't work for the IRA to relax, or to be eccentric either."

"Keep your voice down, Mother! You're slap in the middle of a British street, and there's someone who wants to come by."

Mrs McKearney hurried onto the pavement. She embraced her son. Liam got into a waiting taxi and Mrs McKearney went back into her house, which Maguire was waiting to canvass. Natalie was standing beside him. The woman was still wearing a monogrammed bath towel when she answered the door.

"Hullo. Well, if it isn't Mrs McKearney! Sorry if I called at a bad time. Jack Maguire's my name, and I'd like to speak to you." Mrs McKearney knew who Maguire was, because she had seen a photograph of him, which her son had shown her.

His striking appearance confused her. Had his features been unattractive, her attitude towards her estranged husband's target, would have been as cold-blooded as befitted the tradition of her family.

"Good morning, Mr Maguire," she said formally. "Yes, you have indeed called at a bad time."

"The departure of a loved one, for whatever reason, is always distressing," said Maguire, "and I know how you must feel. I'm not going to stay long. Can I count on your vote? A fat lot of good the other two parties are. Their policies speak for themselves."

"Will you be taking your country's invaders out of Northern Ireland?" asked Mrs McKearney aggressively.

"That very serious matter is under consideration, Mrs McKearney," said Maguire noncommittally.

Mrs McKearney misinterpreted his remark. She thought this t Party intended to withdraw troops from Northern Ireland. That, combined with his looks, softened her. She had always had a *penchant* for blue-eyed men with thick, blond hair.

There was a pause. She continued to rub herbal cream onto her face.

"Are you a Catholic?" she asked, eventually looking at Maguire sideways.

Maguire knew she liked his looks and he wanted her vote. He looked her straight in the eye and smiled. *"In nomine Patris et Filii et Spiritus Sancti.* Maguire's yer man and the blessing of the Pope is upon you!" he said, making the sign of the cross. With the fourth movement of his hand, he slapped her on the bottom.

She gaped at him like a teenager staring at Elvis Presley. After a short silence, she said she'd left a tap running in her kitchen. She and asked Maguire to wait while she turned it off.

When she returned to her front door, she told Maguire that she would vote for him and shook his hand. She also shook hands with Natalie. As she did so she pushed a rolled-up piece of paper into her palm. It was not until she got into the Maguiremobile that Natalie read it. The words were written in pencil.

COME TO MY HOUSE ALONE AT SIX O'CLOCK THIS EVENING
WITHOUT FAIL. IT IS A MATTER OF LIFE AND DEATH.

* * *

"Why have you sent for me?"

It was raining heavily and Natalie was wet.

"Come inside," said Mrs McKearney, who was wearing a bottle green dress and a matching green jacket.

"Whatever you wish to discuss with me, must be dealt with on your doorstep. I'm not coming into your house, and I've left behind a note of your name and address in an envelope marked, 'to be opened only in the event of my disappearance, death or injury to my person'. Tell me what you want to see me about, and get it over and done with, as soon as possible," said Natalie curtly.

She went into Mrs McKearney's house, reluctantly. The look in the older woman's eyes convinced her that she was probably neither armed nor dangerous. Her house was clean and tidy.

On the walls of the living-room were framed photographs of IRA patrols, dating back to about 1939. One of them showed Mrs McKearney's father-in-law, aged about twenty. He was good-looking, and he was standing by a barbed wire fence with a bag slung over his shoulder.

There was a framed photograph of Mrs McKearney's husband on the mantelpiece. The photograph resembled, his father. Added to the photographs was a painting in profile of the Irish rebel, Patrick Pearse.

An orange, green and white flag covered the wall above the pictures. A life-sized crucifix occupied the facing wall, and well-polished Catholic relics adorned the tables.

"Why have you told me to come here?" asked Natalie suspiciously.

"Please sit down."

Natalie sat on the arm of a green velvet armchair, and held

her hands together in front of her. Mrs McKearney poured out two glasses of sherry. She gave one to Natalie and drank the other, which she refilled and drained, before filling it once more.

"I didn't know what sort of man your Mr Maguire was until today. To us, one Brit in politics is as bad as another, and one Brit killed for the Cause…"

The older woman was unable to finish her sentence.

Her voice cracked as if she were fighting tears "… is there no more than a pheasant," asked Natalie.

"What do you mean it's broken?"

"My son has never kept anything from his mother. He's been summoned to Belfast by his father, Ruari McKearney. My husband's an important figure in the offensive wing of the IRA. He is also a man of considerable wealth." Mrs Mckearney continued, "He poses as a Protestant and his income comes from races won by a number of racehorses which he owns. He is also a successful gambler and has inherited wealth. His most famous racehorse is called 'Shamrock Kitty'. Apart from the maintenance of my house and the generous allowance that he gives me, his income goes to IRA funds and the sponsoring of its operations."

"What in the world has that got to do with Mr Maguire?" asked Natalie.

Mrs McKearney poured herself another glass of sherry and drained it. Her mind had become befuddled and her tongue was looser than her husband would have wished it to be.

"My husband has already planned Mr Maguire's execution, because of his pied-piper appeal to the British public. My son is as good at handling a rifle as his father is. He will be present at Maguire's execution, in case anything unforeseen happens. If it does, he will take over the execution himself." Natalie listened in horror, without interrupting Mrs McKearney.

"I know there are others involved, because my son has

connections in Kilburn, where he's been spending a lot of his spare time."

Natalie had already told the police about her experience in the IRA pub and had reported the conversation which she had overheard. The Churchill Hotel, in Belfast, which Maguire had planned to stay in, was going to be surrounded by Special Branch detectives. Natalie was not satisfied that this was safe enough.

"Where does your husband live?" she asked.

Mrs McKearney opened a desk drawer, from which she took a map. She drew Natalie's attention to a stretch of countryside north of Belfast. She showed the younger woman where her husband lived. She explained that he lived in a castle, rather than a house.

"That's where he lives," she repeated, almost proudly. "There's a Protestant pub in Haagan village nearby. He drinks there every day. As he's a perfect mimic, he can imitate the brogue the Protestants use. He's known to the locals as Raymond Morgan. He attends Protestant services in the local church regularly, and will go there on Christmas morning. The pub is very near the church.

"Maguire's execution is due to take place at one fifteen. He will be leaving the Churchill Hotel just after twelve o'clock, before he visits the William of Orange orphanage."

"Do you think that what your friends are doing is right?" asked Natalie.

"I am committed to the withdrawal of troops from Ulster, and the only way to get anything out of the British, is to use perpetual violence.* I've been a Republican all my life, and I would die for the Cause, but nothing, and I repeat nothing would induce me to condone the killing of a fine man like Maguire. He would look exactly like my husband, if my husband had blond hair."

---

* Please note that this narrative precedes the Good Friday Agreement.

"You sound as if you were in love with him," commented Natalie tersely.

"I have only met him once but I know a good man when I see one. Are you in love with him?"

"I am," replied Natalie, in a stilted tone of voice. She added, "How can I prevent your husband committing this act?"

"He has a weakness for beautiful women. His sexual tastes are rather perverse."

"In what way?"

"I can't be specific. He just likes women to do things to him, which are odd," said Mrs McKearney vaguely.

Natalie was tired and bored. She expected direct answers from Mrs McKearney. She was intolerant of incoherence and evasiveness.

"My patience is as limited as my time," she said. "You're going to have to do a lot better than that if this operation is to be averted. What's the best way to approach your husband?"

"I'm doing my best to explain," said Mrs McKearney.

"It's no good your saying you're doing your best, if your best isn't good enough. Try again."

"He likes beautiful women, as I said, and anything that is kinky. It makes me feel ill to talk about it and I'm pleased I don't know any details. It was his strange sexual habits, as well as his compulsive womanizing, that made me ask him to leave this house, although I still love him to distraction. I don't want him to do wrong, but I don't think I know the difference between right and wrong anymore."

The older woman burst into tears.

"I'm not a hard woman, but I don't know how to handle other people's tears, Mrs McKearney," said Natalie, unsympathetically. She added, "What time will your husband be attending the church service on Christmas Day?"

"The service will be at Haagan Village Church, as I said earlier. It is due to start at nine o'clock. It should end at ten

186

thirty," said Mrs McKearney. She continued, "This will leave my husband enough time to drive to the Belfast city centre and assemble the Armelite rifle."

Suddenly, Natalie remembered the film, *The Day of the Jackal*, and feared that whatever security regulations were enforced, nothing would prevent a professional assassin from carrying out an execution, although the Jackal failed to assassinate General de Gaulle.This was because he had lowered his head.

"Is your husband devout?" she asked cautiously.

"No."

"What I am trying to say is — does he have any scruples about what is done in a church and what isn't?"

"When he was a young lad, he cared deeply, about his faith, but now he has no scruples about how to behave in the House of God. If he did have any scruples, he would not frequent the House of the wrong God." Mrs McKearney began to cry again.

"I do wish you'd stop crying, Mrs McKearney," said Natalie, in a matronly tone of voice. "It doesn't help either of us. Perhaps you could tell me about your husband's behaviour towards women. Does he like them to be aggressive or submissive when he has sex with them?"

"In the home, he likes them to be submissive, but outside, he likes them to be kinky and aggressive."

"You're going to have to be more specific than that," said Natalie. "Does he like them to dress up as French maids? Does he like them to whip him?"

The older woman laughed.

"Just do anything," she said at length. "I can't discuss it any more."

"All right, Mrs McKearney, I'll go to Haagan Village Church and I'll see to it that your husband is delayed. I'll need a photograph of him as he is now, from the front and in profile," said Natalie assertively.

Mrs McKearney showed Natalie a photograph album. It was full of pictures of a muscular, dark-haired man, somewhere in his early fifties. He had a well-proportioned, forceful face, large grey eyes and ruggedly attractive features. He did not have the kind of face that one would associate with a professional assasin.

Mrs McKearney told Natalie that her husband carried a leather, Church of England prayer book, with the initials R.S.M. (standing for 'Ruari Sean McKearney' and 'Raymond Stanley Morgan') in gold letters on a bright red background. She added that he occupied a pew to himself at the back of Haagan Village Church.

"All right, I know what to do," said Natalie, adding. "Don't think it's convenient for me to do this. It isn't. I'd much rather be with my family on Christmas Day. I'm concerned about Mr Maguire's. If you are double-crossing me, I will leave an envelope in my bank and another at home.

"In the envelopes, will be documents which will brand you as being an informer against your own people, and in particular, against your husband. The document, will also say exactly who you are and where you live.

"Your son won't get off lightly," continued Natalie. "Terrorists are not treated well in English prisons. I'm sure you wouldn't want your precious, eccentric son to be disfigured, or even worse than that, buggered, which is what happens to most IRA men in English prisons."

After another long fit of weeping, Mrs McKearney forced herself to speak. "I'm not double-crossing you. I'm so confused now. Once I thought I knew right from wrong. Now, I don't."

"So you said," said Natalie, adding, "All I care about is preventing this assassination." She got up to go. She left without saying "goodbye" to Mrs McKearney. She made a statement at a neighbouring police station. She also put a call through to Maguire's headquarters. Miss Bechtold answered. Natalie left a message for Maguire. All she had to do now was to delay Ruari McKearney's plans to execute him.

* * *

Ruari McKearney was extremely good-looking, as was shown in his photographs. He had secretly been an active campaigner for the IRA since the age of eighteen. Unlike many of his fellow Republicans, who tended to spend their money as soon as they earned it, McKearney was thrifty. He also had a considerable amount of inherited wealth.

Like his father and grandfather, who had both been politically active, McKearney was an expert in breeding horses and training them. He was responsible for the breeding and training of a number of horses which became Grand National winners.

His favourite horse was called 'Shamrock Kitty', which he rode himself and it had never lost a race. Liam rode it as well. The money it won was used to buy acres of land, and to support servants and retainers in McKearney's luxurious residence in Northern Ireland. The money was also used to subsidize Mrs McKearney's house in England. Lastly, it was used to boost IRA funds.

Ruari was known in his local community as 'Raymond Morgan'. He posed as a respectable and genial Protestant. No one working, either in his castle-like house, or on his land, suspected that over two-thirds of the Republican offensive were supported by his income alone.

His comrades in the IRA, his wife and his son, were the only people who knew about his influential Republican connections. Apart from them, his image as a clean-living, Protestant Lord of the Manor was inviolate.

Liam, was a professional jockey, as well as a trained marksman. He knew better than to question his fierce father's orders. Apart from McKearney, he could handle Shamrock Kitty better than any other jockey in Northern Ireland.

Liam had been raised as a Catholic and a militant Republican. He had an overtly strict upbringing and didn't want to be knee-capped, even through orders issued by his own father.

McKearney was a ruthless, inflexible and uncompromising figure in the IRA, and was one of its most prominent masterminds. He was by far the most accomplished marksman the Movement had ever had among its ranks. For that reason alone, he nearly always carried out the executions of British politicians himself.

Not once in his life did he miss his target. Not once, with his face covered, as it invariably was, by a Balaclava, was he ever suspected of an execution, let alone detected.

McKearney had two major weaknesses, however, neither of which had as yet impaired his infallibility as a deadly and accurate marksman. One of these, the demon to destroy three Irishmen out of four, was drink. The other, that destroyed two out of four, was women. Women to him were as harmful as narcotics. Although he did not know it at the time, it was a woman who would bring about his ruin.

Liam had not seen his father for some months. McKearney was in his study in his castle-like house in Northern Ireland. The study was encased within a secure, four-foot thick, concrete-walled vault, which not even his cleaners had access to.

To enter his father's study, Liam had to push six different metal buttons, before the solid door could open.

He found his father sitting behind an oak desk, cluttered with rifles and other firearms, that he had taken from his vast armoury to clean.

Some of these guns were for shooting birds at his weekly pheasant shoots. Others were for shooting people and one, an Armelite rifle, its barrel freshly and lovingly cleaned by its owner, had been laid to one side. A person, not a bird, was to be its target. That person was Jack Maguire.

Liam entered his father's study, wearing a jockey's outfit, holding his cap in his hand. He was going to ride Shamrock Kitty. His father had also told him to help him to execute Maguire on Christmas Day.

McKearney was dictating a speech which he wanted a senior cell commander and ammunitions expert to make at the funeral of a hunger striker. He took a long swig from his whiskey flask and spoke into a tape recorder. Liam sensed that it would be unwise to interrupt his father, and stood timidly, like a police constable on duty, prepared to wait all day if necessary.

"Our rules, staunchly adhered to by our beloved martyr just departed, are taken from history. We remember the potato famine. We remember the Fenians. We remember 1916 and the British executions of our heroes. We also remember the British murders of the boys who gave their lives marching beneath the Flag of Green.

"Further, I trust that our dear departed will be an example to all of you on this sorrowful day, and that he will give you greater strength to free our glorious country."

Liam cleared his throat, afraid of using more radical methods of attracting his father's attention.

McKearney ignored his son's presence and continued to dictate, his voice rising to a thunderous crescendo: "After centuries of slumber, our nation shall once again strike, please God, at those who have infringed her liberty, murdered her sons and raped her daughters. Our nation shall strike and strike hard, and make the evil British tyrants go down on their knees begging for mercy and forgiveness!"

"Father?"

McKearney's ranting continued: "With the help of God and his blessed mother, shall all our comrades and our holy martyrs in heaven look down upon our tortured, crucified country!"

"I've arrived, Father," said Liam, who was relieved because he had been able to interrupt McKearney before he started a new sentence.

"Turn round!" shouted his father peremptorily.

Liam turned round, fearing that his father would find something to criticize about his appearance.

"Would you be getting your hair cut, son," said McKearney.

Liam's southern Irish accent was not very pronounced, due to the length of time that he had lived in his mother's house in England. "Jesus Christ wore his hair long, so why shouldn't I?" he ventured.

McKearney thought of picking up the Armelite rifle by its barrel and swinging it violently against the edge of his desk like a golfer. He checked himself. "Jaysus Chroyst may have worn his hair long," he bellowed, "but Jaysus Chroyst didn't happen to be roydin' any of my fockin' hosses!"

* * *

PART THREE

PART THREE

The Salvation of Miss Natalie Klein

Natalie sent a telegram to Maguire, warning him not to go to the orphanage on Christmas Day, just in case her earlier message hadn't reached him.

Haagan Village Church was named after General James Haagan, a Puritan who had fought in Ireland on the British side under Oliver Cromwell. It stood at the end of Haagan Village Street. It was a large, quaint old church, which was attended by parishioners from an area of about twenty square miles.

Its visitors were smartly-dressed, middle to upper-class Protestants, many of whom took part in Orangeman's Marches. A number of them admired Raymond Morgan, whose castle-like house had a Union flag flying from a mast on its roof. He sat alone at the back of the church in his special pew.

Natalie entered the church before the nine o'clock service was due to start. She was dressed conventionally in an Austrian hunting coat with its collar turned up. She was wearing a headband, attached to a veil, which covered her face and which gave her an air of wealth and respectability.

Her coat was modestly buttoned up to the neck. Beneath it, she had on the clothing of an Amsterdam prostitute. She sat down in McKearney's pew. She had recognized his face from the photographs she had seen, and noticed his red Church of England prayer book with his initials engraved on it. He was formally dressed in a tailored brown tweed suit. A middle-aged woman, sitting near Natalie, gave her a strange look, because she had not knelt down as some churchgoers do before a service.

Like anyone caught in the act of being different from other people, she knelt down so hurriedly. She closed her hands in front of her and closed her eyes. She stayed like this for two minutes, during which time she thought of a way to attract McKearney's attention.

Christmas carols were sung throughout the service. Prayers were read. That seemed interminable, and Natalie could not them find in any of the prayer books scattered around. A clergyman delivered a noisy, ear-piercing sermon about thrift and moral decency.

After one of the many prayers, Natalie rose unsteadily to her feet and lurched to the right, forcing herself to fall over. Instinctively, McKearney helped her up. She looked at him sideways and thanked him in a pronounced Northern Irish brogue.

"It's my pleasure, ma'am," said McKearney affably.

"Do you mind if I hold onto you? I'm feeling faint," said Natalie.

McKearney stared at her pretty profile.

"It would be the making of my day," he muttered.

The congregation began to sing '*Once in Royal David's City*'. McKearney joined them, and Natalie was struck by his perfect musical ear. She continued to hold onto him. She could hear the quickening of his heart, and undid part of her coat to show her legs which were covered by black fishnet tights.

Suddenly, for no apparent reason, she was reminded of her visit to the IRA pub in Kilburn, and of the tin-rattler who had asked her if the Marquis de Sade had ever done anything for Ireland. It amused her to think that, among his many debauches when not behind bars, the Marquis had devoted himself to whipping people and to being whipped. He also ordered his valet to whip him in his apartment in Marseille. He scratched the number of lashes which he had received from his valet, on the chimney flue.

An idea flashed through Natalie's mind as the carol continued. She turned her face towards McKearney and unbuttoned her coat further. He extended his hand, which she took in her own and bit hard, until it bled. This excited him and his breathing became even heavier. She put her mouth to his ear and sang, making up the words as she went along:

"In a southern sun-drenched city,
Stood an ancient chimney flue,
Where a valet lashed his master,
Watching how his Hampton grew.
When the master's eyes went wild,
The valet meekly bowed and smiled."

"This is too strong for me," muttered McKearney. He took a long swig from his whiskey flask which was nearly empty. Natalie led him by the hand towards the door of the church, continuing to sing softly in his ear:

"The master ordered, 'whip me harder.
This is like a piece of cake.'
"But when he reached two hundred and sixty,
The valet said, 'I need a break'."
"On the chimney, he inscripted
The number of strokes that he'd inflicted."

Some disgusted members of the congregation stared at McKearney and Natalie as they were leaving the church. A few of them overheard what she was singing. It was ironical that a man, who had maimed and slaughtered thousands, was being led by a woman like a brainwashed sheep.

"I'll take you to the outer perimeter thirty yards from here," said McKearney, adding, "As long as we hurry. I've got things to do."

He led Natalie to a five-foot high gravestone by the wall of the churchyard.

"I'd like you to lie on top of me."

He closed his eyes and quickly ran his hands through Natalie's hair.

She grabbed hold of a heavy stone and hit him on the head with a stone, hard enough to knock him out, but not hard enough to kill him.

No one saw her leaving the churchyard. She drove her self-drive Ford Focus to Belfast Airport and took the next plane back to London.

* * *

The Reverend Wentridge-Toomey was a short, bald-headed man of fifty-five. He had been shaking hands with the members of his congregation, as they left Haagan Village Church. Among them, was a farmer who was an old friend of his.

"I see that scoundrel, Morgan, picked up a tart today," said the minister. "If he must do that sort of thing, he might at least do so in private and not in a Christian church."

The farmer chuckled.

"We all have our vices. Mr Morgan may have a weakness for members of the opposite sex, but he's still a pillar of the community," he commented.

"Even so, I think his behaviour today was a bit much but I suppose you're right. At least, the blighter has the decency to fly the Union flag from his residence," said the Reverend Wentridge-Toomey.

The 'blighter' who had flown the Union flag from his residence, regained consciousness after a few minutes. Although he was confused because of the blow to his head, he looked at his watch and realized how late it was.

He opened the suitcase in the boot of his white Jaguar, which he had parked outside Haagan Village Church. He checked that the Armelite rifle, at the bottom of his suitcase, was untouched and ready to load. He covered it with gift-wrapped presents, eased his weight behind the steering wheel and headed for the Belfast city centre, blindly overtaking and forcing oncoming vehicles to swerve to the other side of the road.

Once he had reached the outskirts of Belfast, he looked at his watch once more. The time was five past one. He feared he might be unable to carry out Maguire's assassination, and went through two red lights. An army patrol car forced him to the side of the road. The driver was accompanied by a colleague.

"What's your game, Paddy? You've been through two red lights," said the patrol car driver, who asked him for his licence.

McKearney handed over his licence, which gave his false name and smiled.

"You realize that you've broken the law," said the patrol car driver. "Get out of your car."

Panic took hold of McKearney. He wondered whether he ought to reverse into the patrol car, to immobilize it. Instead, he decided to act the part of the dumb Irishman. He lost his head, for the first time in his life, and mimicked a southern Irish accent.

"To be sure, I was trying to make a citizen's arrest of the driver who went through in front of me," he said.

"Oh, you were, were you? Now, I'm arresting you. Are you going to get out of your car, or am I going to have to use force?"

McKearney got out of his car.

"OK, Paddy, stand up against the car with your hands above your head."

"A little courtesy wouldn't go amiss, sir. I fly the Union flag from the roof of my house, I'll have you know. You're not talking to a Papist upstart."

The patrol car driver and his colleague searched McKearney's car removed a Colt .38 from his inside pocket.

"All right, Paddy, let's have the shooter and we'll check the boot while we're at it."

"The gun's for self-protection, sir. I've got gifts for my family in the boot. I'm late for lunch already. It's Christmas Day. Can't you show some charity?"

"Not a chance, Paddy, we're going through the lot."

The parts of the Armelite rifle were found in the suitcase in the boot. It was check and mate for Ruari Sean McKearney.

* * *

Liam McKearney, had been staying at the Chaucer Hotel, near the Churchhill Hotel for a few days. On checking in, he had spoken with an American accent and had posed as a tourist. When his father had failed to turn up by ten past one, he realized that he had been detained, and assembled his own Armelite rifle, before climbing onto the roof of the hotel, through a skylight in one of the bathrooms.

Maguire was late leaving his hotel, because he had been told about catering difficulties at the orphanage, which had slowed everything down. He decided to take Vodka, his golden Labrador for a walk.

Liam climbed through the skylight and balanced himself before taking aim. He focused the rifle sight on Maguire's forehead, as he stopped walking to let his dog lift his leg. He had only to pull the trigger and the job would have been finished.

Liam recognized Maguire from his published photographs. He remembered his shock of blond hair and his penetrating, bright blue eyes.

Somehow, the index finger on Liam's right hand would not respond to instructions from his brain, however. It stayed rigid, like that of a body in rigor.

The police and security guards found their way to the bathroom and the skylight from which Liam had been operating. One of them climbed up, pulled him to the floor and tried to disarm him. He was still holding the Armelite rifle and the the index finger of his right hand remained rigid.

The officer kicked him in the stomach, causing him to bleed from his mouth. His captors closed in on him as he lay whimpering, his index finger still ramrod straight.

"I couldn't do it! I just couldn't do it! I couldn't get my finger to bend," he spluttered, speaking in staccato sentences. He added, "The man went out unguarded. He's a fine, grand lion of a fellow!" Liam started to cry. His tears were stimulated by a kick in the kidneys from one of his captors.

Foreign and British press reporters assembled on the scene. The British press, ranging from right to left, had similar wording on their newspapers' front pages:

'IRA PLOT TO SHOOT MAGUIRE FAILS', and in smaller print, "I just couldn't do it! He's a fine, grand lion of a fellow!" blubs gunman.

Thousands of votes, that would otherwise have gone to Labour, went to Maguire on the strength of the headlines alone. This was in his constituency.

Although Maguire's Party had made a lot of gains in his constituency, nationwide opinion polls still showed the Party to be equal in popularity to Labour, now entirely in the hands of the hardline Left. The balance was either forty-nine per cent, or fifty-one per cent and vice versa. The scales had only to be tilted fractionally for a landslide in favour of Maguire's Party, to take place.

* * *

"I've got to take time off, Jack. My father's very ill," said Natalie at breakfast one morning.

"I'm sorry to hear that, Pussycat," said Maguire.

"Do you mind?"

"No. Why should I mind?"

"That's very kind of you," ventured Natalie inanely.

"No, it isn't. It's very kind of you to canvass for me."

* * *

Murphy had hoarded a large stash of heroin behind the bricks in the wall of his room. Natalie had taken it away in her carrier bag. She had originally meant to save the heroin, in case she suffered from a malignant disease in later years.

She knew several pubs in South London which were rough and which were visited by heroin addicts. She disguised herself as a down-and-out and went to a shabby, tattered pub called the 'Warwick Arms'. She had put the contents of her carrier bag into a sackcloth hold-all which she carried over her shoulder.

Four bleary-eyed junkies in their early thirties were standing by a gaming machine in the corner of the pub. One of them, known as 'Badger', was holding a fierce-looking Alsatian dog by the collar. Its owner was desperately trying to raise enough money for a shot of heroin.

The names of the four young men were 'Ted', 'Nick', 'Bozo' and 'Badger'. The latter was addressed thus because of the pungent aroma of unwashed clothes, and stale sweat that surrounded his person.

He was wearing an imitation, black leather jacket, torn jeans caked with dirt and cowboy boots with flapping soles. He had long, dark, greasy hair, a broken nose, an earring in his left ear lobe and three days' growth of beard. A two-inch scar, inflicted by a flick knife, covered his right cheek.

His eyes appeared to be black, as their pupils covered their irises. His complexion was yellowish because he was feverish and jaundiced. At first, Natalie feared that he might be carrying an infectious virus. She was relieved when she found out that all he had wrong with him was cold turkey.

Ted was bald. He had shaved his head deliberately, to flaunt a tattoo on its crown, saying 'Smack is Cool'. He was wearing a T-shirt, black trousers and soiled trainers. He had teeth like piano keys, stank like a skunk and looked like the wreck of the Hesparus. He also had foul breath.

Nick looked fractionally cleaner than his companions. He was wearing grey trousers and an open-necked orange shirt. His greasy, brownish hair was styled in a 'fifties' look and he had tattoos of two athletic-looking youths, locked in an embrace on his right arm.

Bozo, the fourth man, looked equally as nondescript as the others. He was wearing an off-white shirt and dark red trousers. All four men were frantically playing with the gambling machine.

When Natalie approached them, she sensed that they were shy and introverted, beneath their outward image of the hunting and the hunted, that makes some drug addicts so menacing to look at.

She exaggerated her Welsh accent. "Are you winning, then?" she asked Badger.

"No. It's a fuck-up tonight. I can milk this bastard dry most nights, and now my dole's screwed," said Badger, who needed heroin more than the others, and who would have made a badger smell like a rose-scented bath.

"The machine's snarled up on us. It's all take and no give," said Ted, Nick and Bozo, simultaneously. The four hardened heroin addicts eyed each other, not as friends, but as wild animals, working out how to destroy a weaker animal, to stay alive.

Natalie looked at Badger, who was trembling and sneezing. She fidgeted and moved from one foot to the other, trying to put everyone at their ease, by pretending that she knew and understood what junkies had to go through, to survive.

"You shootin'?" she asked Badger.

"Yeah. I've got cold turkey coming on. Another half hour and I'm in the shit."

"I've got a nice supply of smack. I've kicked. I can load you all, but you'll have to work for it," said Natalie, adding, "I'll give you all some smack first, so that you'll be able to do as I ask."

"I'll do a *redrum* for you, if you want, but I've got to have a fix first," muttered Badger.

"You'll all be pleased to know you'll get your shots before you earn them. What's a *redrum*?"

"Backwards for murder," said Badger.

"What I'm going to make you do will be less messy than that," said Natalie. "I've got enough smack to keep the four of you out of the shit for a month. But don't try anything fancy, because I'm armed."

Natalie turned towards the men, away from the other customers, and flaunted an illegally purchased Colt .38. revolver.

"What's the deal?" asked Badger aggressively.

"I've got a car outside. At about eleven-thirty at night, I'll take you all to people's houses. We'll bring the dog. We won't feed him till after the visits. We'll knock on people's doors every night of the week."

"What for?" said Badger mildly.

"It's not for you to ask me what for. You're to say a few things, when the doors are opened. I'll tell you what to say, just before they are opened. I'll give you all some smack beforehand, as I promised."

"Is that it?" asked Ted.

"That's all it is. It's very simple. Do you vote, by the way?"

"I ain't votin' for no one," said Badger vehemently.

Natalie could tell that these men were of lower than

average intelligence, and spoke slowly to them, as if they were foreigners.

"I suppose you all wish to know why I want you to work for me," she said, adding, "You won't really understand my motives, because they are complex. I'm asking you all to work for me because of a bet. If I win, I will get a lot of money. I will give most of the money to charity, of course. That's all I can tell you."

"Where's the stuff?" asked Badger.

"In the boot of my car. I'll give it to you all, before you bang on the doors. I'll also hand you Labour Party leaflets to force on the occupants of these houses I take you to."

A policeman at the end of his last beat, sat at the bar, near the corner, in which Natalie and the junkies, were standing. This was PC Bush, who had a temperature of 102°. As his wife was continuously quarrelling with him, he was anxious to postpone his journey home, for as long as possible, but he promised himself he would not be making any more arrests that night.

"Double rum, barman," he said, "and a couple of aspirins, if you've got 'em. I haven't had flu as bad as this for years."

Natalie winced and whitened when she heard PC Bush's words. So did her companions, but for a different reason. The notion of being caught with a large supply of neat heroin on her hands, was less daunting to her than catching the policeman's germs.

PC Bush suspected that Natalie and her companions were 'hot', but couldn't face the formality of another load of arrests. They lurched shiftily out of the pub. He had almost forgotten about them by the time he staggered home.

The four junkies followed Natalie to the car park, at the back of the pub. She took her sackcloth bag out of the boot of her car. She pointed her Colt.38 at the four junkies in turn. She then took portions of heroin from the sackcloth bag, and gave some to each of them.

"Nothing false, pal, or you lose a kidney." Natalie was a keen reader of James Hadley Chase's novels and found the language used by gangsters appealing.

Badger and the other junkies were too slow-witted to grab the Colt.38 from Natalie's hand, and take the heroin from her.

"Can you prove the stuff's real?" asked Bozo.

Natalie scooped a spoonful of white powder out of the sackcloth bag, and put it into the palm of Bozo's hand which he licked.

"The stuff's fine. Her word goes. We'll do whatever she wants. OK, fellas?"

Ted, Nick and Badger agreed with him.

"It will mean travelling round the country," said Natalie. "You'll have to sleep in the back of the car. I'll go to a hotel and I'll take the heroin with me. You'll have shots whenever I think you need them, but you won't be able to go home every night."

"We don't live nowhere. We crash out under bridges nights," said Badger.

Natalie took a map from the glove compartment of her car, and worked out how best to cover the rough, working-class districts of cities in some of the marginal constituencies. While she was reading the map, Badger developed cold turkey and said he needed an injection. He produced a dirty-looking spoon with congealed egg on it, and waved it in front of Natalie.

She sprinkled some heroin into the spoon. Badger added water to the heroin, from the bottle which he carried with him. He heated the spoon by holding his cigarette lighter underneath it.

He found a vein in his arm which was covered with festering prick marks.

"Have you got everything you need, chaps, water, lighters and hypodermics?" asked Natalie.

"We've got the works. We share the hypo," said Badger.

"That's pretty dangerous and unhygenic but it's your business not mine. What I'm giving you now should just about last you intil the morning. Then, I'll come ack and give you more," said Natalie. She continued, "I hope you'll do this yourseleves. I'm not very good with my hands, and I've got other things to do, besides hanging about, heating up spoons."

"We know how to do it ourseleves, thanks." said Badger. They each injected themselves and Natalie watched them with the conflicting emotions of morbid curiosity and shock. She had been spared the pain of watching Murphy injecting himself, and suddenly felt sad when she saw the junkies doing what he had done in private.

Badger stopped shaking and smiled benevolently at Natalie, after he had had his injection. He passed the syringe to the other addicts.

"I never asked you for your name," he said affably.

"Megan."

"Megan? That's a funny name."

"Lloyd George's daughter was called 'Megan'. It's not such a strange name," said Natalie.

"I didn't know Boy George had any daughters," said Badger.

"Forget it!" Natalie snapped. "We've got things to do, and I'm not pissing about talking rubbish." They waited until nightfall.

After half an hour's drive, the party reached the main city in a marginal constituency, which had finally gone to Labour at the last General Election, after two recounts.

Natalie aimed for the rougher areas of the city and chose an unlit residential street, its litter strewn on the pavement and its walls daubed with graffiti. Many of the inhabitants of the street displayed Labour Party stickers in their windows. These were the people whose loyalty had to be shaken, if Maguire's Party was to win.

"Here you are, Badger," said Natalie, after about an hour, when she noticed him sweating and shaking once more. She handed him some white powder and some Labour Party leaflets. She also handed powder to the other addicts.

She turned on the light in her car so that They could all see what they were doing. Badger rolled up his sleeve to inject into an area which was severely infected, Natalie watched him, despising him. She suspected that he had sold heroin at higher prices to finance his injections. She found this both sickening and amoral.

"It's nice to see you all getting your asses out of your misery," she commented disdainfully. The junkies, who heard her words, ignored her.

"What do we do now?" asked Badger.

Natalie gave each of them a raw onion.

"What do I do with this?" asked Ted, who had spoken for the first time since their arrival in the street.

"You're all to eat some! Then you must breathe straight into the faces of the people you'll be talking to. It's eleven thirty now. Go up to the door of the house with the Labour Party sticker on the window. I want you all to hammer violently on the doors of each house you come to, as if the buildings were on fire. Wait until someone opens the door."

"Are the buildings on fire?" asked Ted.

"No. You can see they aren't. Don't ask silly questions. You're here to carry out my orders. The people, who open each door, will be rude and abusive, partly because of your personal appearances but mainly because of the lateness of the hour.

"Hopefully, the people will open their doors and will try to slam them in your faces. You're to act smartish, all of you, and wedge the doors open with your feet. Then I want you all to lean right into the target's face, so that he or she can smell the onions on your breath.

"Then say, 'I'm canvassing on behalf of the sodding Labour Party. We're so bloody overworked that there are some places that have to be canvassed late at night, and yours is one of them' —

208

be sure to say this very aggressively. Then say, 'I've come to check you'll be voting for us.'"

"I can't remember all that in one go," protested Nick. "Besides, they're already voting Labour because of the stickers in their windows."

"The whole point of the exercise is to pretend you haven't seen the stickers. I'll talk to the person in the house we're coming to. You're all to stand behind me and listen to what I say, and how I say it, then repeat my words outside the next house along but one. I'm going to need the dog." added Natalie slowly as if she were talking to the educationally sub-normal.

"Are you going to hurt the dog?" asked Badger.

"No."

Natalie took a bar of chocolate from her bag, split it into pieces and waved the pieces in front of the dog. It had not yet had its nightly meal, and it leapt into the air, trying to seize the pieces from her hand.

She banged on the door of the first house like the Gestapo. There was no answer. She went on banging, until footsteps could be heard. She threw a piece of chocolate through the letter-box, so that the dog, now in a bad temper because it had been duped, would try to snarl its way into the house.

A fat, slatternly, woman eventually answered the door. She was wearing a pink, quilted dressing-gown and a hairnet; she could have been Ena Sharples's sister. She opened the door hurriedly, fearing the news that a relative had had an accident.

The sight of the dishevelled strangers, clutching Labour Party leaflets, dispelled her fear, transforming it to the aggression that often accompanies relief.

"What do you lot want?"

The dog started barking and wrenched at its lead, trying to get within reach of the piece of chocolate which had landed at the bottom of the stairs. Its teeth were gnashing and its jaw was salivating as if it had rabies. The woman was terrified. She feared that the dog would go straight for her throat.

Natalie blew the offensive smell of raw onions into the woman's face, and jammed her foot in the doorway, to prevent the woman slamming the door.

"Was you asleep, missus'?" she asked gruffly, using a vaudeville Cockney accent which lapsed from time to time.

"I bloomin' well was and all. My hubby's got to leave house at five to go to factory. Control bloody dog!"

"Why aren't you using the definite article?" asked Natalie in a puzzled tone of voice.

"Never mind the way I speaks. Just fuck off, all of you!"

"Don't start giving us no flak, sister. I'm just carrying out my orders. I'm 'ere on behalf of the bloody Labour Party. Unlike some slatterns I could mention, we work round the clock. We have to canvass at this hour, whether constituents like it or not."

Natalie went closer to the woman and gripped her under the arm, until she let out a wail of pain. "We need your vote," she said in a menacing whisper.

"Didn't you see our sticker in the window?"

"Sod that, missus! We haven't got time to look for bits of paper in fuckers' windows."

"Well, now you're here, I'll tell you. Years ago, people working for, the Labour Party always took us to the polls in a car that they supplied. If you send us a car to take us to that polls, we'll vote for you."

"There was a risk that the woman would persuade her neighbours to give her a lift to the polls."

"'Fraid them easy times are over, grandma," said Natalie. "The Labour Party's got better and more important things to do, than dole out bloody chauffeurs for lazy slobs, who can't be bothered to turn up at the polls. What the hell's wrong with going by bus?"

"We'll be wanting a car!" said the woman adamantly.

"A car? A car? The Labour Party doesn't owe you a bloody car. You gets to the polls on Shanks's bleedin' pony!"

"I'm not so sure I want to vote Labour after all. You've dragged me out of bed, so late at night, and you've been really rude."

Natalie shook her fist at the wretched woman.

"When we win, we'll have ways of tracing the names of the people who didn't vote for us. They'll be picked up in vans at the dead of night and will never be heard of again," she added, "We're going to do a few good things when we get in, but we're also going to keep order, like Comrade Stalin and Comrade Castro did.

"We're going to be fair, but if anyone isn't loyal to what we stand for, we're going to lock them up in unheated cells, till they know better. Don't you go putting on no flippin' airs or bleedin' graces neither! A car indeed! What do you expect next, a flippin' 'orse and carriage and a flippin' load of liveried footmen?"

"I'm reporting you to the law and worse than that, to our local paper. I'm not voting for you, not after this!" said the bullied woman.

"Don't you think you're pushing your luck? When we get in, all Facist newspapers, like your local rag are going to be state-owned, like in Stalin's Russia, where at least people are taught to have a bit of respect for socialism," said Natalie.

"I wish you'd all piss off! I need my sleep," repeated the woman. "Me hubby's been laid up with bronchitis for two months and he's too frail to go to work."

"True socialists aren't interested in people's personal problems. They're only interested in the advancement of decent ideals," shouted Natalie.

"Just leave me alone," begged the woman once more. "We're not voting Tory if that's what you're afraid of. After this experience, I'm going to vote for that other lovely man."

"What lovely man? Can't you be more bloody' coherent?"

"His name's Jack Maguire and he's getting my vote."

Natalie slapped the woman across the face. It hurt her far more than it hurt her victim. She regarded her as being decent, and had to shout to prevent herself from crying.

"I'll see to it that you'll be sorry, if you don't vote Labour. We'll find out if you don't, you stupid old bitch!"

"That alone confirms my decision. Your threats don't scare me. I'm going to vote for Maguire, if I have to crawl to the polling station on all fours. I'm going to tell all my friends and neighbours to vote for him, and I'm also goin to tell them about your bullying."

"Bloody posh bigot! Fascist swine!" shouted Natalie.

The woman slammed the door in Natalie's face. Natalie saw her tear down the Labour Party sticker in her living room window and spit on it.

Through her unorthodox and clinically insane methods, Natalie had gained one more vote for Maguire, not to mention the many people that the harassed woman would be telling about her experience.

Natalie, the junkies, the Alsatian dog, the onions, not to mention the Labour Party stickers, moved on to the other houses in the neighbourhood with Labour Party stickers in their living room windows. During the next few days, Natalie took the heroin addicts from one constituency to another.

The same tactics were used and the same results were obtained. Natalie and her companions sometimes canvassed until about one o'clock in the morning.

She drove them all into a lay-by where she gave Badger enough heroin to last for at least eight hours. She then gave Ted, Nich and Bozo their rations, which were far less than Badger's.

Natalie did what she wanted to do, which was to book herself into the nearest five star hotel. She used her mobile phone and got a taxi. She went to the bar and ordered a double gin and tonic.

A feeling of gentle melancholy descended on her without warning. She wished she tell Jack and Hortense about her methods of gaining votes for his Party.

She was tempted tell Maguire what she had been doing and why. Her wiser part told her not to tell him, however. She realized he would have asked her how her 'ailing' father was, and she would have been obliged to tell him the truth.

She believed that what she had been doing was right, but knew that Maguire and Hortense would consider her actions to be wrong.

She asked for another double gin and tonic, together with a snack. After that, she went to her room.

* * *

None of the junkies slept that night. They did not trust Natalie, and feared that she would not come back to the car in time to give them their injections.

Ted was the first to break the long silence. "Why do you think Megan wants us to go to people's houses and quarrel with them?" he asked mildly. "Also, why does she put on that whacky Cockney accent?"

"I think it must mean that she wants them to vote Labour, and she thinks that being rude and making threats is the only way to get them to do what she wants. She's as mad as a hatter," said Badger.

"That doesn't make much sense," said Ted. "Remember, she said that she was doing all this for a bet. Surely, if you want someone to do something, you try to be nice to them, not hostile."

"I feel the same way, but maybe, she doesn't know how to be nice to anyone. She's not even all that nice when she talks to us," said Bozo.

"She's just mad, as I said," contradicted Badger.

Nick, who had said nothing so far, gave his opinion, "What difference does it make, provided we get free fixes?"

"On second thoughts, she may not be a nut after all. I think there's something false and phoney about her. Look at the way she's always changing from one accent to the other," said Badger once more, adding, "Personally, I couldn't give a fuck why she asks us to do these things. I need another fix now and I'd be prepared to bump someone off, just to get one!"

Natalie returned to the lay-by early that morning. The junkies were shivering and having withdrawal symptoms. Badger's cold turkey was the worst. He lay on the floor in the back of Natalie's car, viciously scratching himself all over with his dirt-clogged nails. He had ploughed furrows down each side of his face. He had clawed through his flesh, until he reached the bone, and looked as if he had been through an obscure tribal rite.

Natalie was horrified when she saw the state Badger was in, with loose strips of shredded flesh hanging from his face. She was also shocked by the appearance of the other junkies. She felt nauseated and thought she had taken on more than she could handle.

What plagued her the most was the knowledge that she had kept these desperate men waiting, simply because she had not bothered to come to the lay-by earlier.

"When did the withdrawal symptoms start, Badger?" she asked.

"At about six-thirty this morning, maybe earlier"

"I gave you your last shot at about eleven thirty last night."

"I still had to go through cold turkey starting, as early as six-thirty this morning. You made us all wait like hell."

"Then, in future, I'll get to you by six-thirty and that goes for the others, who need a smaller dose than you do. Here's your ration. Has your dog been fed?" she asked.

Badger hurriedly prepared his injection. Natalie looked away.

"No."

"I thought as much. All you think about is yourself."

"You're a fine one to talk, Megam!"

Natalie gave Badger's dog four packets of a gruel-like substance which contained chunks of dried meat and vitamins. She put the food into a bowl. A well-cared for domestic pet would only have eaten a quarter of the food, but this dog ate the lot as soon as the bowl was put in front of it.

"When did you last feed this dog?" asked Natalie.

"Two days ago."

"I find that nothing short of disgraceful! I'm handing it over to someone who is good to animals."

"Anything to get it out of the way," said Badger. "We can't look after it ourselves. It was my father's dog but after my father died, I took over its care."

"I bet your father had no idea you were a good-for-nothing junkie," said Natalie cruelly.

"I didn't start using until after he croaked. It was my grief that started me on the shit. Now, although I've got over the grief, I can't stop using."

"I'm sorry about your father. I didn't mean to be callous. When did he die?" asked Natalie.

"Three months ago."

"I'm sorry."

"I don't want to talk about it any more."

"All right. Have you taken the dog for a walk?"

"No."

"I'll take it, then. What's its name so that I can call it, if it slips its collar?"

"Smack."

"That's a bloody stupid name for a dog."

Natalie was about to lead Smack away. Ted heated the communal spoon, and made a horrible, moaning noise as he waited for the powder to melt.

"I wish you'd do that outside the car where I can't witness it, Ted," said Natalie. "It's a disgustingly sordid thing to watch."

Nick and Bozo had their injections. Soon they were all ready to be driven to another area. The next major city was seventy-five miles away. Lunch-time would be a particularly inconvenient time for housewives. Natalie and the junkies worked relentlessly, leaving nothing but hostility in their wake.

Their bad reputation soon gained nationwide publicity. They did not need to canvass each rough street in every marginal, for local newspapers, and even Fleet Street newspapers to have such front page headlines as, 'LABOUR DENIES HIRING HEAVIES' and 'THUGS DON'T WORK FOR US', LIES LABOUR'. The latter of the two headlines covered the front page of *The Daily Mail*.

The Tories were beginning to lag behind the other two Parties. A large number of the votes cast by the unfortunates who had been intimidated by Natalie and her recruits, went to Maguire. Many harassed housewives, and their friends and neighbours were more willing to support a civilized pioneer for the underdog, rather than bullies claiming to sympathize with it.

Natalie thought it would be worthwhile to take on those who displayed Tory Party stickers on the windows of their living rooms.

* * *

An industrialized town called "Hammerdean", was the next on Natalie's list. It had a huge population. Hammerdean was a Tory seat. The opinion polls showed the Tories to be slightly more popular than Maguire's Party. Labour continued to lag behind. The voters in other industrial towns on Natalie's list were, if only fractionally, greater supporters of Maguire's Party than the Tory Party.

It was six o'clock on a cold, crisp morning. Natalie returned from yet another five star hotel to her car, in which the junkies were waiting for their fixes. She seemed to be in more of a hurry than usual.

"OK, chaps, get on the spoon and load! First, we'll be doing Hammerdean and we're heading for white working-class areas only. As you can see, I'm wearing a mink coat and am carrying a Dior handbag. Also, I have on a string of imitation pearls and an artificial diamond bracelet." The junkies looked non-plussed.

Samuel Johnson Street was one of several streets which Natalie covered in Hammerdean. It was clean and tidy, and consisted of Victorian houses. These were owned by thrifty, working-class whites, many of whom were racially prejudiced, not so much against nationality, but against colour.

Natalie walked down Samuel Johnson Street confidently. She had hired her outfit from a theatrical shop. There was an abundance of Conservative Party stickers in the living room windows in the houses she passed. She regretted that she and her recruits would have to work harder and faster than they had before.

It was still quite early in the morning. Natalie banged heavily on the door of the first house facing her, which belonged to Mrs Charlotte Power, an exhausted thirty-eight-year-old housewife. She was battered regularly by her husband, who was a history teacher in a local grammar school. He was a National Front supporter.

He thought it would be wasteful for him and his wife to vote for the National Front, if they could vote Tory instead.

Charlotte was the daughter of an abstemious Methodist preacher. She had always voted Tory, because of her views on immigration. Although she was a starry-eyed reactionary, she was timid and submissive towards her husband. She believed that a woman's place was by the hearth, and that it was her duty to allow her husband to use her body, whether she felt in the mood for sex or not.

Charlotte had five small children, all of whom had flu and rattling coughs. They were too young to go to school. They hung around their mother, clinging to her skirt, coughing and spluttering. They gave Natalie an impression of Hogarthian squalor.

George Power, Charlotte's husband, had given his wife a vicious beating the night before, because his evening meal had been burned. In addition, like her five children, she had flu.

When she staggered towards her front door and opened it, she saw an ostentatiously dressed woman, over a decade younger than herself. The woman blew smoke into her face from a cigarette in a nineteen-twenties gold-plated cigarette holder. Charlotte bent over and had a violent coughing fit, from which she took about five minutes to recover.

"I'm afraid I've got flu," she stated.

Natalie would have been less frightened, had Charlotte pointed a gun at her. She had learned to face Badger's repulsive withdrawal symptoms and those of the other junkies. She had been approached on several occasions by thugs carrying flick knives and felons, threatening to slash her face, when she was canvassing for Maguire. Once, she had been pushed over and had cut her head open above the hairline.

She had been threatened with violence frequently and had emerged unshaken and even amused. Charlotte was more dangerous in her view, than anyone she had met before, however. This woman had a cough, germs and probably a fever. She had already stated that she had flu.

Natalie had not been faced with germs so far, during her terror binge, apart from those of the policeman in the pub where she had met the junkies. She turned away from Charlotte, took a swig of gin from a flask and told herself that she would have to complete her job, for Maguire's sake.

In her mind, she saw a flashback of the film, *Taras Bulba* that had impressed her so much as a child. She saw Taras Bulba's son galloping over a ravine, and the pieces of rock kicked into the ravine by his horse's hooves. She remembered her words to her friend, Mark Oppenheimer, namely that she wished she could be thought of as being as brave as Taras Bulba's son.

At the time, she had failed to recognize that a truly brave person does the things that frighten him most, things that may seem trivial to others.

Natalie was about to flee Charlotte's house in terror, but the galloping horse's hooves thundered through her brain once more.

"I'm afraid I must come in, madam," she said in a stilted tone of voice.

Charlotte beckoned her into her living room, which was adorned with wedding photographs, photographs of children and a small framed photograph of Enoch Powell*. All these were on her mantelpiece. Charlotte's children, their faces worn with flu, ran in circles round their mother. She told them to go to bed. They ignored her.

Natalie sat down and put her feet up on an occasional table, flaunting a pile of Tory Party leaflets.

"Any chance of rustling up a gin and tonic, with ice and lemon? I'm canvassing for the Conservative Party," she said, mimicking a Sloane Ranger's accent.

Charlotte started to cough again and wrung her hands.

"We always vote Tory here. I don't keep drink in the house, though. My husband's an alcoholic."

"No drink? But my dear, whatever do you do when you recieve guests? Surely, you don't serve — what's that strange-looking stuff you've got over there — Lucozade?"

Charlotte continued to wring her hands. One of her children was sick on the floor. She burst into tears. Natalie

---

* Enoch Powell: Extreme Right-Winger and racist, notorious for his "*Rivers of Blood*" speech in 1968

desperately tried to fight the hideous fear that obsessed her, by thinking about the pieces of rock, being kicked into the ravine. She forced herself to speak.

"I'm most *awfully* sorry, breezing in on your little home like this. At my public school, our headmistress taught us to be charitable towards the… er… less well off. Well, I think this lounge is an awfully good show. Jolly well done!"

The woman stared at Natalie aghast. The children were still coughing. Natalie continued to blow smoke into Charlotte's face.

"Oh, aren't I being beastly? I had no idea this was Nanny's day off," she exclaimed.

"We haven't got a Nanny," said Charlotte in a flattened, depressed tone of voice.

"You mean you're *between* Nannies? How perfectly mizzy for you!" said Natalie, adding, "I know your situation only too well, as I have so few servants myself, but at least I've got a nursery-maid, so that helps a bit."

Charlotte wiped the sweat from her brow with her handkerchief. Had she been less low in spirits, she would have asked Natalie to leave her house.

"Some tea?" she asked eventually.

"Tea?"

"Yes. Would you like a mug of tea?" repeated Charlotte.

"I don't drink tea. I either drink gin and tonic, champagne or nothing at all. Now, to get to the point, I notice you've been good enough to sport a Tory Party sticker in your front window. I'm so glad you'll be voting for us, which is why I thought I might drop in on you, to express my gratitude on the Party's behalf."

"I had been intending to vote Tory," said Charlotte, "but now I'm not sure I really want to. You're so patronizing and snobbish. If all Tories are like you, I don't want them in office."

"Come now, my good woman, I didn't mean to sound

patronizing. It's just that all the Tories I mix with, live in grander houses than yours. One would expect a Labour voter to live in a humble house like this, but it's a bit of a slap in the eye if she's a Conservative does so."

"That's enough to make anyone vote Labour," said Charlotte, after having another long coughing fit that Natalie thought would never end.

"Damned nasty cough, what! It looks as if you've got something seriously wrong with your chest. I know a cracking good chap in Harley Street who's dashed hot on chests. He only charges a hundred guineas for a consultation, which is nothing nowadays, is it?" said Natalie.

"That's about the total of the housekeeping money I get monthly. If the Tories want to win this Election, they ought to send out people who are more tactful than you. I never thought I could possibly be persuaded to vote Labour, till I met you," said Charlotte, between fits of coughing.

"But, my dear woman, you'd be absolutely bonkers to vote Labour. Besides, you do *own* this charming little house, don't you?"

"Yes."

"Do you realize it's Labour's policy to force owners of private property to surrender their property to the State? You'd still be able to live in this cute little place, of course. Instead of having to pay a mortgage, you'd have a perfectly *beastly* little man, coming round every week and asking you for rent — at least, that's what one of Daddy's chauffeurs says," said Natalie.

"There's a third Party, called Maguire's Party," spluttered Charlotte, adding, "That sounds like the best Party. Do you know anything about Jack Maguire?"

"Not an awful lot, except what the papers say," said Natalie.

"Do you think he's a nice man?" asked Charlotte cautiously.

"I don't know anything about him, except for some of his policies."

"What are his policies on immigration? My eyes aren't so good these days, and I wouldn't be seen dead in glasses. I never get a chance to read the papers."

Natalie looked at the framed photograph of Enoch Powell on the mantelpiece once more, and blew more smoke into Carol's face.

"Well, most papers say he's a bit racist, actually. At least, Daddy's butler says so, but there again, he's as black as the ace of spades and therefore not a reliable source."

"I'm thinking of voting for Jack Maguire," said Charlotte, adding, "My husband never reads the papers, but I listen to the radio a lot when he's at work. Politics is the only subject he listens to me about. I've made up my mind that I'm not going to vote Conservative, I'm going to vote for Maguire," repeated Charlotte assertively.

"Bully for you! I can't force you not to, although I'd like to. I've got to go now and do say 'tootle-pip' to those poor neglected children of yours. Jolly bad luck being caught between Nannies, what!"

"We've never been able to afford a Nanny. I've told you this before."

"I'm sure your dear friend, Mr Maguire, will help you out, now that you've decided to vote for him," said Natalie with a sneer in her voice.

"Who's that thug banging on the window?" demanded Charlotte suddenly. The window was open.

Natalie turned round and saw Badger's torn sweat-drenched face and mad, staring eyes.

"I need another fix!" he shouted.

Charlotte went over to the window and closed it, spluttering and trembling with terror caused by the hideous spectacle of shredded flesh facing her.

"Don't mind him, my good woman," said Natalie, "that's Badger. He's a smack-soak, as you can see, but he works dashed hard for the Conservative Party, once he's topped up, don't you, Badge?"

"For the *Conservative Party*?" gasped Charlotte.

"Why yes, dear, someone's got to. It's mizzy for Badger but his services are indispensable and he's going to drive our supporters to the polls."

Charlotte tore down her Tory Party sticker. She went upstairs clinging to the bannisters, and collapsed on her bed. (She and her husband slept in separate rooms.) She fell into a deep sleep, until her husband got her up to cook his evening meal.

She told him about her experience earlier that day. Though for the wrong reason, he too agreed to vote for Maguire. The Powers told all their friends and neighbours about Natalie's visit.

When she had recovered from her illness, Charlotte took a coach to London, to visit the offices of *The Daily Herald*, an influential national newspaper. The paper printed a long article about unreasonable behaviour displayed by canvassers for both the Labour Party and the Conservative Party. The paper concluded that so far, Maguire's Party was the only Party whose canvassers behaved in an acceptable manner.

When Natalie read the article, she felt a twinge of guilt about her underhandedness. She knew she would never be able to tell Maguire about her effective, if very unsubtle exploits, without losing his friendship.

She and the junkies travelled across the country and worked hard throughout further constituencies, some of which had fractional Labour majorities and some of which had Tory majorities. Natalie put on the appropriate clothing when she was covering both Tory and Labour areas. The junkies, continued to stand by her side, when she was banging on doors, and their appearance was absolutely terrifying.

* * *

This headline appeared above an article on the front page of a Sunday tabloid. The article read as follows: 'The leader of the Opposition, Labour MP, Mr Gareth Curruthers, has firmly denied being sexually perverse.

When he was asked for his opinion about the clothing worn by IRA members, attending the funeral of a hunger striker, he is alleged to have replied, "I find the paramilitary uniforms worn by IRA men at funerals sexually attractive."

However, he furiously denied, having said this at a later date, "I meant that IRA uniforms looked neat and tidy," he told reporters, adding, "I am a happily married man."

Curruthers wore black horn-rimmed spectacles and was sixty-one years old. He was thin, nondescript and bald. His popularity was due to the electorate's dissatisfaction with the Tories in a constituency known as 'Greymills' which was in the north of England.

A Left-Winger, he was preoccupied with the needs of oppressed minority groups, and in particular the Irish. He was gay and had married to save his public image. His wife was reasonably tolerant of homosexuality as well as his sexual perversions. Both of which he denied whenever he was interviewed by reporters. He and his wife stood side by side in publice.

Mr and Mrs Curruthers occupied separate bedrooms at different ends of a secluded bungalow, which was surrounded by an acre of wasteland, and which was protected by a barbed wire fence. In their respective bedrooms, husband and wife received their respective lovers.

Although he was more concerned with ideas than emotions, Curruthers suffered from two incapacitating handicaps. Firstly, he was a depressive. Secondly, he was an alcoholic. His attacks of depression were acute, and when they descended on him, they lasted for as long as ten hours at a time. He suffered from them at least three times a week.

It was when he was in these moods, that his bizarre sexual indulgences got out of control. He confined himself and his lovers to a gym which was attached to his bungalow.

Once he had drunk enough to drown his gloom, his physical needs became more urgent, and his methods of obtaining young men got more extravagant. The young men were financed by Labour Party funds.

Sometimes, weeks would pass, without him indulging in his hobbies, but as the date of the General Election drew closer his activities became more frequent and harder to control.

There were no windows in the gym, and Curruthers was discreet in his binges, once he was within its walls. He usually wore a mask. No-one knew that he had rooms in the bungalow because Curruthers's official residence was a spartan flat in Greymills City.

His sexual binges helped him to work. If he had had a 'productive' night, he was cheerful the next morning and free of his attacks of gloom for at least forty-eight hours.

He was unperturbed by the article in the tabloid paper about his remarks to reporters. His comment about IRA uniforms would be taken as a joke, he told himself. Besides, the photograph of his buck-toothed, grinning wife, her face framed by hair the colour of a raven's wings, appeared on Labour leaflets, under the heading, OPPOSITION LEADER'S LOYAL WIFE, MURIEL. This helped to dispel suspicions about his warped sexuality.

Greymills was a vital Labour stronghold and was as safe as a fortress. It had had a vast majority in the last General Election, and was the strongest Labour seat in the country.

The Greymills Labour Party had a lot of respectable, industrious volunteers working for it. A few Hell's Angels worked for it, however. Among them were soccer hooligans and unemployed youths, who, when not working for Curruthers, indulged in crime to fight the boredom of the dole. These people were inclined towards the Left than the Right.

They had been primed to be polite when canvassing, but once within the Labour Party's headquarters, they shocked upright workers by being rowdy and coarse. Most of them were straight and brought their girlfriends along with them. Curruthers noticed those who were not straight and wrote their names down in his diary.

Natalie had found out a considerable amount about Curruthers's policies, as well as his sexual perversions. She had hired a private detective called Tony Raine. Although he lived in London, Raine travelled to Greymills City by train and had hung out in numerous gay pubs, frequented gay agencies and had bugged Curruthers's bungalow, paying particular attention to his gym.

Raine was fiercely professional. He had even gone so far as to insist on Natalie's signing a contract. He proved to be completelt trustworthy. He was bald but had made up for his baldness by growing a thick beard.

He invariably reported his findings to Natalie at the bar of the five star hotel in Greymills City. Both spoke in quiet voices.

"What I need is a rent boy, speaking with an Irish accent, acting as general manager of Carruthers's male tarts."

She refrained from telling him about her infactuation with Maguire. Instead, she told him that she was working for the Tories.

"I'll find someone of that description. Meet me here this time tomorrow evening," said Raine. Natalie eased a wad of bank-notes into the palm of his hand.

The following evening she drank two double fin and tonics. Raine ordered a pint of Heineken.

"I've found the man you're looking for," he said. "He's got

a strong Belfast accent. He's as gay as cricket and he's very intelligent. Also, he has IRA sympathies and he's very discreet."

"What's his name?"

"Sean Kennedy. He's attractive and wears tight-fitting, leather suits."

"He sounds all right. Bring him here tomorrow night and I'll look him over," said Natalie.

* * *

It had been a tedious, uneventful Sunday morning for the boys entertaining Curruthers in the gym. Meanwhile, in the main office of the Labour Party's headquarters, the Hell's Angels sat at a table banging down their fists and singing a ribald song, called '*Gilda,* * *Gilda, show us your leg*'.

Suddenly, they were alerted by the appearance of an exquisite-looking young man, somewhere in his late teens or early twenties. He was wearing tight-fitting, black leather trousers. A bomber jacket, bearing naval insignia, was zipped up to his neck. He had on a black leather, peaked cap with no hair showing underneath it.

A young man called Joe was sitting with the Hell's Angels. He was gay and stared at the newcomer with a glazed expression of lust on his face.

"Come on, Joe, you're just a bloody poofter!" shouted one of the Hell's Angels, adding, "You bat for the other side; don't you? You're a brown-hatter."

"Lay off Joe, will you?" said another young man who was also gay.

His name was Cecil Buck. He was Joe's lover and he was loyal to him, despite his fear of the more macho boys. The

---

* Gilda Mount was head of the Conservative Party. She was a tempestuous, white-haired woman who modelled herself on Maggie Thatcher She has been mentioned earlier in this book.

newcomer thought there would be a fight, so he advanced towards the noisy Hell's Angel, swinging a bicycle chain in the air. He was chewing gum in the slow rhythmic motion of a lion about to pounce.

There was a long silence. Eventually, the newcomer spoke. The others were struck by his deep voice, rather than by the words he uttered.

The noisy Hell's Angel asked the newcomer for his name. He did not answer. He walked over to the table with a pronounced navvy's lurch and heaved his weight onto it. He looked at Joe and continued to swing the bicycle chain above his head.

The Hell's Angels became nervous. They couldn't work out whether the newcomer wanted a fight, or whether someone among them owed him money. They made the maximum amount of noise, by banging their fists on the table once more. They continued to sing their song which had been interrupted:

"A rich girl uses Tampax. A poor girl uses bumph,
But Gilda keeps two vampire bats and feeds 'em once a month."

The newcomer spat out his gum. It landed on the floor.

"Would you be talking about the bitch who orders innocent Irish women and children, to be slaughtered in their own country?" he shouted, pointing at the Hell's Angels.

"You're right. We want her out," said one of them, the same one who had spoken before.

"That's what I'm here for, to talk to Mr Curruthers about what he proposes to do about it."

"About the British Army?"

"You're onto it. I think his is the only Party who can help us. Where's Mr Curruthers's office?"

"You go through that door over there," directed Joe. "Then you go down a corridor with red doors. His office is the second door on the right and his name's painted on the door."

"Thank you," said the newcomer. "I'll come back when I've had a word with Mr Curruthers."

Curruthers was drinking Cognac, because he had been feeling tired and depressed that day. He was wearing a neatly ironed pair of dark grey trousers, a string vest and well-worn correspondent's shoes. The liquor had exhausted him but it had washed away some of his gloom.

When his depressions were not brought on by tiredness alone, they were exacerbated by the conflict between his two images. One of these was of a sex pervert. The other was of a respectably married politician and public figure. He also feared that he might lose his seat, due to the dodgy publicity that he had received.

Gradually, the alcohol raised his spirits slightly. Because it was a Sunday, he had no major commitments. He looked forward to a day in bed preferably with a male companion. He felt as if he had been given a pre-med before an anaesthetic.

He replied, "come in" to the loud knock on the door leading to his office, which was flung open, banging against a table. On the table, was a framed photograph of one of his lovers. He thought at first that his visitor was the father of one of the boys he had abused. When he saw the delicate-featured figure in black leather, he had a sudden urge to rush over to him and seduce him. The visitor was chewing gum slowly and purposefully, once more. He walked over to Curruthers, toying with his bicycle chain.

Curruthers broke out in a cold sweat.

"Who are you?" he asked eventually.

"Sean Kennedy?" said the young man. His harsh Belfast accent sounded more pronounced than usual.

Kennedy stared at Curruthers. The young man pulled a

copy of *The Daily Worker** out of his pocket. The paper carried an editorial, urging the electorate to vote Labour. Also the paper was adamant that the British withdraw from Northern Ireland.

Kennedy shook the paper in the air like a dish cloth impregnated with varnish, and rattled it in front of Curruthers's.

"You have the hands of a lady," ventured Curruthers shyly.

"I may have the hands of a woman but I have the heart of an oppressed Irishman," said Kennedy. He threw the paper in the older man's face.

Curruthers read its editorial, took his glasses off and gaped at Kennedy. He wiped the sweat from his brow with the back of his hand.

"OK, so you've read the editorial. What are you going to do about Ireland?" asked Kennedy cheekily.

Curruthers stared at Kennedy's thighs and broke into a cold sweat.

"Naturally, we're going to bring the troops home, if we get elected," he said eventually.

"You don't sound all that convinced," said Kennedy.

Curruthers bent over to pick up a tissue which he had deliberately thrown onto the floor. Withdrawal from Northern Ireland was on his Party's agenda although it was not particularly high.

He swivelled round on his chair, so that Kennedy would not see the expression of tortured lust on his face. "Go and lock the door, Mr Kennedy," he gasped.

Kennedy locked the door. Then he advanced towards Curruthers and ran the index finger of his right hand along the outline of the older man's nose. Curruthers broke out in an even greater sweat, than he had earlier, but managed to prevent himself from seducing Kennedy.

"Will you come to my gym this evening?" said Curruthers.

---

* *The Daily Worker*: a communist newspaper

"I'm not a physical fitness type," said Kennedy.

"I'm sure you know roughly what I want you to do in there."

"No I don't."

"Well, I want you to be preoccupied with sexual matters in general," muttered Curruthers uneasily adding, "I need a few boys you included."

There was a long pause, which was finally broken by Kennedy. He was terrified of Curruthers. He thought he was creepy.

"Are you prepared to pay the boys?" he asked.

"Why, yes, Mr Kennedy."

Curruthers did not name a price, however.

"I've got a venereal disease. I got really sore about the British after a rally, and to let it all out, I went wild down a fucking Belfast public convenience," said Kennedy.

Another awkward silence ensued which was broken by Kennedy once more.

"I know four boys who may be able to help you."

"Are they as beautiful as you?"

"You must learn not to ask for too much, but at least the boys are not infected, like me, and I'm sure they'll be prepared to do what you want," said Kennedy.

"How do you know what I want?"

"Word gets round," said Kennedy casually.

"Then bring them to me!" said Curruthers urgently.

"I'll bring them on one condition. That is that you get the British out of Ireland. If you fail to do that, once you come to power, I'll have every limb blown from your body."

"You don't need to make threats like that, Mr Kennedy. Just bring me the boys."

"What exactly are you going to do with them?" asked Kennedy.

"I don't wish to hurt any of them. I only want to do the kind of things that we gays usually do, except with a bit of relish."

"What do you mean by 'relish?'" asked Kennedy in a hostile tone of voice.

Curruthers blushed profusely. He fought to find words but none came. Eventually, he managed to express himself with the stammering repetition of a three-year-old boy.

"I… don't really know how to put this to you, Mr Kennedy. I don't want you to get the wrong idea."

Curruthers clawed self-consiously at his blotter and was silent.

"Would you get to the point, please? I've got better things to do, besides sitting around, listening to British politicians who can't string a sentence together," said Kennedy rudely.

"It's not easy to tell you what I want, in so many words," began Curruthers. "I want this particular thing to be done, because it reminds me of something that is noble."

"Get on with it or I'll leave the room," said Kennedy.

"It's basically because I associate in a way all this with heroism. I like boys to wear *these* clothes."

"Which clothes?" asked Kennedy impatiently.

Curruthers looked flustered. He produced a photograph from the drawer of his desk. It showed a Provisional IRA funeral march. The pallbearers were wearing berets, dark glasses, black, polo-necked sweaters and leather jackets. He passed the photograph with shaking hands to Kennedy, who looked at it briefly and handed it back to him.

"What you are asking me to do is very odd," said Kennedy mildly. "Besides, who supplies you with this clothing?"

Curruthers beckoned Kennedy towards a locked cupboard in the corner of his office. In the cupboard, was an aluminium chest with a combination lock on it. The older man opened the chest and spilled its contents onto the floor.

As well as IRA uniforms, it contained manacles, chains, whips, strange-looking suction tubes and other instruments of torture.

Kennedy did not look as surprised as Curruthers had expected him to.

"Do you intend to whip the boys?" he asked.

"That's all part of it."

"I'm not sure whether I'll be able to persuade them to do what you want but I'll talk to them."

"You've got to do your best, Mr Kennedy. I try to get a group of my own boys together, and use all this gear when my spirits get low. I've got six boys working for me on this project alone."

"Project?"

"Yes. I like to call it that. My boys don't know who I am because of the mask I wear. I can give you two computerized cards, which open the outer and inner gates, leading to the gym where I work. I'll give you directions and if your boys agree, I'd like you to bring them along tonight. That way, all the boys can meet."

"If that's what you want, I'll try to arrange it" said Kennedy in a sullen tone of voice." He added, "How much are you going to pay them?" Curruthers named what to Kennedy was a resonable price.

"I think you're a raving lunatic," said Kennedy, after a pause, "Besides you're making mockery of what the heroes in these glorious uniforms represent."

"I'm sorry I offended you, Mr Kennedy. When I use the uniforms for perverse purposes, I don't mean to mock or degrade the dignity of the men who fought, and who still fight for Ireland. I do these things, because it excites me to associate something perverse with what is fine. I like to see the boys marching up and down the gym, to the slow beat of the tune of an Irish rebel song, called *The Wearing of the Green*."

"This is insane!" exclaimed Kennedy.

"The song has a rousing tune which is played at a dead march pace. It is often played at IRA funerals. I'm going to play it over loudspeakers. That, together with the er… well… my kinky habits, provides me with the greatest erotic cocktail that I can ever hope to have."

Outwardly, Kennedy appeared to be reasonably satisfied with some of the older man's words.

"I'll co-operate with you," he said, "but I still think there's something ridiculous and sinister about the way you entertain yourself."

"Do you think I will get elected?" asked Curruthers suddenly, as if he were actually confiding in Kennedy.

"You *will* get elected. If I didn't know that, I wouldn't bother to waste my time, agreeing to do all these whacky things for you," said Kennedy.

* * *

When Kennedy turned up at the bungalow, accompanied by Ted, Nick, Bozo and Badger, Curruthers's first reaction was one of shock and disgust. However, as he looked at the addicts more closely, he felt that the barrier between their ugliness and the contrasting beauty of Kennedy himself, was inexplicably thin. He concluded that attraction and aversion lay side by side.

Natalie had already introduced Kennedy to the junkies. They were all in a café in Greymills City.

"I want you to do a different kind of job, now, boys. If you don't do as you're told, I will withraw your junk rations I'm going to introduce you to a man called John Donaldson. Here's a photograph of him. He is going to whip you. He won't hurt you though. As you're all itching and scratching yourselves most of the time, between getting cranked up, you'll find the whipping will relieve the itching."

Natalie continued, "You'll have to put on funny-looking clothes and perform bizarre sexual duties. I'm sure you know what I mean by that, the things you had to do to pay for your fixes, before I first met you. I'm referring to male prositituion."

Badger said he couldn't care less what happened to him, as long as he could have his heroin injections. The three other junkies agreed with him.

"Good," said Natalie. "Mr Donaldson wants to heat up your gear for you, and give you your injections himself. He thinks that the way you prepare you injections, with just one needle, and one spoon, is very unhygienic. You'll end up getting hepatitis, thrombosis, gangrene and God knows what else.

"We've managed all right so far," said Badger.

"Yes, I know but things are different this time," said Natalie vaguely adding, "I've got a set of clean, disposable syringes. Before you do whatever Mr Donaldson asks you to do, he has very kindly agreed to inject you all, personally. He was a doctor before he retired, and he knows how to do these things better than you do."

"The man in the photo looks like Gareth Curruthers, the Labour Leader, except he's bald," said Badger. (Curruthers always wore a toupé in public.)

Natalie ignored him.

Curruthers had agreed to inject the junkies himself, and Natalie had paid Kennedy to make a film, showing Curruthers giving the junkies their injections.

Kennedy had been told be Natalie, to play the film to the massive audience on the eve of polls, in the Labour Party headquarters in Curruther's Greymills constituency.

Kennedy had taught himself to use a video camera. Once he had drilled a hole in one of the walls in the gym, he inserted the camera lens into the hole, having supported the camera on a pile of books on top of a table. There was no one else in the bungalow, as Mrs Curruthers was busy, campaigning on her husband's behalf.

Apart from Curruthers and the four heroin addicts, there were other ten young men in the gym. Everyone in the room was wearing an IRA uniform, except Curruthers who was dressed as a woman. This time, he had not bothered to wear a mask. He wore neither a wig nor make-up and when the camera zoomed in on him, his features were unmistakable.

An empty box, six-foot long, representing a coffin, lay on the floor. The video camera got a close-up shot of Curruthers heating up the white powder in the clean spoons, having disinfected the skins of the addicts with a cotton wool swab at the injection sights. He then injected each of the junkies, who queued up like Dickensian workhouse waifs pining for their gruel.

Once the boys had recieved their shots, they assembled in two regimented lines, on the instructions of Curruthers. They went through the bizarre marching ritual, which was accompanied by the slow but rousing tune, sung by The Dubliners, a group specializing in Irish rebel songs. As planned, the song being played was 'The Wearing of the Green'. Occasional whipcracks could be heard through the walls of the gym but the cries of pain from their consenting victims, were partially drowned by the lachrymose, stirring refrain:

"I met with Napper Tandy and he took me by the hand.
He said: "How's poor old Ireland? How does our country stand?"
She's the most distressful country that I have ever seen;
They be hanging men and women for the wearing of the Green."

Kennedy was not easily shocked, by what he saw through the drilled hole but on this occasion, he was aghast. He had never witnessed anything on such a sickening and vile scale, as the actions performed by Curruthers and the boys. The things Kennedy observed that night were more extreme than those he had seen in any pornographic film or show.

He fainted. Within about two minutes, he came round. It was the continuation of the marching song that had woken him.

Between the acts of depraved bestial degradation, the two

regimented lines marched backwards and forwards past the camera, followed by Curruthers, who cracked a whip in rhythm to the song.

Then the even more extreme perversions started to take place. Each was more harrowing than the one before it. The camera had not fallen from its perch when Kennedy had fainted. He had overcome his initial shock and watched the carnal carnival with morbid curiosity. He had filmed all he needed to film.

Ted, Nick, Bozo, Badger and Kennedy staggered out of the gym and got into Natalie's car. Kennedy left no address and told Curruthers he would be bringing his boys back the following night. He had no intention of doing so. Natalie turned on the ignition and drove off.

"It was all a bit rough, Megan," Badger said mildly.

"It's a good song, though. Can you sing it?"

"I can indeed but I'm trying to drive a car now," said Natalie.

"You won't make us go back to that perve tomorrow, will you?" said Bozo.

"No. As of tomorrow, you'll all be free. I'll give you what I've got left of your heroin. It's now up to you to distribute it among yourselves. After that, there'll be none left. Maybe, you could get it from wherever you got it from before you met me. You could always go on the game though. No form of prostitution is as nasty as what you had to do tonight."

"So are you just dumping us?" asked Badger.

"Yes. I'm giving you seventy-five pounds each and I'm leaving you here at Greymills Station. You've all been very good but now the time has come for us to part."

She handed a cheque for £500 to Kennedy, who got out of the car and disappeared into the night.

His services were by no means over.

"That's very sad," said Badger, as Natalie's car came to a halt. "But tell me one thing – why are you so eccentric?"

"Because, sometimes they make 'em eccentric, Badger dear — so long!"

* * *

Natalie made two copies of the video which Kennedy had recorded. She deposited one in a safe at the National Westminster Bank in Camberwell Green and kept the other in her suitcase. As she watched the disgusting film in the privacy of her bedroom in another five-star hotel, she was surprised by the fact that she was no not at all shocked by what she saw. She felt extreme morbid curiosity, and that in turn was replaced by attraction for the clothing worn by the boys. The attraction was enhanced by the background song.

Natalie had a capacity for self-discipline, and she forced herself to suppress her erotic fascination for something with such sinister associations. Besides, she had been on her own for long enough. She longed for the company of the Maguires. The fact that it was two o'clock in the morning did not deter her from dialling the number of the house where she knew she would be welcome.

* * *

Maguire had been addressing factory workers all night. Hortense and Miss Bechtold were alone in the house, when she (Hortense) was woken by the phone.

"Yes, who's that?" came the shrill, anxious voice, the accent more markedly French than usual.

"It's Natalie. I'm sorry if I woke you up."

"Where on earth have you been? You didn't go to see your family at all. Jacques rang your father who said he hadn't seen you for some time. What have you been doing all this time? We've been very worried about you."

"I'm sorry. I should have told you. I've been ill, very ill and staying with some friends," lied Natalie.

"Are you now fully recovered?" Hortense's tone of voice suggested that she was not convinced she was being told the truth.

"Yes. I'm better. Well, to tell you the truth it wass something to do with a man."

"Ah, now I understand you! You should have told me that at the beginning."

"May I please come and stay in your house for a while? I really want to see you and Jack again."

Hortense was used to Natalie's abrupt methods of suggesting herself, and instead of thinking she was rude, she considered her charming.

"You know very well you will always be welcome, and I won't ask you a lot of difficult questions, because I know how unpleasant this sort of thing is. If you want to confide in me and tell me about this man, I'll always be there to listen. You *do* know that, don't you?"

There was no answer Natalie was in tears.

"Are you still there, Natalie?"

"Yes."

"I will leave the front door unlocked. I won't be up to see you, though. Everyone will be in bed."

"Thank you. What bedroom will you be putting me in? I don't want to wander round the house waking everyone up."

"The bed is made up in Arianne's room. She's staying in her aunt's house. Also, don't have one of your four o'clock in the morning baths. They get on Miss Bechtold's nerves and she's often complained about them in the past. You can stay with us for as long as you like. You know that, don't you?"

"You're very kind. I'd like to stay for the weekend. Also, I'd like to do some canvassing for Jack. There's something else I want you to know."

"Yes?"

"I think much more highly of you than you will ever know."

There was a pause. Hortense thought that Natalie was

being genuine but was puzzled by her intensity. Natalie broke the silence tersely. "I'm coming now. I won't wake you up when I get to the house. Bye!"

Natalie left her two navy blue suitcases in the hall of the Maguires' house. One contained her clothes and make-up, the other, her pills.

Maguire returned to the house at six o'clock that morning. When he saw the two suitcases with the silver initials N.K. staring ostentatiously at him, he reacted with a mixture of pleasant surprise, relief, that the owner of the suitcases had come to no harm, and anger because he had been let down and lied to.

Hortense spoke to Natalie at length at breakfast in the kitchen. Natalie lied repeatedly to the older woman, and her task was made even more difficult by having to speak French.

Maguire found the two women at the kitchen table.

"You *are* mean, Ma," he said. "You never told me Natalie was coming to stay, and you didn't give me a chance to look forward to it."

Natalie was touched by the remark and kissed Maguire on the cheek. It was the first time she had felt proud of her exploits. She remembered her conversation with Hortense when they had first met. "We must all find Napoleon within ourselves," Hortense had said, at a time when Natalie needed strength. The younger woman had sought inner strength and had found it.

Maguire interrupted her pleasant thoughts. "You know you've caused me a lot of trouble, Missy. You lied to me. You told me you were going home because your father was ill. When I heard nothing from you, I rang Selwyn up. He said he wasn't ill, as you had led me to believe, and that you hadn't gone home at all. Next time you disappear, you should have enough consideration to tell us what you're doing and where you're going, because for all we knew, you could have had an accident."

"You're right, Jack. I ought to have kept in touch with you. I'm sorry."

"So am I," Maguire replied. His dry remark amused Natalie. When she laughed out loud, he softened.

She looked at him sideways, her eyes happy. She felt no envy for Hortense, only admiration for her. Both Jack and Hortense were doing what was right. Natalie had chosen wickedness in the interests of justice. Hortense had chosen honesty as she knew no other path.

Natalie thought fleetingly about the two sisters in the 1787 edition of the Marquis de Sade's novel, *Justine*. She saw much of the virtuous sister, Justine, in Hortense. Natalie identified partly with Justine's sister, Juliette, who committed one crime after another and who gained nothing but good fortune in return.

Miss Bechtold entered the kitchen hurriedly and faced Maguire.

"The night editor of *Maguire's Voice* wishes to speak to you urgently," she said.

"Put him through and put the phone on the kitchen table, please."

Miss Bechtold did as she was told, took a pile of cereal bowls and cups away from the table to make way for the phone, and left the room.

"Yes, Stephen?" (That was the *Maguire's Voice's* night editor's first name.)

"It's about our Anti-Heroin Campaign which is to be started in Monday's first edition." (The night editor's voice was loud and clear, so Natalie could hear every word he uttered.)

"What about it, Stephen? You said this was an urgent call. You approved Monday's front page headline, BABY ADDICTED TO HEROIN, didn't you?" said Maguire impatiently.

"Yes. Naturally, I did. We were going to have a picture of the baby underneath the headline. However, there's been a change of events. One of the team has just got a significant scoop from Greymills City. It's pretty sordid. We feel this would be more suitable for Monday's front page, than the baby story," said Stephen.

"Greymills? That's Gareth Curruthers's constituency, isn't it? Let's have the story and keep it brief, for mercy's sake."

"An unemployed heroin addict, somewhere in his early twenties, stabbed three other addicts to death in a men's public convenience at Greymills Station. He then gave himself a massive overdose of heroin, enough to supply his needs for at least a week. The man's syringe was found embedded in his neck. The police are convinced that he killed the three other addicts, to get more heroin off them, so that he could keep the lion's share of the drug for himself."

"I couldn't care less what he killed the others for! Have you got a picture of the man with the syringe embedded in his neck?" asked Maguire.

"Yes. It's as close up as Manning (a bright, ambitious photographer on *Maguire's Voice* could get," said the night editor.

"Good. Shove the picture on the left hand side of the front page."

"Yes, Mr Maguire. I've thought of a series of headlines, but I felt I ought to consult you first, in case you thought there was something more appropriate. What about 'Evil Cancer Worsens?'"

"No, Stephen. That sounds too much like a late night film. What about, 'Hang the Bastard Who Gave It To Him'."

"All right, sir. Should we put an exclamation mark after that?" asked the night editor timidly.

"What the hell for? This is *Maguire's Voice*, not the bloody *Soviet Weekly*."

The night editor laughed out loud. "If we use so many words, there won't be any room for your own photograph, sir," he ventured.

"You'll have to work that out of yourself, Stephen."

"Very good, sir."

"I take it you've got the names of the syringe man and the men he murdered," said Maguire.

"Yes, sir. The syringe man's name was Eric Samuels but he was known as Badger. The others were Edward Mason (known as Ted), Nicholas Ward (known as 'Nick') and Bill Oliver, known as 'Bozo'."

"There's just one more thing but we haven't got enough facts to make a story out of it yet," added Stephen, "A clean-shaven boy with a Belfast accent was seen speaking to all four heroin addicts at an earlier date."

"So what?" said Maguire irritably. "He was probably asking for directions. I don't see what that's got to do with it."

"Perhaps the man with the Belfast accent had sold the heroin to them. I think it's worth sending someone along to look into it," said the night editor.

"*Screw* the boy with the Belfast accent!" said Maguire, adding in a quieter tone of voice, away from the mouthpiece, "For Christ's sake, Natalie, that was one of Hortense's favourite vases you've just knocked off the table. You're a bloody nuisance."

"The man with the Belfast accent is, as I said, worth following up," persisted the night editor, although it was not his job to tell his proprietor where to send reporters.

"The man with the Belfast accent is not worth following up, Stephen," rasped Maguire. "He's not relevant to the story, unless for any reason, he comes back into the limelight,"

"I know it's not my place, but I still think there could be more to it than that, sir." There was a pause, because the night editor was a bit in awe of Maguire. He added, You ought to know this, though." Maguire sighed heavily into the mouthpiece. "What, Stephen?"

"An eye-witness thinks the man's first name is 'Sean'."

Maguire sighed even more heavily into the mouthpiece, to show his frustration.

"I think you'll find that quite a lot of men with Belfast accents are called 'Sean'," he said, his voice raised.

"But Mr Maguire…"

"Goodbye, Stephen!"

* * *

Hortense was going through a list of canvassing sheets when Natalie entered her study.

"Hullo. Have you come to give me a hand?"

"I'm in trouble, Hortense," began Natalie. "I'd like to stay here with you for ten more days, to help you both, but my mind is so disturbed that I'd be a hindrance to you. I need at least ten days to think something over. I've got a hard decision to make and when I've made it, I'll come back."

"Is it because of that man you were talking about?" asked Hortense.

"Yes."

"Is it unrequited love?"

"It's very much worse than that. It's unrequiting love."

"Can you tell me anything about it? It will make you feel better," said Hortense kindly.

"I'd like to tell you but it's so unpleasant, I can't."

"I understand. You know where to come when you've sorted it out."

"I don't know what to say, except how unworthy I feel of your friendship," said Natalie pompously.

"Think nothing of it!" Hortense went back to her canvassing sheets. As she leafed through them, she sang a song of Edith Piaf's called '*Padam*'. She liked to sing this song when she was happy. After Maguire had proposed to her, she sang it while she was unwrapping the flowers which he had sent her. He watched her without her knowledge. In spite of his fortitude, the song sometimes brought tears to his eyes.

'*Padam*' became quieter as Natalie walked from the house and got into her car. She headed for Camberwell.

* * *

Elliott was busy when she descended on him at *Klein and Elliott's*, but he wasn't singing like Hortense. Two pallbearers had left the firm for a week without his permission. He was kneeling, doing a demeaning carpentry job. He swore as the hammer hit one of his finger-nails.

"Stop that. I need to talk to you," said Natalie impatiently.

"You've been away for weeks on end and you've left me on my own. Then you turn up and bark orders at me. All I ever get from you is one long, thunderous flood of orders."

"When I was away, I was working hard, fighting to stop us being nationalized. You'll never find out what it's been necessary for me to do, to help us both and to help my family. I'm exhausted. I need a rest, even if it's only for a few days."

"All right. Where do you want to go?" asked Elliott reluctantly.

"I want to go to Marseille."

"You mean now?"

"Yes."

Marseille was Natalie's favourite place. Its atmosphere delighted her, as well as its *bouillabaisse* restaurants surrounding its harbour, and its backstreets worn out by time and crime. She was fascinated by its foul-mouthed prostitutes, its gutters swimming with used syringes, the sordid dregs of the dregs, the wafts of garlic, the permanent sound of an accordion, and the street fights which often took place near the harbour and in the backstreets.

The street fights attracted Natalie because she liked to

place bets on the combatants and shout encouragement like a common street woman, at the combatant she'd placed her bet on.

She liked to watch the *Legionnaires* picking up the toughest women in the roughest bars. She liked seeing the streetfighters being arrested and dragged screaming into police vans, their faces covered in blood and the sirens wailing.

She liked the white holsters which the *gendarmes* carried their guns in, contrasting with the colour of the blood on the faces of their prisoners. She loved the perpetual sound of car horns and most of all, the opportunity to swim across the harbour, when she was midly inebriated after a heavy dinner. It was then that she liked to watch the reflection of the city's lights on the water.

She had decided that, after her death, she would have her ashes scattered over Marseille harbour. She had made out a will, in which she had stated her wish.

On her visits to Marseille, she was completely happy, as if she had been injected with an opiate. Because Elliott was so good-natured, he wanted her to be happy, and he always agreed to accompany her to Marseille, although he did not like the city particularly. When Natalie was happy, however, he too was happy and in an obscure way, he eventually grew to have pleasant associations with Marseille.

"All right," he said, "we'll see to it that the shop is manned in our absence. We will leave for Marseille on the earliest plane tomorrow morning."

* * *

Nôtre Dame de la Garde is an imposing, fortress-like church at the top of a steep hill overlooking the city of Marseille. To get to it, one travels up a long, mountainous road. From the church itself, there is a magnificent view of tiled, pink-tinted buildings against the outline of a bright blue sea.

In front of the church, there is a gold mosaic with a design of the Virgin Mary in the centre. This confronts visitors and somehow invites them into the building.

The crypt has a ceiling covered with gold mosaics. The confessionals are in the crypt. There are intricate oak carvings outside them. A misleading notice saying, *'Un prête est en permanence a votre disposition'** stands nearby.

Natalie feared that she would go off her head, if she failed to tell someone about her crimes, although they had been committed because of her love and intense attraction to Maguire. She had tried to make an appointment to see a French psychiatrist. This was because speaking French was somehow unnatural and less daunting than speaking English.

However, she had lost her temper in the offices of the British Consulate, due to the slow-wittedness and lack of cooperation the staff there.

She abandoned the idea of getting in touch with a French psychiatrist. All she wanted was an ear and the opportunity to hear her words in the air, floating into the consciousness of another person. She got drunk, hired a taxi to take her to Nôtre Dame de la Garde and decided to take on a man of the cloth.

A bus carrying a group of provincial English tourists, many of them either middle-aged or retired, was unloading as Natalie went into the church. Her instinct on looking at the confessional was to open it, to see whether there was someone inside it. She deliberately refrained from opening it, however. "Is there anyone at home?" she asked loudly. There was nothing but a grid and no-one sitting behind it. The more nervous she became, the noisier and clumsier became her behaviour.

"God knows what makes a Catholic tick!" she said, intentionally to herself, although her words echoed round the crypt.

* A priest is permanently available for you

She ignored the English tourists who stared at her aghast. If she couldn't release the words describing her crimes, the thought of suicide crossed her mind.

Natalie pressed her lips against the grid of the confessional. Her words started to fall on the air, like poison that had to be released from the body, if its owner were to survive. They came in French, which was less painful than English. It took her fifteen minutes to confess her crimes. Her 'listener' neither expressed sympathy nor shock.

"Well, what's your opinion?" said Natalie, addressing the anonymous person on the other side of the grid. She didn't see why she should call her 'listener' 'vous', if she couldn't see a face.

"Have you no tongue?" she demanded.

There was a silence.

"I demand an answer!"

She rattled on the door of the confessional. The noise she made was like that of an unfastened shutter in a violent wind.

She turned round and was about to leave the church. The astonished English tourists were facing her. Her natural exhibitionist streak brought on by alcohol, had come into its own. She shouted at the tourists in English.

"Where the hell's the man?"

The tourists were dumbfounded. They continued to stare at her. She loved being the centre of attention.

"No wonder the Vatican's going bust!" she shouted. "It's a scandal that the confessionals are unmanned. If the Catholic Church wants the show to go on, it should see to it that these priests work in shifts. A Borgia Pope would soon have got these people cracking!"

Some of the tourists hissed at Natalie to prevent her shouting, but she ignored them. She ranted more zealously than before about how the Vatican should run its affairs, regardless of the fact that she knew nothing about the subject.

"Excuse me, my name is Timothy Nicholson. You're in

trouble, I see." The man, who identified himself, had a thick, untrimmed beard and was wearing off-white, ill-fitting shorts, showing lily-white legs, bitten to pieces by mosquitoes. His appearance disgusted Natalie.

"Can't you see the joint's a shambles?" she asked.

"I'd like to get to know you better. I'm a sociology teacher. I'm from Lincolnshire."

"Are you now?" asked Natalie irritably and added. "The Vatican is run by a bunch of half-witted cowboys."

"It's no good blaming me. It's nothing to do with me."

"Why are you chatting me up?" asked Natalie.

"Well, I'm into weird ethnic groups and strange people who don't fit in."

"Indeed?"

"Are you free tonight?"

"No. I'm going back to London."

As she walked down the hill towards the city, Natalie felt exorcized, partly because of the comical side of her visit to the church, and partly because she had heard her words flying through the air like a bird, whether they had been listened to or not. She no longer had a guilty conscience. That evening, she swam around the perimeter of Marseille harbour. after having dinner with Elliott.

* * *

Maguire's Party headquarters were crowded the night before Polling Day. The walls were draped with the Party's mauve and white flag. When Maguire came into the hall, his supporters gave him a standing ovation. They chanted his name for about five minutes.

Maguire raised his right arm appreciatively. Then he mounted the platform. He went to the table in the centre of the platform, where his wife and children were sitting. His agent,

Paul Briggs, pushed a microphone into his hand. The chanting of his name died down.

"Before I talk to you tonight, let me say first that I don't need this." He handed the microphone back to Briggs. "I would like to introduce my wife and family to you, because without them I would never be where I am now."

"Come, come, you are far too modest!" exclaimed someone near the front of the hall.

"No, not modest, just truthful."

Then he introduced Hortense about whom he spoke warmly. He introduced each of his children.

"It looks as if you've got your Cabinet lined up with you already, Jack!" This was the voice of Gladys Bingo, who was sitting in the front row with her mother. She was about to say something else but broke into a hacking smoker's cough. This was followed by more chanting which irritated Maguire. He banged the table for silence, with the palm of his hand.

"Ever since I became associated with this constituency as the candidate for the Maguire Party, I have done my best to help individual constituents with their problems. I have been able to get things done, things that needed doing."

"I pledge myself to help, not just a privileged few but everybody, and I repeat everybody." At this point, Maguire raised his voice dramatically, "the skivvy, the navvy, the mucker, the raker, the butcher, the baker, the candlestick-maker, all those who need guidance, those whose will to live is boosted by a kindly word and a friendly pat on the back." He continued, "As it is, the sick are turned away from NHS hospitals and doctors' surgeries, because richer patients occupy beds free of charge, when they can well afford private medicine."

"The unemployed often turn to crime in their idleness. The elderly are often neglected and alone."

Thunderous applause ensued. Maguire waited for the

250

applause to die down, hoping that his audience would not slow things down by chanting again. They didn't.

"We *will* fight unfair privilege!" he said, banging the table with the palm of his hand once more, "and we *will* fight complacency! We intend to get this country back to where it belongs. If I become Prime Minister, I intend to keep every one of my promises."

To Maguire's dismay, the audience broke into the new National Anthem, *Once to Every Man and Nation* which dragged on slowly, as he raised his eyes to the ceiling in dismay.

"I don't see that this is an occasion to get carried away," he remonstrated. "We will continue to fight to end discrimination against women, which still exists and which is an important subject to speak about tonight. There was further applause. He waited for it to die down.

When I first bought *Maguire's Voice,* I was shocked by the lack of female workers on the paper. 'Why aren't there more women working here?' I asked. 'Because there are lots of bundles for them to lift,' one of the managers replied. 'When did *you* last lift a bundle?' I asked. 'Not for some weeks,' was his glib reply. Far too many women have been kept out of jobs on the notion that they can't lift bundles."

A further ovation followed, comprising shrill female voices. Cameras clicked. A television camera encircled Maguire. He went on speaking when the noise had died down. "When will society stop treating a woman on her own in a public place as a freak?" When only silence greeted his words, Maguire continued, "Hotels are among the worst culprits. Women are often ignored at reception desks, given the worst tables and made to feel as if they are looking for trade in the bars.

"If I become Prime Minister, we will name the worst offenders and the stars will be knocked off the value of the institutions which offend.

Both men and women applauded. Maguire waited patiently before speaking once more.

A solitary man in the back row muttered angrily, but was silenced by the stares of those who were loyal to Maguire. He added, "To return, if exhaustively, to women's rights, if I become Prime Minister, a secretary's wage will be equal to that of an executive's. Secretaries' wages are low because of the belief that they are frivolous and are only interested in men. A secretary *will* be able to afford to buy luxury goods. She *will* be able to afford to get her hair done, without having to borrow money. She'll be able to get it done from her own wages."

"That's the right Jack!" Gladys Bingo called out. She was even more drunk than Natalie had been in Marseille.

"Things will be very different," said Maguire, noncommittally. Then he covered a number of other controversial issues, unleashing a cocktail of Leftist and Rightist values, which baffled his audience, as well as mesmerizing them. He was bitterly critical of both the Tories and the Labour Party.

When he had finished speaking, he left through a side door, accompanied by his family. He had been working the previous night and had had a long day. His driver collected the family in the Maguire mobile. Maguire slept deeply until he and his family arrived at the house they rented during election campaigns.

* * *

Maguire's Party won the General Election on a landslide. The obscene film about Curruthers's private hobbies was shown to his supporters in the crowded Labour Party headquarters at Greymills City, on the Eve of Polls. The news of the film's existence, spread through the country with Concorde-like rapidity and had a startling effect on nationwide voters.

Natalie Klein's unorthodox activities played a major part in the landslide. However, Maguire's victory was equally due to his popular personality. Even if Natalie had not committed her crimes, he would have won anyway, but with a less comfortable majority.

Maguire, his wife and his family stayed the night in the house they rented. He, his family and supporters were glued, mesmerized, to the only television in the house.

After about an hour, it became clear that Maguire's Party were winning.

* * *

The Greymills Labour Party headquarters had also been crowded on the Eve of Polls. Sean Kennedy had to get to Greymills City in time to divert Curruthers from his Eve-of-Poll address to his constituents. He had paid a Greymills video company to bring a video recorder to the Labour Party headquarters. The film was to be played on a cinema-sized screen. Kennedy rang Curruthers from London. The older man was in his bungalow watching television.

Kennedy told him he would come to the bungalow, pick him up and drive him to his Headquarters, in the absence of his own driver, who was ill.

"I'd like you to stop off at my bungalow to have a drink with me before my Eve-of-Poll address. Incidentally, where have you been all this time?" asked Curruthers, "What became of those boys?"

"They all walked out on me. They thought that your requirements were too heavy. Also, I've had a bad cold and haven't had anyone to look after me." Curruthers accepted Kennedy's explanation.

"I'll expect you at the bungalow at five-thirty," he said, "Don't be late. Where are you now?"

"I'm in London. I'll get the next train from Euston. I'll be with you at five-thirty," said Kennedy.

A chalked notice on a blackboard apologized for any

inconvenience caused, due to a woman who had thrown herself under a train. Suddenly, Kennedy realized he had forgotten to record Greta Garbo's *Anna Karenina,* which was being screened that night on BBC 1. His absent-mindedness made him short-tempered. He paced up and down on the platform, swearing and elbowing aside crowds of waiting travellers. He saw a uniformed man whom he decided to use as a scapegoat for his frustration.

"Why does it take so long to drag a dead body off the tracks and get the bloody trains running again?" he barked.

The man whom he addressed was startled. First, he looked at the platform. Then, he looked at Kennedy but there was something about him that made him feel uncomfortable. He failed to look him in the eye.

"Look me in the eye when I'm talking to you, man!" shouted Kennedy. "When's the next train to Greymills City?"

"It's no good asking me. I don't know nothing about railways, do I?" said the man.

Kennedy pinned him against a wall, showing advertisements. His head banged against a poster advertising the film, *A Clockwork Orange.* "If you don't know anything about railways, why the hell are you wearing a railwayman's uniform?" demanded Kennedy.

"I'm not wearing a railwayman's uniform. I'm wearing a flippin' busman's uniform!"

* * *

"Come in, Mr Kennedy!" exclaimed Curruthers, when the young man eventually arrived at his bungalow. "We've still got a few minutes left before I'm due at Headquarters. Some tea?"

"Yes, please. Two lumps of sugar, please. That photograph of such a handsome man over there in the corner of the room, is that your father?"

"Yes," replied Curruthers, walking towards the photograph, a little nervous of Kennedy.

"What a fine face he has!"

"Yes, he had a fine face. He's dead now." Curruthers eased the picture off its hook, to examine it more closely, as a wave of nostalgia came over him. Kennedy used the opportunity to put a heavy sedative into his tea. It was enough to knock him out for a few hours, but not enough to kill him. Curruthers sat down and drank the tea. "Funny taste, this tea," he muttered.

"To be sure it's fockin' disgusting! The tea-bags must be years old, but until you mentioned it, I was too polite to complain. Haven't you got any tea that's in date?"

"No," said Curruthers suddenly he fell to the floor.

"Are you all right?" asked Kennedy.

"No. I don't think I can stand up."

Curruthers lost consciousness. Kennedy dragged him by his feet to his bedroom and locked the door from the outside. It was nearly time for his Eve-of-Poll address. His supporters were beginning to fill the hall which was draped with red cloth. When Curruthers showed no sign of appearing, Kennedy mounted the platform and walked towards a table, in front of a large screen that had been erected next to a video recorder. He banged the table for silence.

"Comrades! Ladies! Gentlemen! And decent working people! First, I expect you're wondering why our dear brother Curruthers isn't here yet. He's been held up. The Russian Ambassador and he are having a brief talk about arms reduction and the scrapping of Cruise missiles."

Lukewarm applause ensued.

"Next, I expect you'll be wondering who I am. My name is Sean Kennedy, I'm the new secretary to brother Curruthers, and I'm here to entertain you till he arrives."

"I don't half like that leather outfit!" said a fifteen-year-old-girl with peroxide curls. "You're Irish, aren't you?"

"Aye, daughter."

People in the audience clapped and chanted the words, 'Brits out.' Kennedy raised both his arms in a gesture of goodwill, until the clapping and chanting died down. He continued, "First, I'm a great believer in personalization. A politician, particularly if he's a decent, democratic fellow like brother Curruthers, shouldn't be shown to the world as a wooden, two-dimensional character, making speeches from behind a desk.

"He should be seen as an ordinary human being, as a man with hobbies, a family man, and above all, he should be seen as one of us, one who has dedicated his life to fighting injustice, and one who, unlike all the other conniving British politicians, wants to free Ireland from the neo-Nazi jackboot."

Kennedy was interrupted. He knew there was a large Irish contingent in Curruther's constituency. A group of middle-aged women, drunk on cider, started singing,

"Oh, come to my heart, Sean Kennedy.
There is room in my heart for thee."

"I appreciate your support, but to return to what I was saying I'd like you all to see brother Curruthers, not as your future Prime Minister, but as a people's man, a man of the litter-strewn streets, a man playing darts in your local, a man at the disco and at the fish and chip shop. I could go on but won't.

"Here in my hand is a video. It's a home movie, showing our leader at home, surrounded by his friends and relaxing with his hobbies. The film is a fine and moving one. While we're waiting for brother Curruthers to turn up, we'll watch it. In it, we will see him as the fine, home-loving human being that he is. He's even given the film a name. It's called *The Wearing of the Green.*"

"Show it!"

Kennedy eased the video from its cover.

"Show us the film!"

"To be sure, a little patience wouldn't go amiss, now." He put the video into the recorder, and waited for the sound of '*The Wearing of the Green*', which preceded the visual part of the film.

It began with a close-up of Curruthers dressed as a woman, preparing the heroin injections for the four junkies. The camera had shown a close-up of his face, to which he was holding the spoonful of powder in concentration.

It then showed him injecting the drug into the four junkies' veins. The majestic, dirge-like song continued and the sexual perversions, which were becoming increasingly more vile and more revolting, were shown.

A woman in the front row, sitting next to her nine-year-old son, gasped in horror and covered her son's eyes.

"Wanna see it! Take your hands away, Mum!" whimpered the boy, who was tired, over-excited, and whiny. He yearned, like all children, to witness forbidden material.

His mother let out another startled cry, louder than before, and dragged him out of the hall, boxing his ears every time he turned to look at the screen.

Kennedy disappeared through a side door. He hired a taxi and took the next train back to London. He bitterly regretted the fact that he would never witness the audience's reaction to the film.

As the film continued, the Irish rebel song, '*The Wearing of the Green*' was drowned by the pandemonium that had broken out in the Labour Party Headquarters. "Shame! Pervert! Traitor! Filthy smack pedlar!" These were the mildest words of abuse that members of the audience, who had once been strictly loyal to Curruthers, were now shouting about him.

One woman, who had once been a hardened Glaswegian, raised on her mother's immoral earnings, in the slums inhabited mainly by the unemployed, passed out as the material shown on the screen became more repulsive than even the vividest imagination could have envisaged. Hissing from the audience was replaced by booing. Booing escalated to rioting.

Newspaper reporters, trying to photograph the scene in the crowded hall, were jostled by the crowd, but were still able to take pictures of the screen. As the screaming and shouting died down, Curruthers's formerly loyal supporters gradually left the hall in droves. Occasionally, they chanted, "We'll all be voting for Jack Maguire." The film was still running when the hall was empty.

The news of Curruthers's sexual perversions and alleged involvement with heroin addicts, dominated the national press on Polling Day. As yet, no one knew exactly who Sean Kennedy was but not many socialists in Curruther's constituency voted Labour that day. Those who did vote, and who had voted Labour all their lives, voted for Maguire.

* * *

The Maguires had been in Number 10 Downing Street for three days. It was ten o'clock at night. Hortense was tired and had gone to bed. Maguire was with Natalie in his study, watching *News at Ten*. A news bulletin from Rome announced that a Mafia attempt had been made to assassinate the Italian Head of State.

"Now on the home front," began the newsreader, "It is suspected that there has been some foul play on the part of someone in the Election campaign of former Opposition Leader, Mr Gareth Curruthers." The newsreader continued, "Mr Curruthers, who resigned immediately after the General Election, was featured in a bestial, pornographic film, believed to be a forgery. The film, which was referred to as *The Wearing of the Green*, showed perverse sexual activities of men wearing provisional IRA uniforms. The film was shown to Mr

Curruthers's constituents and former supporters on the Eve of Polls.

"Further it is suspected that one man, rather than several, is responsible. The culprit's political beliefs are not yet known, but police believe he is either mentally deranged, or a member of a splinter Irish rebel organization, wishing Curruthers to be defeated, despite his expression of support for the withdrawal of British troops from Ulster. The newsreader continued,

"This man is still at large. He is thought to be armed and dangerous. He is being sought in connection with drugging Mr Curruthers's tea, with a barbiturate dose strong enough to kill him, to prevent him from delivering his Eve-of-Poll address.

Mr Curruthers is in hospital but he is responding well to treatment, after an emergency stomach pump, and his condition is said to be satisfactory."

"Satisfactory to whom?" asked Maguire, although he was baffled by the story.

The announcer continued: "The man is thought to be approximately eighteen years of age. He is about five foot four inches tall. He wears black leather and a leather peaked cap. He has delicate, effeminate features, speaks with a Belfast accent, and is known as 'Sean Kennedy'. This may not be his real name, however."

A police artist's impression of Sean Kennedy filled the screen. The man looked attractive.

"Lastly, he has been seen on numerous occasions, driving a silver Ford Focus, registration number FBL 705K," said the news announcer.

Maguire switched the set off by remote control. "That's your car," he said and looked very surprised. "I don't understand. Do you know this man, Sean Kennedy?"

"Yes, as well as one can know anybody, I suppose," replied Natalie, smiling complacently.

"What kind of company are you keeping, Natalie? What the

259

hell do you think you're doing? Consorting with dubious Irishmen and being involved with the screening of a pornographic film, with intent to pervert the course of justice?" Maguire threw his cigar butt away.

"I don't understand how you could waste your time being so irresponsible," he added. "Don't you see that now this man has been seen driving a car, registered in your name, it will look as if you had hired him to dope Curruthers knocking him out, and show his constituents a film which, incidentally, is really very unpleasant. Do you know where Sean Kennedy is?"

"I don't know where he is but I hired him," confessed Natalie.

"Why the hell did you *do* it, Natalie?"

Maguire gaped at Natalie.

"Because, through my own unhappy experiences, that right only comes about through doing wrong."

"Who are you to judge how right is obtained, by your own experiences, which are few? Do you think that my past experiences have been happy? What about my childhood? All you've ever had to suffer is the memory of some idiot calling you a 'coward', for some reason I don't understand, and the wrongdoings of a couple of bent psychiatrists. I'm a better judge of how right is brought about than you. I've lived almost twice as long as you have, and believe me, right is *not* brought about by doing wrong."

"I've got to interrupt you. The Marquis de Sade wrote about two sisters, Justine and Juliette. Justine did nothing but right and suffered in return. Juliette did wrong and was rewarded. It's her I identify with, not her sister."

"I'm not interested in those bloody sisters!" rasped Maguire. He took off his jacket and loosened his tie. Even as Prime Minister, he had not given up this habit. It had always made Natalie feel lecherous.

"You may not be interested in the sisters, but their respective philosophies are important and show how the Marquis de Sade must have seen society."

Maguire paced up and down the room. "I don't want to hear another word about the bloody Marquis de Sade!" he shouted.

There was a long silence.

Natalie looked at the carpet. She could feel Maggie Thatcher's imprints on the carpet, when she was Tory leader. Then her eyes followed Maguire as he continued to pace up and down.

"I had to do it! I had to!" she shouted, wringing her hands. "I wanted you to become Prime Minister. I did it for you because I love you, and I lover her too."

"Don't think I'm not grateful to you for your loyalty, but you should have asked me before you did these silly things. On top of it, there was that film. What connection did you have with it, Natalie?"

"I didn't know what was in the film when I told Kennedy to put it on," lied Natalie. "I thought the film was merely about Curruthers beating up his wife."

"I know nothing about the technicalities behind what Kennedy was doing, although, he knew how to set things up and organize others.

"Obviously, he knew how to set the video up for all to see." Natalie paused.

"It's time I was honest with you, Jack. I tracked down Sean Kennedy and paid him for his help on all these matters, in order to screw Curruthers and make room for you!"

"I don't think you understand how very serious this is. You haven't seen the film. I have. In a minute, I'm going to show it to you."

"Oh, no, please don't! I hate obscene films," said Natalie hypocritically.

"It's time you grew up, Natalie. Curruthers's abnormal fetish about men in IRA uniforms is nationwide knowledge."

"Why does he do that sort of thing?" asked Natalie mildly.

"How the fucking hell should I know?" said Maguire adding, "What I do know is the fact that he is mentally ill!"

"Is he now?"

"He has been shown in Curruthers's constituency, injecting certain men with heroin. He has also been seen giving it to men, hired to wear IRA uniforms. There are several men in this film, four of whom are now dead. The names of the dead correspond with the people mentioned in *Maguire's Voice*.

"Oh, I see."

"You say 'Oh, I see'. You'd better hear this. One of them killed himself, as you probably know. These people put the IRA uniforms on, when they needed heroin," added Maguire, if somewhat obscurely.

"We are talking at cross-purposes," said Natalie. "I'm rather naive, I know, but surely if a man were suffering from the withdrawal symptoms of heroin, his first reaction would not be to put on an IRA uniform. It would be to go out and buy the stuff." Natalie suddenly got the giggles.

"You haven't listened to a word I've said. It is thought that either Curruthers supplied these men with heroin in return for sexual services, by someone who wanted another Party to win in Curruther's constituency."

"I can't keep up with any of this. I don't know anything about IRA uniforms or heroin." lied Natalie once more, "All I know is that a commie gave me the film, and told me that if I wanted to get rid of Curruthers, I was to show it to his constituents. I passed the film to Sean Kennedy."

"How did you get talking to the commie?" asked Maguire.

"We were both in a pub. We were pissed."

"I had no idea you were capable of such crass stupidity, Natalie." Maguire regarded Natalie with his familiar, suspicious, fox-like stare, his head raised. She stared at the carpet once more. It had not been cleaned recently and had been heavily dented by Maggie Thatcher's high heels. Neither Maguire nor Natalie spoke for about five minutes.

Eventually, he said: "I'm showing the film to you, whether you like it or not. If you've seen any of these people or recognize their faces, you're to let me know."

"No, please! I don't want to see it! I've said so already."

"Because you don't want to see it again. Is that why?"

Natalie blushed profusely. Maguire inserted the film. "Of course, I haven't seen it before," she lied once more, adding, "It sounds horrible." Maguire ignored her and asked, "Do you recognize any of these people?"

"No. Only Curruthers but it's probably a forgery."

"I don't believe you. Was it you who drugged Curruthers's tea?"

"I give you my word it wasn't me. I've done some terrible things in my life, but I would never do something as evil as that!"

"It was very stupid of you not to have had a look at the film, and also to have accepted it from a stranger."

"Yes, it was stupid," muttered Natalie.

Another silence followed. Natalie looked at Maguire and Maguire looked at Natalie. He was so revolted by what she had done to help his Cause, that his first impulse was to call the police.

However, her dog-like affection for him and his wife, confused him and prevented him from being directed by his instincts. The soppier side of his otherwise tough nature caused him to feel a numb sense of forgiveness, even an urge to reform Natalie's character. He felt angry with himself for not being ruthless and not turning her in. He allowed himself to weaken.

"I can still be your friend, can I not?" asked Natalie, in a rather pathetic tone of voice.

"You know very well, you will always be my friend, and I yours. Your heart was in the right place, even if your hands were not," said Natalie kindly.

"John!" When Natalie had gone to bed, Maguire was still pacing up and down, shouting for one of his sons. The young man didn't hear his father calling him above the sound of running bath water. Maguire called again.

"Yes, Dad?"

"Come down stairs at once."

"I'm in the bath, Dad."

"Then get the hell out and come down this instant."

"Yes, Dad."

"Did you know what Natalie was doing?" he asked, as John shuffled into the room, wearing a bath towel dressing gown.

"Yes. She phoned me on the Eve of Polls. What are you so concerned about? You wanted to win, didn't you?"

"I'm disgusted to hear a son of mine talking like that. I brought you up to be decent."

"By the time Natalie told me what she had been doing, it was too late for me to stop her. Besides, you won, so what are you bothered about?" asked John.

"Won! Won! After what's happened, I don't see myself as having won, not fairly, and the only way to win is the fair way. By the code of ethics by which I was brought up, I *ought* to resign."

"You're taking this too far," said John. "All right, because of Natalie's misdeeds, you won on a landslide. You would have won anyway." The young man stared at his father, trying to read his mind. He added, "Besides, the country needs you. If you resigned, think of the lives that would be ruined, the millions of people who would be disappointed. What alternative is there to your Party? The Tories, under whom working conditions are like those in the workhouse days, or the Stalinist Left?"

Maguire pondered for a while and didn't comment, either on the validity or the flaws of his son's argument.

"Get out now, John," he said, "I need to be alone."

* * *

Natalie stayed in Number 10 Downing Street with the Maguires for another two weeks. Weekends were not spent at Chequers but at their house in the country. After the arrests of Dr Buttercrow and Dr Morganton-Bradshaw, and the closure of what was formerly the Bodmin Moor and Jersey clinics, one of the once Bodmin Moor inmates had been reported missing.

Helicopters scanned the moor, hovering with telescopic equipment over the mineshafts. A body, initially thought to be that of the missing inmate was found in one of the more shallow moorland shafts. Dental records confirmed the body to be that of Dolores Murphy, whose landlady had originally reported her missing, because she had been way behind with her rent.

* * *

Natalie was having dinner with the Maguires. Hortense, John and Arianne were present. Maguire had forgiven Natalie for her "stupidity" and dishonesty. She was sitting on his right-hand side, joking flirtatiously with him, happy because she knew that she was the centre of his attention. Every time she cracked a joke, he delighted her by responding with the seductive laugh that had made him so popular. It stimulated her to tell him anecdotes, many of them comic and outrageous and some of them ribald.

"Excuse me, Mr Maguire," interrupted Miss Bechtold, as she entered the dining room. "Chief Superintendent Joseph

Blair and Detective Constable Peter Adams from Scotland Yard have come to see you."

Natalie hated being interrupted and continued to eat in a sulky silence.

"What do you want?" asked Maguire.

"They want to know if Miss Natalie Klein is staying in the house, and if so, they want to speak to her. They are in the drawing-room."

Natalie rose to her feet.

"There's no hurry. You can see them when you've finished your chicken," said Maguire.

She looked across the table at Hortense, who smiled, as if the arrival of the two policemen was of no consequence.

"I'd better see them, now," said Natalie.

Maguire waved his right hand in the air and shrugged his shoulders.

"Off you go, Nat," he said.

He continued to eat his chicken with his fingers. He was bored and exhausted.

* * *

Chief Superintendent Blair and Detective Constable Adams were sitting uncomfortably on an Empire chair by an occasional table with chessmen on it. The Maguires had moved their Empire furniture and the tables supporting chessmen, to number 10 Downing Street.

"Are you Miss Natalie Klein?" asked Blair.

"Yes. What do you want?"

"Do you recognize this woman's face?" he asked. Blair showed her a photograph of Dolores Murphy, looking more like a criminal than a victim of a savage murder.

Natalie looked at the photograph. Then she looked at the chessmen on the occasional table. In a subconscious effort to be cocky, she moved one of the white knights out. The white knight shook in her hand. She banged it aggressively onto a square, and its carved ivory sword broke under the pressure. She put her hands in her pockets.

"No, not off-hand. I don't think I've ever seen her before, but I haven't got a very good memory for faces," she replied.

Blair put his face close enough to hers to be able to kiss her. His eyes bored into her own, as if they were trying to drive them back into their sockets.

"I think you *do* recognize her, Natalie. After all, you were in love with her brother once, weren't you?" said Blair.

"If you are referring to Seamus Murphy, who died in a road accident, I can assure you I never met his sister. He was ashamed of introducing his girlfriends to members of his family. He may have had a picture of her by his bed, but I never look at women's photographs by men's beds. I'd be too frightened of recognizing a rival."

Natalie hoped her remark would amuse her interrogator. It didn't. She picked up the second white knight and moved it out.

"Would you like a game? I'm prepared to play without my queen, if it will put you at your ease," she said arrogantly.

"I would advise you not to waste your time and ours, by being frivolous, Miss Klein. Dolores Murphy visited you several times after her brother's death. The man you live with, Mr Charles Elliott, finally reported her to us, because she was becoming a nuisance."

"I never saw her personally. It's true our firm dealt with the disposal of the late Mr Murphy's remains, but only Mr Elliott deals with that side of the business. He has more contact with the clients than I do. I've got rather an unfortunate manner when I'm ill at ease, so I keep away from them if I can. I try to stick to admin work."

"Why do you think Mr Elliott complained that Miss Murphy was harassing and upsetting you personally?"

"It's his way of saying she was harassing him, but he was trying to sound like a gentleman, because he is a gentleman."

"What was she harassing him about, Miss Klein?"

"First, she wanted Mr Murphy to be buried. She was dreadfully drunk and aggressive, by the way, or at least that's what Mr Elliott said. Once Mr Murphy had been buried, she changed her mind and demanded that his body be exhumed and cremated. On top of that, she refused to pay us. If you were an undertaker, I bet you'd call that harassment!" shouted Natalie.

"There's no need to shout. I am not deaf. Are you trying to tell me you never met her?"

"No, I never met her. Mr Elliott said she'd been pestering him several times a week with abusive phone calls. Eventually, she stopped, because he threatened to take her to court if she continued to be a nuisance. He said she had been upsetting other clients as well. If I'd met her, I'd have sent her packing."

"You did meet her. And you did send her packing, but you killed her first before you packed her," said Blair.

"You must be raving mad! I've never met the woman, as I said."

"I think you'd better come along to the station with us. There are one or two things that need to be cleared up."

Maguire came into the drawing-room, accompanied by Hortense. "What the hell's going on?" he asked. "Why are you touching my chessmen? What have you done to my white knight? Where's its sword, sir?"

"We're very sorry about this, Prime Minister. I regret that we will have to take this lady to the police station. There are one or two questions that we need to put to her."

"What about, for Christ's sake?"

"We are arresting her for suspected murder."

"I hope you know what you're talking about."

"I know my job, Prime Minister. I voted for you. I hope you know yours too."

"Will you allow me to say 'goodbye' properly to Mr and Mrs Maguire?" asked Natalie.

"As long as you don't take all night," said Blair.

Natalie kissed Hortense on both cheeks. She said 'goodbye' to Maguire and hugged him. He picked up a porcelain bust of himself, which he had kept on his desk. "I want you to take this with you," he said. "You've always said how much you liked it."

"I can't take this away from you."

"You may keep it until you come back. Hortense and I want you to be reminded that, though you may be a fool and a wrongdoer, a coward you are not."

"All right, Prime Minister. You will have to excuse us now. Come on, young lady. There's no way you can get out of accompanying us, so we won't cuff you. That will mean you can hold that blithering china job — pardon me, Prime Minister — for the rest of your life if you want to," said Blair.

* * *

Natalie was found guilty of the murder of Dolores Murphy, as well as other offences, some major, some only minor. She was charged with first-degree murder, attempted poisoning to pervert the course of justice, being involved with making a film designed to deprave and corrupt, trafficking in hard drugs, and other more trivial offences. She was found guilty on all counts and sentenced to life imprisonment. In court, she disassociated Maguire from her illegal methods of electioneering.

* * *

Jeremy Klaytor completed his slow, uncomfortable journey in the London Underground tow-cart. The wagons moved in fits and starts and aggravated his rheumatism. His fellow travellers delighted in spitting at the convicts, working in the

Underground, two of whom manned each wagon. Klaytor found these people immature. He thought it was in order for adolescents to abuse the convicts but he considered adults who indulged in this activity, to be childish and vulgar.

After two hours, he got out at Harley Zone One, and went straight into the hospital which was linked to the underground tow-cart station by a tunnel. He waited in the reception area of the makeshift cancer clinic for half an hour, before being seen.

"Mr Klaytor! Do come in, sir," said the senior consultant, Dr Lipman. The tone of his voice was not compatible with an impending announcement of bad news, so Klaytor waded boldly into the subject which tortured him.

"Is my son still ill?" he asked, putting his hand on the consultant's shoulder.

"No, sir. We have splendid news. See these?"

Dr Lipman produced four different scans and held each one against an illuminated screen.

"What does all this mean?" asked Klaytor.

Dr Lipman smiled, respecting Klaytor's stoicism, as well as his position as Keeper Elect of the Maguire Vault.

"The cancer has gone," he said. "If it had not been for the money Mr Maguire had put into cancer research, it might never have been cured."

There was a pause. Finally, both doctor and layman embraced.

* * *

Highgate Cemetery was not as wet and windy as it had been when Klaytor left it. There was a light breeze and a pale, watery sun was just visible through the dense clouds. Klaytor's son, Michael, had not yet got to know his father. He was only five years old. He had always looked forward to the visits of the friendly, sympathetic person who came regularly to his bedside. He did not know that the man was his father, but he had always wanted to run away from the hospital with him.

He had never been out-of-doors, and stared at the bleak surroundings with a smile of delight on his face.

Klaytor led his son by the hand into the inner chamber of the vault and lifted him onto his shoulders so that he could see Maguire's gold effigy. Michael wandered round the vault, fascinated by the statues. Klaytor raked the leaves outside while his son explored. Raking was something he liked to do himself, without the help of the Vaultmen.

As he worked, he whistled a strange old tune. He thought the tune was that of a song called '*Greensleeves*' but was not certain. His whistling was in such perfect pitch that the notes could have been plucked by a lute or a lyre.

* * *

'*Once to Every Man and Nation*' was still being played in the isolated women's prison. Beverley Pell, the youngest of the two warders, had been staring through the door of Natalie's cell once more. She turned to Ethel, the older warder.

"The old lady seems to be beckoning me. She keeps laughing out loud," she said.

"That's because she doesn't know she's here. She is also drugged. She's reliving her childhood. She's perfectly happy."

"She's still beckoning me. I think she wants something. She has a really mischievous look on her face."

"Go in, and see what she wants, dear," said Ethel.

"Yes, 100623?" said Beverley crisply.

The prisoner had a wild, mad expression in her eyes. She had been hearing the galloping horse again. Like alcohol, the auditory hallucination made her feel elated and victorious.

"What do you want, Klein?" asked Beverley.

The old woman laughed wickedly.

"An ice-cream, please, miss."

"You can't have one. Any other requests?"

"Yes. I've got a message for you." The old woman looked round shiftily, as if she were about to play a practical joke. She let out a strange laugh and pointed at Beverley.

"There's a very good-looking boy in the cinema who'll fuck you for a shilling," she said.

Beverley smiled charitably.

Natalie was holding Maguire's bust with an effort. It had become heavier as she became frailer. She saw herself standing in front of her parents, reciting Tennyson's poem, *The Charge of the Light Brigade*, which she had been made to learn, because she had tried to prove that she was not a coward. She heard Hortense's voice saying, *'You are not a coward.'* She heard the horse galloping towards the ravine once more.

'They that had struck so well
Rode through the jaws of death…'

Her parents were waiting for her to remember the next line.

The image of her elder brother, Gomer, appeared in her cell. He winked at her and prompted her as he had once before. *'Half a league back again'.* He walked backwards and disappeared through the wall. Natalie saw herself throwing a brick at a sports car and cackled maniacally at the sight of the dented panel on the passenger's side.

The horse's hooves were becoming louder but much slower, as if something that had to end one day, had ended.

Natalie thought she was moving towards the ravine but she was not afraid. Maguire was standing on the other side. He seemed to be saying: *'Tibya izvyenili.'** She extended her arms in greeting and dropped the bust. Both warders rushed into her cell.

---

*   Russian for 'You are forgiven.'

"Klein 100623, say 'yes' if you can hear me," requested Ethel, who felt the prisoner's pulse and found nothing.

Natalie's serene, open eyes were deceptively alive, as was the smile of joy that had frozen on her lips. It was as if the young soul imprisoned in the frail, decaying frame had found as much personal glory as the man whose porcelain bust lay smashed on the floor.

Ethel looked pleased when she saw that Natalie had died. She took two gold coins, both with an engraving of Maguire's profile on them, and spun them in the air in a gesture of triumph. She slapped them onto Natalie's eyes.

In the aftermath of a nuclear holocaust, it was natural to cling to ancient traditions, and even more natural to show reverence towards someone who had just died.

"This is my lucky day," said Ethel. "I'm going to the offices of *The Sun*."

"I remember you saying something about that. You're going to sell the information Murphy's sister had about Natalie, aren't you?"

"That's right. I've got the filthy evidence on tape, ha! ha!"

"Well, what did Murphy's sister know about Natalie?"

"You'll have to read about it in *The Sun*," said Ethel. "Do you realize that their sales are going to be boosted so much by this story that they will probably be issuing their readers with free radiation-proof black rubber mackintoshes?"

The younger warder looked confused.

"I never really understand when you talk about things like that."

"Don't worry. A paper like *The Sun* will give you a bloody revolting ride for your money!" replied the other.

THE END